To
Catch
a
Kiss

Other Avon Contemporary Romances by
Karen Kendall

SOMETHING ABOUT CECILY

KAREN KENDALL

To Catch a Kiss

AVON BOOKS
An Imprint of HarperCollins*Publishers*

This is a work of fiction. Names, characters, places, and incidents are products of the author's imagination or are used fictitiously and are not to be construed as real. Any resemblance to actual events, locales, organizations, or persons, living or dead, is entirely coincidental.

AVON BOOKS
An Imprint of HarperCollins*Publishers*
10 East 53rd Street
New York, New York 10022-5299

Printed in the U.S.A.

Acknowledgments

This book could not have been completed without the help of my wonderful critique partners Dorene Graham, Jenni Grizzle, Heidi Umbhau, Wendy Wax, and Karen White; nor without the hard work of Micki Nuding, Sara Schwager, and everyone on staff at Avon Books.

Heartfelt thanks to Charles Fannon, Captain Operations Division, Police Services of Alpharetta, Georgia, and Michelle Barnes, CEO of Barnes Information Services, Inc.

I owe a debt of gratitude as well to special effects artist Redd Froge, Purveyor of Cheap Thrills, who provided me with information and anecdotes about the industry.

Though I've tried to avoid them, any mistakes I may have made regarding either police or special effects work are my own. I take full responsibility for them.

Chapter 1

SOME WOMEN KEPT BASKETS OF POTPOURRI on their desks at work. Jazz Taylor kept a basket of latex noses. She also collected chins, foreheads, and ears. Special-effects work called for strange accessories, a flexible personality, and often odd hours.

"Don't squirm," Jazz said for the second time. She sighed in exasperation. "You're going to give my Venus de Milo cellulite." She carefully used the edge of a rubber spatula to smooth plaster-soaked bandages over her model's buttocks.

"But it feels disgusting," her victim whined.

"I know. But think of it this way: a part of you will be immortalized. People in movie theaters all over the country will see it."

The model snorted. "I'd rather the public got familiar with my face."

"Well, you know what they say," Jazz reminded her. "Start at the bottom and work your way up."

"Why can't you just chop up a department-store mannequin, or something?"

"It's not the same," Jazz said patiently. "I need a more full-figured body for the Venus."

"Oh, so not only do I get the spatula treatment, but you're calling me fat. This job sucks."

"Curvaceous. Sexy. *Not* fat. The Venus de Milo was the epitome of female beauty in ancient Greece."

"Yeah? Well, from what I hear, the men were all gay. This stuff better peel right off, like you said."

Jazz shrugged. "If it doesn't, I'll cut you out with my chain saw."

The studio phone rang as the girl's eyes widened to the size of dinner plates.

"Kidding," Jazz told her. "I'm only kidding. Calm down." She added more plaster to the model's posterior, letting the answering machine get the phone.

"Hi, you've reached Taylor FX Studios. We're unable to answer the phone at the moment, but please leave a message and your call will be returned promptly." Her voice on the tape sounded tinny and artificial.

"Jazz, my dear, it's your father. Are you there?"

Her hands froze in position.

His voice continued, clipped and British even after thirty years in the States. "I realize that it's been some time."

Jazz sat down, hard, on a paint-spattered stool.

"Please pick up, my dear. This is rather an emergency. I'm in a spot of trouble." Her father's voice sounded gravelly, rough, not his normal smooth, persuasive tones.

Jazz groaned. Then she wiped her hands quickly on an old towel and reached for the receiver. "What do you want, Myles?"

Police Officer Tony Sinclair bumped his way through the potholes, loose gravel, and puddles in the parking lot of the old warehouse. His unmarked car, which he'd just run through a neighborhood car wash, was fast becoming spattered with mud. He sandwiched his vehicle between a sixties-era Volkswagen bus and a battered Eldorado. The sleek Taurus looked too conservative and conventional in this setting, like Tony himself.

Freakin' probation, he thought with disgust. *Just my damn luck.* And what had happened was beyond any mortal man's control.

Today marked the first day of his disgrace, until the nasty upcoming hearing in front of the Board of Police Commissioners.

He sighed. Things would never be the same. He'd have to dodge the infrared beam of the captain's hairy eyeball until the old goat retired. He could still hear the captain's voice, reverberating with the pronouncement of doom.

"Sinclair," he'd growled, "you're a goddamned disgrace to your father's memory."

Worse, Tony hadn't even been able to defend himself. He shoved it out of his mind and opened the car door, setting one wing-tipped foot, then the other, between two mud puddles.

Two artsy types wearing denim and clunky black shoes watched him with patent curiosity as he crossed the lot. The man sported a bandanna and beard, the woman a clove cigarette.

Tony sniffed hungrily. It wasn't the real thing, but it was close enough. It had been twenty-two days, two hours, and thirty-six minutes since he'd had a cigarette. He tried to feel empowered and disciplined. He felt edgy instead. Slanting an avaricious glance at the full packet of smokes the woman held, he creaked open the aged wooden door of the warehouse and stepped inside.

The hallway was long, gray, and dingy. Plain Sheetrock displayed its seams. Seventy-five-watt bulbs hung from their wires in metal cages. A paper sign pointed the way to several art studios, Taylor FX being one of them.

Tony turned right at the end of the hall, then left at the end of the next, following more paper signs to a heavy black-metal door with a square plexi window. He knocked.

What would this Taylor guy be like? Tony was actually looking forward to meeting the man who'd created so many puppets and odd creatures for Atlanta's theater and television productions. He had a real gift.

So what was he doing working in a dump like this? You couldn't create characters for one of the longest-running children's shows on television and not be paid decently.

In response to his knock, the heavy door swung open, and a slight girl in paint-spotted, baggy overalls asked, "May I help you?" She held a gooey spatula in one hand.

Tony stared at her, taken by this little pixie. Her brows were raised over large brown eyes, the dominant feature in her small face. Her hair was also brown, and clasped into an untidy curly mass on top of her head with one of those plastic clawlike things. She had a small, firm mouth, nude of lipstick, and Tony found it entrancing.

"Baking cookies?" he asked conversationally.

She looked at the spatula. "Not exactly," she

said with a quirky smile. "What can I help you with?"

"I'm looking for J. Taylor."

The girl considered him. "What studio are you from?" she asked.

"I'm not from any studio." Tony stood patiently while she looked him up and down. He wasn't used to being appraised this frankly and found it a little unsettling. Well, women had to go through it all the time, so he'd take his turn.

"And your name?"

"Tony Sinclair, APD." He watched her stiffen ever so slightly. Interesting.

Jazz took a step back. *Shit!* What had her father done now? Why was this six-foot-four, blue-eyed, dimpled hunk of beefcake on her studio doorstep? And why did she find him as attractive as he was alarming? She hated cops.

"I suppose," she said slowly, "that you'd better come in." She turned her head to call into the studio. "Alicia? Do you mind if we have a visitor?"

"Whatever," the sullen model grumbled.

Reluctantly, Jazz signaled Tony to follow. She turned away from him, voiding the image of bronze skin flashing against white teeth and white cotton, shoulders so broad they almost touched both sides of the doorframe, and casually cocked hips presiding over long, well-muscled thighs. Yowsa!

She'd love to have the man on a calendar page, nice and two-dimensional. In the flesh, and after Myles's call, he was daunting.

She knew he'd come to question her about Myles, whatever trouble he was in. Why did her father seem to be allergic to an honest day's work?

She cast a quick glance back at Officer Sinclair and got an eyeful of hot male again that unbalanced her. The guy positively pulsed with machismo: if he ever wanted another career, he could headline at Chippendales.

Sinclair's eyebrows rose as they walked between a pair of enormous, three-toed, iridescent green dragon feet to enter her work space. Good—now she could watch *him* be caught off guard.

Jazz suppressed a grin as she watched him register that her dragon's yellow toenails were as big as his hands. He looked up the legs and into the belly, which protruded above the doorframe.

"Officer Sinclair, meet Donovan."

"He's one big lizard," Tony responded.

Donovan's beefy tail extended to the second story, where it was anchored to a support beam by a chain as thick as a man's wrist. His torso was as wide as a couch and his neck formed a giant loop to the right, swooping high over the doorway and curving down so that visitors were face-to-face with the dragon's humongous head when they stepped inside.

While Sinclair was still riveted, Jazz stepped toward Donovan's control levers.

The creature's huge blue eyes began to roll, his nose extended toward her visitor, and the dragon gave a loud sniff.

Sinclair didn't bat an eye. He turned to see her working the levers and smiled reluctantly. "You're good, sweetheart." He saw a flash in the brown eyes, and belatedly he remembered that "sweetheart" wasn't exactly a PC term. Oh, well.

Tony tore his gaze from her face and stared beyond her in fascination. The walls of Taylor FX were painted a warm Pompeii red, and the place was populated by odd creatures, great and small. His gaze swung higher, to an enormous boulder, made of painted Styrofoam, poised to fall upon his head. On another wall hung a medieval shield the size of a coffee table, with two crossed swords above it.

Three space aliens were clustered on the next wall, their arms around each other's shoulders in a friendly fashion. Their eyes, Day-Glo orange, blinked on and off like Christmas lights.

A huge dinosaur head and neck hung farther down the wall, as if it had been shot, stuffed, and mounted in a huntsman's lodge.

"How long do I have to stay gooped up in this stuff?" a female voice called from the back. "You only booked me for two hours. I've got a lunch date."

"Let me see if the plaster's hardened." The girl in the overalls stepped behind a plastic curtain and rapped lightly on something.

Nosiness was part of his job, so Tony poked his head around to see. Miss Overalls was thumping a nude girl on her mummified butt. He blinked and retreated fast. What the hell?

"Mr. Sinclair, this is Alicia Davies, model and aspiring actress. She's got a part, so to speak, in Lon Adams's new movie."

"I can see that. Congratulations." He turned back to Miss Overalls, who'd rejoined him. "Now, would you mind telling your boss that I'm here to see him?"

The girl wiped her hands on a towel and eyed him levelly.

"I am the boss," she said. "I'm Jazz Taylor."

Tony took in the racks of hand tools, buckets of

paint, shelves holding power saws, sanders, drills, and other equipment. A level. A pneumatic nail gun.

Then he looked back at the diminutive girl. She had the figure of a teenage boy and couldn't weigh more than 110 pounds. "*You're* J. Taylor? In charge of special effects for the *Vortex* series? Oscar nominee for your work on *Starlight*?"

She nodded. "Can you excuse me for a moment, while I parole Alicia from the plaster? Then I'll be right with you."

Tony nodded dumbly as she disappeared behind the curtain again.

"Thank God," he heard Alicia say, and presently there were sounds of a shower being turned on.

Jazz soon appeared with a perfect mold of the woman's torso and rear end, and set it on the worktable next to him.

Tony eyed it, blinked, and then looked back at Jazz. She wore leather work boots with her overalls, and her only jewelry was a pair of dangling silver earrings. She should have looked "butch" and unfeminine, but instead she looked . . . adorable. It was not a word which usually came to Tony Sinclair's mind, and it surprised him.

But Jazz Taylor *was* adorable, with her clean-scrubbed face, those huge brown eyes, a pert little nose, and all that curly hair escaping from its clasp on top of her head.

She didn't look capable of constructing facsimiles of decomposing carcasses for Hollywood directors, and she couldn't be the daughter—and possible accomplice—of a master art thief.

Tony shook himself. Of course she could be; appearances were deceiving. And this girl was nothing if not an expert at appearances. Her whole livelihood depended on props and theatrics.

He steeled himself against her big velvet eyes. "Ms. Taylor, I've come in reference to your father, Myles Taylor. I'd like to question him in connection with the High Museum case." Not to mention another troubling matter: the romantic liaison between Myles Taylor and his Aunt Ellen.

Jazz swallowed once, otherwise, she betrayed no emotion.

"The High Museum burglary? You think my father was involved?"

Tony said smoothly, "I just want to talk to him, because of his, er—background."

Jazz didn't dance around the issue. "Because of his past record, you mean. You think he did it." She dug her hands deeper into her denim pockets and hunched her shoulders. "I haven't seen him in well over a year." A tiny wrinkle appeared in the middle of her forehead—hmmm, a possible lie—but she looked forlorn. Forlorn and defensive. Out of nowhere came an alien urge to take her in his arms, kiss her, and smooth that wrinkle away.

He must be losing his mind! Or else quitting smoking was creating other oral fixations.

"You're not too close with the old guy, then."

Jazz met his eyes directly. "No."

Her mouth hardened but Tony saw a flash of vulnerability, and it struck a chord of empathy deep within him. He missed his own father like hell. But he had loved Sam Sinclair, admired and respected him. What would it be like to feel shame about your parentage? And alienation?

You're a cop, not a goddamn shrink. Get on with it.

"I'd just like to talk to your father," he said gently to Jazz. "Do you have an address for him, or a phone number?"

The girl sighed. "I can give you his last address, but there's no telling if he's still there. Five months is a long time for Myles to stay in one place."

"It would help me, anyway."

Tony found himself wondering how old she was. Jazz didn't look like she could be more than twenty-five, but that was amazingly young for what she'd accomplished. And the money thing was bothering him. Budgets for the types of shows she'd worked on were high, so where were the trappings of success? Tony mulled it all over as she ran lightly up a rough wooden staircase for Myles's address.

Every step she took pulled the denim of her overalls tight against her small, firm bottom.

It was a very nice one.

He forced his gaze to the back of her slender neck, brushed by curling tendrils of hair. What was it about her? He hadn't found Alicia, naked under the plaster, this distracting.

Jazz wasn't the most beautiful girl he'd ever seen. She didn't smell like some femme fatale perfume, and her lips weren't done up in the shade of a cherry blow-pop. But Tony wanted to brush his fingers lightly against the smooth skin of her neck, to nibble on that small, sensual bottom lip of hers, brush his eyelashes against her own. He wanted to taste her, to watch the breath catch in her throat as he—

"Here you go," she said, interrupting his unruly thoughts with Myles's address scrawled on a purple square of paper.

He took it, murmuring his thanks as he inhaled the fresh scents of laundry detergent and a simple, woodsy shampoo. Tony forced himself to take a step back.

The last person he could come on to was Jazz

Taylor. Not only was she involved in this investigation, but that one little wrinkle in her forehead had his radar on alert.

He had a hunch she was hiding something.

Chapter 2

"I AM *NOT* HIDING YOU," JAZZ TOLD HER FATHER. He wore the usual silk ascot, knotted casually at his neck. His cream-linen trousers were a little more rumpled than usual, and his Gucci loafers merely glinted instead of reflecting the room around them. Myles had to be in trouble if he hadn't bothered to have his shoes shined.

"But my dearest child—"

"I'm your only child."

"And therefore my dearest."

Jazz rolled her eyes.

"I'm begging you, on bended knee."

Jazz threw a pointed look at his legs, which were straight, crossed at the ankle, while he lounged in her only decent chair.

"Merely an expression. Your floor is filthy."

Jazz folded her arms.

Myles smiled with all the boyish appeal he could muster, an aging angel in Versace. Except, she hoped, most angels had dispensed with delusions of grandeur and didn't wear pinky rings.

"Myles. You have five minutes to explain to me what you're doing here and prove that you weren't in on the High Museum heist."

"I swear it on a tower of Bibles, dearest Jazz; I had nothing to do with the robbery. You've got to help me."

"I don't have to do any such thing. Why I let you in here, when I'm not even speaking to you, beats me. And sheltering you from the police is not only insane, it's criminal."

"You love your papa, as a good girl should, that's why." Myles put a hand up to smooth his hair, and cast a critical eye around her studio. "Really, my love, this is awful. I know of a wonderful decorator. She'd have this monstrosity transformed in a trice."

"I like my monstrosity, Myles. I make monsters in it. It's a work place, not a showplace." Jazz advanced on her father and leaned over him, hands now on her hips. "Nice attempt at a subject change. Why are you here? What's going on? Be straight with me this time," she warned, "or I swear I'll turn you in."

"Now, dear heart," Myles crooned, "there's no need to speak so severely."

"Yes," she sighed, "there is. Spill it, Myles."

Myles twitched and fanned himself with an envelope from the desk. "Do you mind if I freshen up first? This bloody Atlanta heat is making me perspire."

Jazz fixed him with a stern gaze. "What's making you sweat is having to talk to me. And you'd better start, because one of Atlanta's finest was snooping around here this morning. I still have his business card, and I'm losing patience with you."

Her father looked at her mutinously.

"Myles . . ." Jazz said in a tone of warning. She put a hand on her cordless phone.

"All right, all right," Myles said, testily. "Look, I didn't do it. The robbery at the High was pulled off by someone else. Idiots."

"Why do you call them idiots?" Jazz scrutinized her father. She didn't think he was lying, but he clearly knew more than he'd told her.

"They broke the glass on a Monet study, for Christ's sake! Could have cut it to ribbons. And they sliced two Renoirs out of the frames—

crooked. Damaged them beyond repair." He shook his head, muttering invective.

"What's the matter, Myles? You're upset that they didn't handle the job with your consummate professionalism?"

"Yes, dammit. Jazz, they're blaming *me* for this butchery! Me! You may not be proud of my career, but I handled my jobs with skill, and I was one of the best. *Never* would I have botched it up like that."

Jazz almost smiled at his outrage, but he'd caused her too much anguish over the years. Kids at school had taunted her unmercifully about having a father in jail. Her sour grandmother had barely been able to hold her head up in their community. And he'd even affected her career choice: she'd wanted to study painting and restoration, but what museum would have hired her, with a renowned art thief in the family?

They'd called him a master thief in the years before he'd been caught. After a first jail term of several years and then a second, the papers had dubbed him the Old Master. The name was a wry compliment, and he was quite proud of it. Jazz felt differently.

"Myles, if you had nothing to do with this, then why are you running? Surely it's not going to help your case any."

He looked at her owlishly, and said nothing. With his aquiline nose, slicked-back wave of hair, and the ascot, he looked as if he'd stepped out of an old portrait himself.

"Then all we can do," she said finally, "is let you take your chances with the police. If you weren't there, they can't convict you, even with your background."

"Er—"

"You have an alibi, right?" Jazz quizzed him. "You were somewhere else? Your prints aren't anywhere in the museum . . . ?"

"The police are really not a good idea, sweet."

"Why not?" Jazz asked. "And don't call me 'sweet.' " She was feeling anything but.

"Er," he stalled, avoiding her eye. "I had nothing to do with the actual burglary."

Jazz looked at him in stunned silence for a moment. "Okay," she said carefully, afraid her temper would get the better of her. "But you knew about it?"

"Let's say I'd been asked to be a consultant."

"Consultant," Jazz repeated wrathfully. "Brilliant."

"But I turned them down, love. I swear it. I told them I had retired."

Jazz wasn't entirely sure she believed him. "Then you must have an alibi. What is it?"

"I was with Ellen, my lady love. But she was unsettled after we were paid a visit by a pair of rather unsavory gentlemen, and she left the country for a sojourn in northern Italy. So she won't be obliging the police with a statement."

"Unsavory gentlemen? You mean thugs. This gets better and better! No alibi, and thugs. When are they going to show up *here?*"

"They won't," Myles said confidently. "I left an extraordinarily tangled trail."

"Uh-huh." Jazz eyed him with growing unease.

Myles quirked one eyebrow at her. "Anyhow, the long and the short of it is that these people are now trying to frame me for the burglary. And they'd probably like to bump me off so that I won't go telling any tales about them. I object to this little scheme, of course; it's most unreasonable."

Jazz put her head down on the blotter covering the desk. Then she banged her forehead against it several times. "I don't"—thump—"believe"—thump—"this." Thump. The blotter felt cool and reassuring against her skin, but it offered no solutions.

"At any rate," Myles continued, "with my running from these people, and my lack of an alibi, things won't look so good to the police."

"No," Jazz muttered against the ink-covered paper. "They won't." She balled her hands into fists. Just when her life was starting to go right, when success was striking, Myles had to show up and jeopardize it all.

She'd told him a year ago that she wanted no relationship with him if he didn't go straight for good. Now, here he was, on her doorstep and in trouble again. He hadn't gone straight, precisely, but . . . he hadn't gone completely crooked again, either. While he hadn't reported the criminals' plans to the authorities, he hadn't agreed to work with them, either.

"Okay," she said to her black sheep father, "we need to come up with a plan."

Tony leaned back against the vinyl seat of the Taurus and tried to banish the image in his mind. He was an officer and a gentleman, and shouldn't be entertaining lustful thoughts about a suspect. Yet Jazz Taylor's lithe body swayed before him, and damn if her overalls hadn't shrunk to Barbie size. Funny how her T-shirt had miraculously disappeared, too, leaving her breasts to poke impudently through the straps of the denim.

He banished the image, annoyed, but it was too late. Part of him was alert and wagging like a police dog's tail. He brought it to heel. What the hell was wrong with him? Fantasizing about a woman in *overalls*, for God's sake. Next he'd be adding a hard hat and reflective vest. He liked his women in skirts. Skirts and high heels, preferably. With childbearing hips. Skinny and athletic wasn't for him.

Tony rolled his head on his shoulders. His neck ached. Surveillance was such a bore. He'd been sitting outside the arts warehouse for two hours, and he needed to take a leak.

He got out of the car to utilize a tall hedge nearby. It was uncouth, but necessary. Tony unzipped and had gotten about half the relief he needed when a quavering voice called out behind him.

"Young man, do you know anything about changing a tahr?"

Tony froze and prayed that the old lady was half-blind. He put one hand up to his brow and pretended to be peering over the hedge. With the other, he did a quick shake 'n' stow, then scuffed his feet around to hide the sound of the zip.

"Excuse me?" he asked politely.

Turning around, he found himself navel to nose with a pair of watery blue eyes behind Coke-bottle-thick lenses. Silver-blue hair shimmered above them. The woman was four-foot-nothing, and upholstered in a loud flower print.

"Mama and I were just on our way back from

the covered-dish suppah at church when our front right tahr blew out," she told him. "Could you take a look?"

"Er," said Tony. How did he explain that he was working?

"My car's right over this way," she continued, "and I don't think Mama's feeling too well. The peas must have disagreed with her."

Judging by the age of her daughter, Tony was surprised that "Mama" was still alive. With a sigh, he realized he might as well knuckle under. She belonged to the generation of Southern ladies who still expected chivalry from strange gentlemen they met by the side of the road. He took her arm as she tottered back to her Crown Victoria. "I'll be happy to take a look."

The woman in the passenger seat had to be two years older than Moses. Tony would have sworn that the only thing anchoring her soul to earth was the broccoli-cheese casserole in her lap. Her wig had slipped to one side, and a slight, ever-so-genteel string of saliva connected her chin to the lace collar of her dress.

Tony swallowed and produced a smile. "Evening, ma'am."

A faint whistle of air from her windpipe greeted him. Her daughter climbed slowly back into the driver's seat and handed her key ring to him. "There's a jack and a spare in the trunk," she instructed him. "Thanks evah so much."

Tony looked down at the keys dangling from a pink crocheted heart. He looked back to the sweet old face smiling expectantly at him. "Not at all."

By the time he had jacked up the Crown Victoria (occupants resting comfortably inside), changed the offending "tahr" and stowed it, and graciously accepted half a plate of leftover oatmeal cookies, Tony was streaked with perspiration, grease, and the dregs of his goodwill.

"Ah you sure you won't take the casserole, young man?" the old lady pressed. "Such a sweet boy you ah, and you young people need your vegetables."

Tony blanched. Several flies had settled comfortably on the nubbly green mounds in the dish. "Mama" continued to whistle through her windpipe, oblivious. He was positive Mama's soul would flit upwards to the Hereafter if they moved that broccoli-cheese casserole even an inch.

The little old lady reached trembling hands for it.

"No!" Tony shouted. All he needed next was to haul Mama to the mortuary today.

Her daughter jerked back in surprise, myopic blue eyes registering offense.

"I-I—" Tony stuttered. "I'm allergic to broccoli. Thank you, though. I promise to eat a salad tonight."

"All righty, then."

She rolled up her window and started the engine. Slowly, the car rolled forward. Tony watched her make a hair-raising left into traffic, then finally turned his attention back to the arts complex. The door was ajar slightly, and his eyes narrowed. Damn—what had chivalry done to his career today? Yesterday it had gotten him probation and an ethics hearing. This had to stop.

Tony moved toward the door and noticed, in the mud, two sets of footprints headed inside. One set was made by small work boots. The other set was larger, and bespoke designer loafers. Men's.

"Gotcha," Tony muttered, and wrenched open the door.

Jazz smeared her father's face with heavy foundation and rubbed it in with a sponge. She'd pushed him into a battered pink salon chair in a mirrored alcove, where she performed a cosmetic transformation. She brushed his narrow face with loose powder, ignoring him when he sputtered and sneezed. She added some blusher to each cheek, outlined his lips with a burgundy pencil, and filled them in with a tube of Plum Pleasure lipstick.

Next she went to work on his eyes with a pencil and some shadow.

"Surely not blue, my love!" Myles protested. "It's so passé."

Jazz glowered at him. "Myles, you're really not in a position to be picky, okay?" She kept working. *This is not my life. It can't be. I was a fairly normal child, despite my father's occupation.*

She began to brush his eyelashes with mascara. *There was no sign, when I was playing with Barbies and drawing box houses under smiling suns, that one day I'd be breaking the law and transforming my daddy into a transvestite.*

She chose a wig from an assortment she kept and threw it on Myles's head. It splayed there, resembling a bleached blond amoeba, until she tugged and teased it into place.

"Ghastly," Myles moaned.

"Quiet, you!" Jazz ordered. It was then that she heard the rapping on the door. Her eyes widened. "Myles," she hissed, "find a dress big enough for you in that wardrobe, and some shoes. And put this on!" She threw him some body padding with large breasts.

Then Jazz quickly twisted off the lid of a large

plastic container and plunged her hands into it. They came out gray and gloppy, and she headed for the door.

Officer Sinclair's face appeared in the plexi window, sending an unexplained flash of heat through her midsection.

Determined cheekbones, eyes a serious blue, a nose for trouble: Sinclair was a sexy road sign that spelled d-a-n-g-e-r. Why was the blasted cop back?

Tony banged on the door again, impatiently. How long was Jazz going to keep him waiting?

Her face appeared in the dusty pane of glass, and she held up her gunky hands apologetically, with a sweet smile.

Tony held up his badge, with no smile.

"Just a minute," she mouthed through the glass.

Tony nodded, signaling that he understood she had to wash her hands before she opened the door. Nice stall tactic, he had to admit. Meanwhile, she'd be hiding the old man somewhere. The thought occurred to him that Donovan the dragon was big enough to hide two or three men in. Well, Tony didn't care if he had to crack open Donovan's belly with a sledgehammer and birth Myles Taylor by Cesarean—but he'd find the man and question him today.

He leaned against the wall and folded his arms, fighting irrational anger at the fact that she'd lied to him. As he waited, Tony looked about the dingy gray hallway. Bits of unused cable lay on the floor, along with an empty cigarette package. Marlboro Lights. Tony ground his teeth and averted his gaze.

Twenty-two days, seven hours, and forty-two minutes since he'd last had a cigarette. He had willpower of steel, he told himself. Positive affirmation. *Oh, stuff your positive affirmation*, the craving told him. *Have just one cancer stick. There's a 7-Eleven around the corner. You can buy a pack, smoke only one, and throw the rest away.* With difficulty, Tony ignored the thought.

He turned and launched his fist toward the door again, but it opened before he made contact.

Jazz stood in front of him. "Hi. Didn't expect to see you again so soon."

"I'll bet you didn't," Tony said. His anger faded as he drank her features in again. Delicately arched brows, high cheekbones, impossibly long lashes. She was breathing a little quickly, and he was sure of what she'd been up to. "Can I come in?" He noted an almost imperceptible hesitation, then she moved aside.

"Of course," she replied. "Want a cup of coffee?"

He wondered what it was costing her to behave so casually, and felt unwilling admiration for her. "No thanks." He didn't want to take anything from her that he didn't have to. That included beverages offered in the name of false hospitality. "Miss Taylor, this morning you told me you hadn't seen your father in a year."

Small but perfectly rounded breasts rose and fell under her thin T-shirt as she took a quick, deep breath. He cursed himself for noticing she wore no bra. Her hands began to shake, and she shoved them into her pockets.

"Miss Taylor?" He waited for an answer, a confirmation of her earlier statement.

"What I told you this morning was true. Are you accusing me of lying?" Jazz raised her chin an inch.

"Nobody's accusing anybody of anything." Tony's voice was even and professional, but his eyes narrowed. "However, I want you to understand the consequences of aiding and abetting a criminal suspect. If you're hiding your father, you're guilty of obstruction of justice and can be prosecuted."

Jazz folded her arms. "I don't know where he is." But her eyes blinked rapidly. "And just because he has prior convictions for art theft does not mean that he robbed the High Museum. Has it occurred to you that he may have changed his ways? Retired from the business?"

Tony's mouth twisted. "Is it pure coincidence, Miss Taylor, that a legal search of his abandoned apartment turned up a Degas painting under his bed?"

Her face drained of color.

So that was news to her, was it? "You'll forgive me if I don't take your word for it—I'd like to have another look around."

"Sure," Jazz ground out. "I'll give you a detailed personal tour. There's no one here but . . . my assistant and me." She led the way to a small room in the back, first. It was lined floor-to-ceiling with mirrors. A grimy pink-vinyl salon chair leaned a bit drunkenly before a long countertop, cluttered with tackle boxes full of cosmetics, strange tubes and vials, wigs, brushes, rags, and God knew what else.

Tony raised his eyebrows and took it in silently, shaking his head. "Where's the bathroom?"

Jazz shrugged and pointed. "Right in there."

He crossed the room purposefully and opened the door. The tiny room smelled of disinfectant . . . and a waft of something else. Tony inhaled deeply. Yes, there it was again. Men's aftershave, and a hint of cigar smoke. He scanned every inch of the bathroom, from the dusty top of the over-commode linen cabinet to the grout between the hexagonal tiles.

The window was slightly cracked, and that's where Tony found what he was looking for: a cigar butt, trapped between the screen and the wooden frame. *Cuban*, he noted. *Extraordinary quality.*

He fought the fierce urge to put it to his lips and suck the remaining tobacco essence out of it. *You can't take a drag on the evidence, no matter how hard it is to quit.*

Tony sighed and removed a plastic bag from his pocket. He scooped the butt into it, careful not to leave his own prints, then shoved the bag into his jacket pocket. He stepped out of the bathroom, his face blank. "Do you smoke, Ms. Taylor?"

"No." Jazz looked at him sharply. "Why?"

"Just hoping to bum a cig off you, that's all."

"You're out of luck, sorry."

"And your assistant? Does she?"

Jazz shook her head firmly. "No."

Her posture was militant, her little feet slightly apart, arms folded across her chest. She was paint-spattered, but adorable—and she was damned well hiding her father. Where was he?

"That's all on this floor. I'll take you upstairs," Jazz told him.

Tony could still smell the tantalizing cigar smoke, and his pocket almost physically itched as he followed his reluctant guide up a flight of un-

painted wooden stairs and into the loft that
served as her office. It was an airy room with a
small skylight, and Jazz had hung brightly
framed renderings of her projects on two walls.

Jazz stopped stock-still, and Tony ran into the
back of her with a muttered apology. Though
slight, she was full of unexpected curves, and he
smelled her sweet, woodsy shampoo again.

She hesitated, then waved her hand toward the
desk in the rear, and the large, middle-aged
woman with frizzy hair who sat behind it. "My
assistant, M-Millie," she said nonchalantly. "She
helps me with everything from accounts receiv-
able to electronics. Millie, this is Mr. Sinclair,
APD."

Tony had to bite his tongue, hard. *This* was the
man Aunt Ellen was involved with? He didn't
know whether to laugh or cry.

The figure reminded him of Klinger, from the
old *M*A*S*H* series on television. He could feel
nervous tension radiating from Jazz's small figure beside him, and once again his protective instincts surfaced—he didn't know why.

"Millie" simpered at him. "Charmed, Mr. Sinclair." She batted her lashes.

Tony scanned the makeup job Jazz had done
on her father, and was impressed. Only the jaw-

line was the same as in the police photo of the ascot-clad Taylor he'd snagged from his partner.

With no time to pluck eyebrows or glue on fleshlike appliances, she'd softened her father's angular face by gathering curls around it, smoothed his skin with natural-looking foundation, and plumped his narrow lips with one of those hideous purple shades now in vogue. If this was what she could accomplish in a few minutes, Jazz must be a wizard given two hours.

Tony glanced unobtrusively down at Millie's crossed legs and prim pumps peeking from under the desk. Yep, about two inches of curly black hair between hemline and ankle. Just one of those little details it was hard to take care of in five minutes.

Tony kept his face expressionless. "Game's over, Myles. You're looking lovely enough to take downtown, so let's go." He spared a glance for Jazz. The corners of her mouth drooped, and the big brown eyes were downcast.

"I beg your pardon, sir?" Millie, playing it to the hilt, put a hand to her breast. "I don't go anywhere with strange gentlemen. 'Tisn't safe these days. For all I know, you have dastardly designs on my—"

"Virtue?" Tony finished dryly. "What little you ever had, Myles, has long since evaporated."

"How dare you, sir!"

"Don't insult my intelligence, Myles—and spare your daughter any further embarrassment. Let's go—both of you."

Chapter 3

"**B**OTH OF US?" MYLES DROPPED HIS LADYLIKE, falsetto tones.

"Yes," maintained Tony.

Jazz and her father spoke simultaneously.

"But she's innocent!"

"But he's innocent!"

"He's retired, Sinclair," Jazz continued. "He had nothing to do with the robbery, as I told you. And the people who did it are after him; they want to kill him." She put a pleading hand on Tony's sleeve.

Tony went very still, and his breathing quickened.

Jazz felt a zing of unexpected pleasure at the contact. Sinclair's pulse beat a strong tempo un-

der the damp cotton, and heat from his skin radiated into her palm. What would it be like to touch
him without the barrier of his shirt?

She snatched her hand away, and Tony cleared
his throat.

"I find it hard to believe that Myles is innocent
when you've gone to all this trouble to disguise
him from me."

"But—"

"And if there are assassins after him," Tony
added smoothly, "you'll both be very reassured
by the steel bars that will protect him down at the
station."

Jazz had no comeback to this piece of reasoning.

Neither, it seemed, did Myles. He stood up,
minced across the floor in his high heels and
polka-dotted dress, and offered his wrists to Tony.

"Manacle me, then, but spare my daughter!
The poor child was only acting out of loyalty."
His voice resonated with melodrama.

Tony eyed him with distaste. "I'm fresh out of
handcuffs at the moment, Myles. I'll have to rely
on your inability to run in spike heels."

Myles looked put out for a moment, then
shrugged philosophically.

"As for you," Tony turned to Jazz, "I warned
you of the consequences of aiding and abetting a
fugitive."

She nodded. She wanted to kill Myles for getting her into this—but she couldn't really blame Sinclair for doing his job.

As they drove silently in the Taurus for a while, Jazz closed her eyes to think. She had to find a way to clear Myles, and she would have a very tough time doing that from jail. Could she escape? She wondered what her chances of survival were if she opened the car door and rolled out onto Interstate 75. Nil. If she didn't die on impact, she'd be flattened into roadkill by the other speeding cars.

What were her other options? Not for the first time, Jazz wished she'd been blessed with bodacious, melonlike breasts and long, golden gams that could wrap 'round a man like a python and make him gasp for mercy.

She sighed. Her breasts were more the size of limes; her legs were in proportion to her five-foot-two-inch frame, and they were milky white to boot. Sleazy seduction in the name of freedom was probably out of the picture.

The only way out of this situation was an articulate appeal to Tony Sinclair's sense of justice.

Hah. Cops, in her experience, followed the letter of the law, which often had nothing to do with fairness. Procedure was king, with justice just a vague cloud on the periphery.

A vague cloud was drifting from Myles's side of the backseat to hers, but it didn't smell like justice. It reeked of tobacco, very fine tobacco. He had lit up a fancy cigar, which dangled between his Plum Pleasure-coated lips.

At a strangled sound from the front seat, Jazz met Sinclair's cop blue eyes in the rearview mirror. They were narrowed and furious. His hands had white-knuckled on the steering wheel.

"Taylor," he growled, "do you mind?"

"Not at all, Sinclair." Myles passed the cigar forward. "Like a puff, would you?" He crossed one hairy leg over the other and leaned back comfortably. Jazz averted her eyes from the sight.

Tony swerved onto the shoulder of the road and screeched to a halt. He flung himself out of the car and ground the cigar under the heel of his shoe.

Myles squawked in outrage. "That was Cuban!"

"Shut *up*," Jazz hissed at her father.

Tony stalked back to the car and got in, slamming the door shut.

"Bloody hell, Sinclair! That was a twenty-dollar

stogie!" Myles's rhinestone earrings vibrated in offense.

"Don't I know it." The rearview mirror reflected a look of pain on Tony's rugged features.

"Then why—"

"Unless you want to die painfully in the next three seconds, don't smoke in my car," he ground out. "I'm trying to quit."

"Police brutality!" howled Myles.

Jazz clapped a hand over her father's mouth, and again hissed into his ear. "Stop it right now! Let me handle this, or you'll rot in jail for a crime you didn't commit. Do you understand?"

Myles nodded, and she released him. "Mr. Sinclair," she began.

"Tony," said Tony.

"Okay." Jazz took a deep breath. "I know I misrepresented the situation to you, but I didn't actually 'abet' my father. I only disguised him. It's not the same thing at all."

"How do you figure that?"

Jazz was encouraged that he would even enter a dialogue on the subject. She smiled eagerly. "Well, it didn't aid him at all. You recognized him right away."

"No thanks to you."

"Actually, what I did was hobble him for you,

with the spike heels, so he couldn't run away. You pointed that out yourself."

"I did," Sinclair admitted.

Jazz's heart pumped hard in her chest. She was making some headway. "So, I didn't aid or abet a fugitive, according to the strict letter of the law."

"You told me you hadn't seen your father in a year."

"That was true. I hadn't—until an hour ago, when he showed up at the studio."

"Did you know he was coming?"

"Well, yes," Jazz said. "But you didn't ask me that."

Tony frowned into the rearview mirror.

"So technically, you have no real reason to take me to jail."

"You're splitting hairs, Ms. Taylor."

"Jazz. And yes I am. But lawyers do it every day—they win or lose cases just on verbal hairsplitting. And I'm sure my lawyer would win this, if you want that hassle." She held her breath.

Tony drove in silence for a while. He rubbed his jaw.

"Well?" Jazz pressed him.

"I think it's a question of intent," he said.

"That's an assumption on your part. Assumptions have no place in this argument. We're talking about actions, here—whether I aided and abetted. And besides, Myles is innocent. How do you expect me to prove that if I'm sitting in jail with him?"

"I see your point."

"Excellent. Then you'll let me go."

"No."

"Why *not*?"

"Because I think your father is in this up to his ascot-wrapped neck, so I'd hate to see you expend any further effort upon his behalf."

"I'm innocent until proven guilty!" interjected Myles.

Sinclair cast him a look of contempt. "Did I mention that you have the right to remain silent?"

"No. And I would argue that it's really a wrong disguised as a right—"

"Exercise it," Sinclair commanded.

Myles sniffed, folded his arms, and gazed sullenly out the window.

Jazz relaunched her attack. "What you believe, Tony, is really immaterial. Myles is my father, and I intend to prove he had nothing to do with the High Museum burglary. Wouldn't you help your own father in this situation?"

Sinclair gave a short bark of laughter. "Believe me, it would never have arisen."

Jazz stiffened. "Oh, is he such a saint, then?"

"Yes. He was."

She eyed the back of Tony's head, curious. His neck and shoulders were rigid, and his mouth in the rearview mirror was set in an uncompromising line.

"Your father's no longer living? I'm sorry." Jazz couldn't imagine life without Myles, even with all of his eccentricities. She turned to look at him as a honk sounded, and a Mack truck drew up next to his side of the car. Its driver leered down at her father, licking his lips suggestively.

Myles blew him a kiss.

Jazz closed her eyes. *Life would certainly be less embarrassing without Myles.* "What did your father do, Tony?"

"He was a cop. A great cop. He was shot on a bust when I was eight."

"I'm so sorry," Jazz repeated softly.

The shoulders in front of her shrugged. "It was a long time ago."

"That doesn't make it any less painful." Jazz thought of her mother, who'd been gone since she was six. "It's hard to live up to a saint."

Tony's blue eyes met hers in the mirror. "You have no idea," he said, and looked away.

"You'd be surprised." Jazz bit her lip as her mother's beautiful face appeared to her, lines of forgiveness accentuating the huge hazel eyes.

Memories of her childhood washed over her as the car sped down the highway. She recalled going to visit Myles in jail, and talking to him through a pane of glass. Showing her latest drawings to him for his approval. Asking Mama if Papa was a bad person, and if not, then why was he in jail? Mama said sometimes even good people did misguided things. Things that weren't right. And then they had to pay for them. Jail was for grown-ups what time-out was for kids, Mama explained.

Jazz wondered if it had really been mortification that had killed her, not cancer. "Your father is a good man," Mama had emphasized before she'd died. "He's a good man, darling."

"Then why do people say he's a thief?" Jazz had asked.

Her mother had hesitated. "He *is* a thief, honey. And I want you to promise that you will never, ever steal anything yourself."

"I promise," Jazz had told her. "But why does Papa steal things?"

"Papa," her mother sighed, "has a mistaken notion that he has to replace the heritage I lost when I married him. My parents cut me out of their will the day I became Papa's wife."

"What's a will?" Jazz asked.

"Ah. Now that's a very important question. A will, my darling, is what gets you through life. It's your reason for being. But many people think it's a piece of paper that guarantees you material things, like money."

"So there are two kinds of wills?"

"That's right. And the more important kind is the one you can't see—you can only feel it."

"Oh. But Papa thinks the other kind is important, too?"

"Yes, but it's not. Remember that."

Jazz came back to the present as Tony switched lanes to exit the freeway. Mama had been a saint, never losing patience with Myles as Jazz did. She tried to remember when she'd stopped calling him "Papa." When had embarrassment taken over and made it necessary for her to create distance between them? Probably the second time he'd gone to jail—when the police and social worker had taken her to live with Grandmother Sophronia in the huge house that smelled like mothballs and disinfectant. Jazz had wailed and hollered, and her grandmother had looked as if she wanted to do so as well, but was too proper. The police weren't very sympathetic to either of them.

Jazz balled her hands into fists as Sinclair pulled the Taurus up in front of a big, ugly, concrete building and unbuckled his seat belt. She wasn't going to wail or holler to this guy—but she was going to change his mind, if it killed her.

"Look," she began, "before you condemn us both, hear me out."

Sinclair turned in the seat, albeit reluctantly. Folding his arms on the headrest, he waited for her to continue.

"Myles is innocent, and I'm the only one who believes him. Give me a week to prove it—to at least build a case for him. If I haven't by then, I'll turn myself in, and you can charge me with aiding and abetting him."

Sinclair's lips twisted. "You must think I'm very gullible."

"No," Jazz said. "I think you might be fair-minded." She gazed at his strong jaw, sensual mouth, the dark shadow of razor stubble over his cheeks and cleft chin. He had smooth chestnut hair that she'd love to tousle a bit. Eyes the color of a midnight sky in Georgia.

She shook herself. His eyes, for God's sake, were also the color of a police uniform. The color she'd hated since she was a child. What was the matter with her?

"Fair-minded," repeated Sinclair. "What's my guarantee that you'll show up in a week?"

"You have my word on it."

He laughed.

Jazz folded her arms defensively. "What's wrong with that?" She tried not to notice how attractive his eyes were when they crinkled in amusement.

"Jazz, you are the daughter of a renowned criminal."

"He's a thief, not a liar!"

"Ah, so you admit he's a thief."

"No! He's retired."

"Indeed I am," put in Myles. "And when I was in the business, I was an honest thief."

Tony put his head into his hands, his shoulders shaking. "An honest thief? What exactly do you mean by that?"

Myles's brows knit together for a moment, then his forehead cleared. "I mean that I was a candid thief. Will that do?" His eyes twinkled.

Tony shook his head. "Candid or not, I don't believe you've retired. What are you living on? You don't exactly qualify for social security, Myles."

His prisoner reddened slightly. "Well, you see—"

"I support him," said Jazz. "He gets an allowance."

"Which is a little disgraceful," her father was quick to point out, "so I've got to get married."

Tony became dangerously still. "Is that so."

"Marriage to a wealthy woman is the only solution," Myles declared. "And Ellen won't accept my proposal unless I've retired for good. So, you see, I have."

Tony stared at him in ominous silence.

"Someone's got to pay for my polo lessons," Myles reasoned.

"Has it ever occurred to you to get a job?" Tony asked.

Jazz shook her head at him.

"Oh," said her father airily, "I'm simply not cut out for employment."

Tony snorted and turned to Jazz. "That's it. Even if he didn't rob the High Museum, he deserves to be in jail."

"But wait! He does love Ellen. It's not just the money."

"Well, it was at first," Myles pointed out.

Sinclair's face darkened.

"*Shut up*," Jazz told her father.

"I'm simply being candid. When I married your mother, my dear, it was all for love. I didn't give a damn about her money. When I met Ellen, I'd deliberately sought her out for the money, but then I fell in love. It's poetic justice, that's all."

"Do you know why I started to check you out, Taylor?" Sinclair asked in lethal tones.

"Because of the burglary," Myles replied.

"No. Because Ellen Whitaker Northrop Banks is my aunt. She raised me. You are scum, Taylor, and I intend to make sure you don't marry her. Got it?"

Cold tension circulated throughout the car, rendering the air-conditioning unnecessary.

After a long silence, Jazz cleared her throat. "We're getting sidetracked from the main issue, here. You may not approve of my father, Sinclair, but you don't have any major problem with me. Give me a week. I swear to you I'll show up again. Please, give me a chance to prove that Myles didn't rob the High Museum."

Tony looked at her, long and hard. She could feel him assessing her, trying to decide whether or not he could trust her word.

She met his gaze steadily.

Just when she knew for certain he wouldn't

fold, just as a wave of desperation threatened to subsume her, an expression of helpless frustration crossed his face, and he closed his eyes for a moment. "Okay." He sighed. "A week."

Chapter 4

SINCE SHE WAS WITHOUT FLOOZIE, HER BAT-tered VW van, Jazz rode MARTA, Atlanta's mass transit system, back to the northern suburbs where she worked. From the MARTA station, she took a cab to the arts complex, folding and unfolding the twenty-dollar bill Tony Sinclair had pressed on her to pay for the ride.

"If you don't take it," he'd sworn, "I'll burn it with my lighter."

"You can't pay for my cab!"

"Yes, I can. I hauled you down here."

"Look, Sinclair, I've got my own money—"

"I don't see a purse on you."

It was true. In the confusion, she'd forgotten it

in the studio. "Well, then, Myles will give me cab fare." Jazz turned to him, but he shook his head regretfully.

"All washed up, my love."

She sighed in exasperation. "You've got twenty-dollar cigars on you, but no cash?"

"The stogie fit nicely into my bra," Myles explained. "Very handy contraptions, these things. Pinch like the devil, though. The girdle's even more beastly. Cuts off the bloody circulation altogether."

"Tough," Jazz retorted unsympathetically. "We women have cut off our circulation, twisted our spines, clogged our pores, and been painfully plucked for hundreds of years so that we could compete with guns, horses, cars, and now television, for men's attention."

Sinclair was openly laughing. "You forgot the Internet."

"That, too," Jazz fulminated. "I should have done a wax job on your legs for good measure, Myles."

Her father looked alarmed, and stepped closer to Tony. "Malice is unbecoming, my love. Go back to your studio, then—forget about your noble sire. I will do penance in a girdle for the male sex. I will be the sacrificial goat upon the altar of Female Vengeance. I will pen an official apology, an ode to the women of the world. But spare me! Do not wax my legs."

"Are you finished?"

"It rather depends upon your answer."

"Myles, come here."

He dodged behind Tony. "I demand police protection."

"What a change of heart," Sinclair said dryly.

"Myles, I just want to kiss you good-bye. I may not see you for a while."

"Well, why didn't you say so?" He popped out and proffered his rouged cheek.

Jazz pecked it. "Now you behave yourself, do you hear? Otherwise, I'll have to cut your allowance."

Myles nodded meekly, and Tony snorted in disgust. "Come on, let's get you inside." He grasped her father by the polka-dotted arm and hauled him to the glass doors of the station.

Jazz met those cop blue eyes as Sinclair threw a last glance her way. "I expect to hear from you in exactly seven days," he called. "Don't make me come after you."

A shiver ran down her spine. What would it be like, to have a man like Tony Sinclair come after her? It just might be exciting. Especially if he came after her with no shirt over his obviously broad shoulders and muscled torso. What if he searched for her with no shoes on, either, and just the top button undone of some nicely faded 501's . . . ? Oooh, mama. Why hide?

Jazz blinked. She was mentally undressing the cop who was throwing her father in jail. She was a sick, twisted woman.

She looked down again at the twenty-dollar bill Sinclair had given her. What kind of cop gave an offender a week of freedom and cab fare home? He sure wasn't like any other police officer she'd ever met.

It wasn't that the ones from her past had been cruel, but they'd always represented a loss of freedom, whether it was her father's or her own. They'd just been caught up in procedure. They followed the letter of the law.

Jazz remembered one policeman who'd been very kind. He'd brought her a teddy bear when they took Myles away. But then he took her to Grandmother Sophronia's house.

Grandmother had tried to throw the bear away, stating that it was infested with germs and fleas. When Jazz sobbed for it, Grandmother held the bear gingerly by its ear tag and hosed it down with disinfectant before returning it to her. After that, it didn't smell right. Jazz missed the imaginary germs and fleas.

The cab finally arrived at the arts complex, and Jazz smoothed the accordion folds out of Andrew Jackson's face. She gave Andy to the cabbie and told him to keep the change.

Sinclair led Myles to a plastic chair in the bustling station and commanded him to sit. He glanced quickly around to make sure Captain Rathburn wasn't in sight, and then approached the desk officer, Johnson.

"Hey, Ted."

Johnson's eyes flashed surprise and condemnation before he disguised both behind his habitual bland expression. "Sinclair."

Other officers stared and snickered before turning back to their business. Tony ignored them. "Give Sneller a buzz for me, will you, and tell him to meet me out front." With a warning glare at Myles, he exited the station and waited for his partner, wishing fiercely for a cigarette.

A couple of minutes passed before the doors opened. Everything about Eugene "Bagel" Sneller was round and doughy. He had veins full of yeast circulated by a cream-cheese heart—Tony was certain of it.

His myopic eyes blinked behind small round

spectacles, which periodically slipped down his button of a nose. Two whole-wheat bagels dangled from Sneller's set of cuffs, and no less than five silver squeeze packets of Philadelphia spread gleamed from his waistband.

"You're a brave man, Sinclair," he opined.

"Captain Rathburn's still on the warpath, eh?"

"I'll say. How the hell'd you get mixed up with his daughter?"

Tony ground his teeth. "I didn't."

"Uh-huh."

"Sneller, you know me better than that. I wouldn't even look at a seventeen-year-old girl!"

"How'd it happen, then?"

Tony expelled a long, frustrated breath. It would feel good to get it off his chest. "I'm sitting there filling out forms, and I notice I'm out of paper clips. So I go to the supply closet, open it, and there she is! One teenage tramp in a G-string. She slicks her tongue around her lips and reaches for me. I slam the door on her and run."

Bagel's eyes had gotten impossibly rounder, and his mouth had fallen open.

"I go for some coffee, and then return to my office, thinking the coast is clear. I sit down at my desk, and damn it if she's not under there. I realize it when she unzips my pants! I yelp in surprise and jolt upright just when Captain Daddy walks in. What would you have done, Sneller? Huh?" Tony opened and closed his fists in agitation.

"Okay, man, calm down. That's bad, very bad." His partner shook his head. "I don't know what I would have done." He unlocked a bagel from his cuffs and pulled a packet of cheese from his holster. "Here, take this. It'll make you feel better."

Tony shook his head. "No thanks." His stomach was in knots just thinking about the whole fiasco.

Bagel shrugged and twisted off a chunk of the bread, squeezing some cheese onto it. "So the girl ambushed you, huh."

"Yeah," Tony said in disgust. "Miss Lolita's had some kind of crush on me for months. I used to help her with her math homework when she'd come to the station, but when I figured it out, I tried to avoid her. I guess she looked up my schedule."

"I never saw it this way before," Bagel said around a mouthful, "but I guess I'm glad I'm not a stud-muffin like you." He chewed reflectively and pushed his glasses up his nose. "Don't look disgusted like that. It's true. You got the dimples, the macho build. The chicks dig you."

Tony shifted in discomfort. "It's a damned nuisance. I've got to get my career back on track, and that won't be easy with the captain wanting my head on a pike—not to mention my nuts in a jar."

He put a hand on Bagel's shoulder. "In the meantime, I need you to do me a favor. There's a character wearing a dress in there, name of Myles Taylor."

Sneller choked. "The thief? Guy we've been looking for in connection with the High burglary?"

"The same. I brought him down, but do me a favor and book him. I don't want to run into Rathburn right now." He began to explain the details.

Bagel interrupted with an exclamation. "Disgusting!" He looked down at the chunk of bread he'd just broken off. "Someone threw a cigarette butt into the dough. I almost ate it."

Tony's nose twitched. "Here—give me that."

"What are you doing?" Bagel's nose wrinkled as Tony inhaled the ashy, smoky scent in the bread. "You're sick, you know that?"

Tony grimaced at him. "You have your habit, and I have mine. Except you're not trying to quit. It's been twenty-two days, eleven hours and twenty-one minutes since I last had a cigarette."

"Yeah? Well, don't even think about lighting

up that bagel. I want it as evidence, to get my money back."

Sinclair relinquished the bagel reluctantly. "Fine. I've gotta get out of here before Rathburn sees me, but I'll be in touch."

Chapter 5

*J*AZZ ENTERED THE WAREHOUSE AND DUG IN her pocket for her key as she walked down the familiar dusty hallways. When she reached her studio, however, she realized she wouldn't be needing the key.

The metal door sported heavy dents where it had been kicked by boots, and it stood open about three inches. Her heart slammed against her ribs and Jazz stood stock still, unable to breathe for a moment. Then she took a deep gasp and the air returned to her lungs in a mini-tornado, swirling with shock.

Run. Hide. See who it is. Her brain issued a series of conflicting orders. *Think. Kill the jerks. How dare they?* For a fleeting moment, she wished for a big, strong protective man to take care of the situation. Someone like Tony Sinclair.

Then she was furious at herself. What was she thinking? Forget about the blue-eyed beefcake. She had to take charge of this problem, and now.

Chances were that whoever was in her studio was after Myles, and when they didn't find him, they would leave. This had nothing to do with her.

Jazz heard rustling inside, and she crept closer, making out two different voices.

"Dang!" one articulated. "Women always keep strange stuff in their handbags, but if this chick don't beat all."

They were going through her purse. Jazz clenched her hands into fists.

"What's she got in there, a tampon?"

"Naw, that ain't nothin'. This is somebody's nose, Pug! Gives me the creeps."

"Lemme see that. Aw, Bones, it's made outa rubber, like that dog poop from Hong Kong."

"I don't care what it's made of. It's sick. What kinda chick walks around with a nose in her pocketbook? Oh-ma-Gawd. This here's a ear. I don't like this one bit. This woman's po-sessed by the devil!"

"Don't be gettin' your shorts in a wad. Lemme see the ear."

"Look, it's pointed at the top. D'you think she done sliced it, like that Van Go guy? Chick's got a chain saw over yonder, an' plenty o' knives. Check out them swords up there."

"Naw, I'm tellin' ya, it's fake, just like that big old dragon. She uses all this stuff for movies. Dresses up people just like Halloween."

"Halloween's for devil-worshipers, too. I don't like this one bit. Let's get outta here."

"We gotta find it first. It's here. He takes it everywhere he goes, and he was here."

Jazz inched the door open gradually and peeked inside. What were they looking for?

The man with her purse was a lanky, greasy weasel in brown-polyester Sans A Belt pants, Hush Puppies, and a string tie. The other was a human pot roast with a fringe of grayish blond curls around his head and a double chin. His black trousers cleared the tops of his shoes by a good two inches, revealing mismatched socks.

Jazz frowned. These guys were stooges. She didn't appreciate them breaking into her studio or rummaging through her purse, but it sounded as if they could be useful in proving her father innocent. The problem was, there were two of them, and however dorky their appearances, they were still bigger than she.

If only she could reach Donovan's control levers. She crouched by the large worktable just inside the door and kept an eye on the thugs.

"Let's go through the stuff on that counter," Pug the pot roast said. He ambled over to the pink salon chair and began sweeping things off the surface in front of the mirror.

"I'm tellin' you, man, I don't have a good feeling," whined the skinny stooge, Bones.

Jazz crawled under the worktable, inching herself along on her belly.

"Look at this! Girl's a devil-worshiper and a prevert. She's made a mold of a woman's backside." Bones held up the offending object and licked his lips nervously.

Jazz wriggled past an old credenza she used for storage and got to the corner where the studio controls were hidden by a large screen.

"Nothin' over here," Pug announced. "I'm gonna head up those stairs. Looks like there might be an office up there."

Good, that gets you out of the way for a minute. Jazz worked Donovan's control levers slowly, and brought the dragon's head around.

Bones whirled at the slight noise and gaped.

Jazz had maybe three seconds before she lost her advantage. She sent the dragon's head hurtling forward, hoping to pin the man against the wall, but adrenaline had her overcompensating, and Donovan's nose slammed into Bones's forehead, instead of his chest. He dropped like a stone.

Jazz clapped a hand over her mouth. Oh God! Had she killed the poor man?

Pug popped his head out of her office. "I found it! Huh? What the heck-fire?" He looked down the stairs at his cohort's motionless body. As he huffed his way down, Jazz knew this would be her only chance. She shot Donovan's head forward again.

The pudgy man dived down the rest of the stairs, his eyes wide with terror.

"Oh, Lord, what are you doing to me? The d-d-dragon's come alive. How is that possible, Lord?" He cowered against the wall.

Jazz worked another lever and Donovan's long red tongue flicked out. He roared and rolled his eyes.

Pug screamed as Donovan approached to sniff him. "Lord, save me!"

Jazz choked on a mad giggle, but it continued to rise in her throat until she collapsed helplessly in laughter. She heard Pug pick himself up and bellow with outrage. Then his heavy footsteps hurtled toward her hiding place.

Quick! She needed a weapon. She grabbed the first thing within reach—her nail gun.

Pug reached the screen and threw it aside. He lunged at her before he could stop himself, and the head of the gun sank into his soft belly. His war cry died in his throat.

"Hi there," said Jazz. "I won't say I'm pleased to meet you, but I *would* like to know why you're here."

Pug's eyes bulged.

"Oh, come now. If you can talk to the Lord, you can talk to little old me."

He produced a sickly grin, but no explanation.

"Did you know," Jazz told him conversationally, "that this is one of the most powerful nail guns made? It drives three-and-a-half-inch nails instantly into pressure-treated wood."

"That ain't plugged in," Pug quavered, finally finding his voice.

"It doesn't need to be. It's fuel-cell-operated. Would you like me to prove it? I can start by nailing your intestines to your spine."

"No! Okay, lady, I believe you. Don't hurt me."

"Tell me why you're here."

Pug's thick tongue licked his lips. "To, uh, sign up for some drawing lessons?"

Jazz raised her brows. "You're a terrible liar." She heard his companion groan and flicked him a glance. "You," she ordered Pug, "go stand by the wall. I need to check on him." She backed the nail gun out of his fleshy midsection and gestured with it.

He did as he was told, Jazz following close behind. "Raise your arms," she ordered. When he'd done so, she carefully nailed his waistband and the pocket flap of his trousers to a crossbeam, immobilizing him.

Then she hurried over to Bones. She put two fingers against his inner wrist and found the pulse was there, faint but steady. She sighed in relief.

Now, how could she ensure that neither of them got away until she could get Sinclair back here? She thought quickly, then dug through various cabinets until she found an old green cleaning bucket. She filled it a third of the way full with water, and then dumped a bag of Quik-Dry Plaster into it and stirred.

When the chemical reaction made it warm, she clamped the nail gun under her arm and hauled the heavy bucket over to the prone form of Bones. Jazz set it near his feet and removed his shoes, wrinkling her nose at the resultant odor.

She cast a glance at Pug. "Don't you move an inch."

He glared at her, saying nothing.

Jazz set down the nail gun, grabbed a jar of Vaseline, and coated Bones's feet and calves. Then she folded his legs at the knees, and plunked one foot, then the other, into the bucket of warm plaster. He moaned and turned his head slightly, but that was all.

Jazz jerked her head up as she heard the rip of fabric, and then heavy feet running for the door. Pug was hauling it for freedom, exhibiting his Porky Pig boxers through the holes in his pants.

"Stop or I'll shoot!" she bluffed.

Pug scrambled for the doorknob, and hurtled out of the studio.

"Damn!" She'd lost a hostage, and he'd probably taken the "it" they had come to find. She narrowed her eyes. That meant "it" was small enough to slip into a pocket.

She knew it wasn't money, because Myles usually ran through his substantial allowance within the first week he received it, and had been known to squeeze her for more.

Drugs? No. Myles had many faults, but substance abuse wasn't one of them. Jazz continued to mull it over as she retrieved her cordless phone and Tony's business card.

Bones moaned again. Jazz rolled up a towel and slid it under his head before dialing the cellular number.

* * *

Sinclair slid his prescription to the pharmacist across the red laminate. "I need a box of Nicorette, please." He was feeling almost physically ill from craving nicotine.

The clerk took the paper from him and turned to the white-metal shelves behind the counter. Tony drummed his fingers and looked to the right.

Beyond a vast array of condoms in all colors and sizes, a colorful display of hemorrhoid creams, and assorted feminine protection, there was another pharmacy window. A lady in pink jogging pants and a "Hello, Kitty" T-shirt walked up to it, placed her order, and nodded at him politely. Tony nodded back.

His clerk and the one who'd apparently been waiting on "Hello, Kitty" returned from the back of the shelves, arguing in low voices. Tony pricked up his ears.

"Well, technically he was here first," his clerk said.

"Yeah, but I've never seen him before, and Mrs. Ogden is a regular customer."

"Are you sure we didn't get a shipment in today?"

"Yeah, I checked. Nothing back there."

"Is there a problem?" Tony asked.

"Well . . ." the clerks looked at each other. "We

only have one box of Nicorette left in stock, and you're both asking for it."

Tony looked at Mrs. Ogden and shot her an apologetic smile. "Technically," he repeated, "I was here first."

Mrs. Ogden's face fell. "Oh, but sir—I really, really need it."

Tony shifted from foot to foot uncomfortably. His head was pounding, and his fingers itched for a cigarette. "I do, too."

"Sir, I don't want to get personal here, but if I don't quit smoking, my husband has threatened to leave me. I've *got* to have this box of Nicorette."

Tony closed his eyes.

"You wouldn't want to contribute to wrecking a marriage, would you, sir?"

He shook his head. What could he do? She was throwing herself upon his mercy. *But if I don't get this prescription filled this instant, I'm going to commit a murder. This is the millennium. Mrs. Ogden and I have equal rights to Nicorette!* "I—" Tony began.

"Oh, *please*, sir."

Tony's cell phone began to shrill.

"Take it," he sighed. *Chivalry is going to be the death of me.* He pressed the TALK button. "Hello?"

*   *   *

"Sinclair!" Jazz exclaimed, as he answered. "It's me, Jazz Taylor."

He'd recognize her voice anywhere, though he'd only met her twice: it was sexy, but with a lilt that was at odds with her precise enunciation. "Your father's fine," he told her. "We got him a cell with a nonviolent offender."

"Great, thanks. I've got a small problem, here."

"What kind of problem?"

"He's about five-nine, 140 pounds, and sealed to the knees in a bucket of Quik-Dry Plaster."

"Come again?"

"Stringy little mustache, too."

"Jazz, what's going on?" he asked with exasperation.

"Two men broke into my studio looking for something that belongs to Myles. I knocked one out, and held the other prisoner with my nail gun, but he got away—and I think he stole whatever they were looking for."

"I'll be right there."

"I was hoping you'd say that." Jazz pressed the OFF button on her phone and turned to look at Bones, who moaned again.

"Are you all right?" She bent over him.

"My head . . ." he mumbled. "Oh, my head." He put a hand up to his temple and winced. "Have I been drinkin' agin', or did a dragon hit me?"

"A dragon hit you."

"Good. I mean—oh-ma-Gawd, I can't move my legs!"

"Well, no." Jazz said it almost apologetically. "You got plastered."

"You said I ain't been drinkin'."

"You haven't."

"I'm paralyzed!"

"In a manner of speaking."

Bones opened his eyes and saw her. Then he twisted and inspected the bucket in which his legs were trapped. "You're the she-devil what has the noses in her pocketbook!"

Jazz merely raised her brows.

"What you done to me?" he demanded.

"Why are you here?" she retorted.

"What you done to Pug?"

"Wouldn't you like to know." An evil idea took hold of her, and she grinned.

Bones's face went from greenish to white. "You killed him."

"No, I'm not a murderer."

Her hostage visibly relaxed.

"I prefer slow torture, myself."

"Huh?" He pushed himself up on his hands.

Jazz gave him a friendly smile and disappeared behind her plastic curtain. She popped out after a moment with a latex man's "gore"-encrusted hand, "chopped" at the wrist.

Bones screeched in terror and bolted upright in the bucket. "No-no-no-no-no! Oh, Pug, my best buddy. Oh, Gawd!"

"Why did you two break into my studio?"

"She-devil! Bride of Satan!"

She nearly rolled her eyes. God, he was stupid. "Call me whatever you want, Bones, but answer the question."

"Vampire!"

"Uggh." Jazz shuddered. "I draw the line at that. I have *not* drunk any of his blood."

Bones blinked at her and began to whimper.

Good grief—she hadn't meant to reduce the poor man to drooling, quivering Jell-O. "Look, Bones. I haven't really done anything to him."

His eyes bulged in their sockets, then rolled toward the truncated hand.

"It's not his, see?" Jazz extended it toward him, but he screamed again, threw his torso to the ground, and began to drag himself to the door.

"It's made out of latex!"

"Help!" Bones shrieked. "Get me out of here!"

"Rubber! It's only rubber!" Jazz went after him, since he had almost reached the exit.

Bones hauled himself up the doorframe, wrenched open the door, and fell straight into the arms of Tony Sinclair.

Chapter 6

"*G*OING SOMEWHERE?" ASKED TONY.

Bones began to blubber.

Tony drew his brows together and pushed him to arm's length. "Pull yourself together, man." He hauled Bones, bucket and all, back into the studio and sat him in the pink salon chair. Then he whirled to Jazz, his concern all for her. He grabbed her by the shoulders.

"Are you okay?"

"I'm fine," she told him, for all the world like she trapped burglars in her studio every day.

Tony lost himself in those sweet brown eyes of hers for a moment, then scanned the rest of her face and body. No scars or signs of trauma were visible, though her overalls were filthy from the knees down.

Her shoulders felt small and firm under his hands, and he wondered what the rest of her would feel like. That mouth—that angel's mouth of hers—smiled up at him.

"I think I did pretty well at taking care of myself." Her stance was even a bit cocky.

Tony scowled. "You should have gotten the hell out as soon as you saw them, and called me immediately. You put yourself in needless danger."

Jazz stiffened. "I take care of what's mine." She shrugged out of his grip. "Whether it's my father or my studio."

"You're a civilian, Jazz. You should let the police handle things like this."

"Pardon me, but all the police have ever done is make my life miserable!" she flared at him.

"I'm sorry to hear that. We're really on your side, though, when you're not trying to deceive us."

"Look, I called you, okay? Beefcake to the rescue."

"Hey!" Bones interrupted them. "Instead of arguing with her, you should arrest her. She cut off my buddy's hand!"

"Would you care to explain?" Tony asked Jazz.

"Here, catch."

Tony caught the rubber hand neatly, as if it were a softball. "Cool."

"I was using it as a . . . persuasion tactic."

"You little devil, you."

"She-devil," Jazz nodded. "Bride of Satan."

Tony laughed and rolled up his sleeves. "I've got much better interrogation methods than that."

Jazz eyed him nervously. Tony's tanned, muscular forearms spoke for his ability to knock, beat, squeeze, or pound a confession out of anyone silly enough to hold out on him.

He wasn't going to beat up Bones, was he? After all, she'd already done the man enough physical damage. "Uh, why don't I get us all some iced tea while we consider various questioning techniques."

Their hostage eyed her uneasily. "You'll poison it."

"No, I won't. I want to keep you alive, so you'll tell us why you're here. Now, do you want iced tea or not?"

Bones considered for a moment. "Sweet or unsweet?"

"Which would you prefer?"

"Sweet. Thanks for the 'orspitality."

"Anytime. It's the Southern way." Jazz went to

the battered old refrigerator in the back of her studio and retrieved a gallon jug of premixed tea. Only in the South could you buy it like milk in the grocery store.

She filled three tall glasses with ice cubes and tea, garnished them with mint leaves, then handed them around.

"Thanks," Tony said.

Bones just nodded at her while he gulped to the bottom of the glass. "Ahh."

"More?" Jazz held out the jug.

He held his glass out, and she filled it. She watched a pint slide past his bobbing Adam's apple.

"Now, we were about to discuss methods of interrogation. Tony, as the experienced person in this arena, why don't you start?"

Tony sat forward, his elbows on his knees. "Well, I have a number of techniques. Number one, Bones, is honesty. You can just tell us what we want to know. Why are you here?"

Bones just folded his arms and stared at him blandly.

"Okay, technique number two is to grab the suspect by his skinny string-bean throat, smash him against the wall, and ask the question again."

Bones's eyes grew round, and he gave Tony a

sickly smile. "You cain't do that if you're a cop. It's illegal."

"So is breaking and entering," said Tony. "Besides, I'm not on duty, and not here in an official capacity. I'm just here to help out a friend."

Bones gulped.

"But," Sinclair continued, "unnecessary violence has never been my style, and I'm sure that since you're such a friendly fellow, you'll tell us what we want to know."

"So what's technique number three?" Jazz was anxious to get things rolling.

"We can't use number three."

"Why not?"

"It only applies if the suspect is a woman. You seduce her, and then get the information through pillow talk afterward."

"That's pretty slimy," Jazz told him. "And it can't be sanctioned by the APD."

"Right on both counts." Tony grinned.

Jazz felt an outrage all out of proportion to her relationship with this cop. How could he do such a thing? What a scumbag. A low-down, dirty, belly-dragging—but very sexy—snake.

"I personally have never used technique number three," he announced. "But it's important to mention it."

Relief washed over her.

Bones belched. "Can I have some more iced tea?"

"Of course." Tony filled their prisoner's glass to the top again.

"Now we enter the realm of psychological techniques. There's simple badgering. There's the good cop/bad cop routine . . ." Tony droned on and on, until Jazz began to pace in frustration, and Bones started to squirm.

"Uh. I gotta pee."

Tony kept lecturing.

After a couple of more minutes, Bones said again, "I really gotta pee." He pressed a hand to his abdomen.

"There's a psychological give-and-take to interrogation," Tony said, ignoring Bones's announcement.

Jazz rolled her eyes. Who would have known that such a gorgeous guy was such an awful bore? "Tony," she broke in, "Bones has to go to the bathroom."

He turned, brows raised, and shot her a wicked look from those cop blue eyes. A look full of meaning. Then he droned on.

Jazz began to revise her opinion as she realized the pontificating-bore stuff was an act, meant to pass the time until Bones's need got so urgent that he broke down.

"Let me get you some more tea," she said sweetly to their hostage.

"Lady, what I really need is the john."

"The john, as you call it, is bolted to the floor. I'm so sorry, but I can't bring it to you." Jazz pushed the glass at him. "Here you are. Fresh mint leaves."

Bones held out for another few minutes. Then, his voice squeaky, he tried again. "Lady, please."

"You had no problem getting to the door before. Why can't you get to the bathroom?"

"That was adren—whatchamacallit—I was scared."

"Adrenaline?"

"Yeah, that. I can't move now. Lady, please, put me on that dolly you've got there in the corner."

Tony fixed her with his blue gaze again. "Don't you do any such thing, Jazz."

"I'll wet myself!"

"All you have to do," Tony told Bones, "is tell us what you and your friend were looking for. Then I'll let you go."

"I can't!"

"You can."

"The boss'll shoot me dead."

"Not if you don't tell him that you told us. Why would he ever have to know?"

"He'll find out."

Tony shrugged.

"Please, lady, bring me a coffee can! I ain't picky at this point."

"No coffee can."

"My back teeth is floatin'! Have mercy."

Jazz tried to look as merciless as possible, though she did feel sorry for him.

Tony went to the paint-spattered sink and turned on the faucet so that a trickle of water could be heard, splashing happily into a bowl and then running down the drain.

Bones's face turned yellow, and with a cry of anguish he howled, "All right! All right, I'll tell you. Sal sent us to get some little black book belongin' to Myles Taylor. A book o' people all over the world who ain't picky about where their art comes from."

"Sal? Sal Cantini?" Tony asked.

Bones nodded miserably. "Now, please!"

Tony retrieved the dolly, rolled it to the pink salon chair, and lifted Bones's bucket of plaster onto it. Then he wheeled the man into the bathroom, propped the seat up, and closed the door behind him.

He looked at Jazz and brushed his hands together. "That was pretty easy. Sang like a canary."

"Yeah, and I bet he pees like a racehorse. So who's Sal Cantini?"

"Sal specializes in racketeering, drug-dealing, and money laundering. His hobbies include pimping, murder, and the occasional round of golf."

"Why would a guy like that get into the art-theft business?"

"First of all, it's lucrative. Second, he may be trying to better himself and get out of the common-criminal arena."

Jazz put her head in her hands. "Are you saying he's a social climber?"

"Snobbery exists even in the underworld. Sal may want to show he's 'arrived,' and is ready to rub shoulders with a higher class of thief."

"A higher class of— For Pete's sake!"

"Yeah," said Tony. "Soon he'll be wearing ascots."

Jazz narrowed her eyes at him.

He looked all too innocent. "So, when Bones is finished in there, we need to see if he knows where the stash of art from the High Museum is being stored. I hope he's decided to talk to us."

"What if he clams up, now that he's peed?"

Tony grinned. "Ever made Ex-Lax brownies?"

Chapter 7

"MY PARTNER'S IN THE NEIGHBORHOOD, SO he'll take him downtown." Tony sat on Jazz's stairs with his hands loosely clasped over his knees after calling Bagel.

Jazz tried not to look at Tony's hands, so big and square and competent. She tried not to look at the tanned triangle of chest that the opening of his shirt revealed. And the more she tried not to look, the more some invisible magnet kept dragging her gaze back. Dark, springy hair curled against that forbidden triangle of . . . of *cop flesh*.

She reminded herself that he was a drone of the establishment. That he was the enemy. He had tossed her father into a cell, and he wanted to keep him there and block any future happiness

Myles might have with Ellen Whitaker Northrop Banks. What warped twist of fate had made him her nephew, for God's sake?

Sinclair gazed at her speculatively. "How do you think my aunt got tangled up with your father?" he asked.

"I resent your using the words 'tangled up.' "

"Well, he *is* a criminal, Jazz."

"Myles is not a criminal! I told you, he's been framed. What do you think Bucket Bozo is doing here? My father obviously wasn't working with *him*."

"Hey!" Bones objected.

They ignored him.

"There's no honor among thieves, Jazz. They double-cross each other all the time. Maybe Cantini—or your father—decided he wanted a higher cut of the profits."

"My father always preferred to work alone. Why would he suddenly decide to collaborate with a mob boss? It's not his style."

Tony shrugged. "How should I know? Look, it's the judge who's keeping him in jail, based on hard evidence like the Degas under his bed. All I did was turn him over."

"But you think he's guilty."

"I know he's guilty. And I intend to get to the

bottom of this and take his partners down with him."

"That's pretty arrogant of you, Sinclair. Arrogant and pigheaded, and wrong. You're just acting out a personal vendetta, because you don't want your aunt to marry him."

His eyes snapped; his jaw tightened. "Personal vendettas have no place in my police work. Has it occurred to you, little girl, that you're just being blind about your father? He's got a record as long as my arm, and he's been romancing a trustee of the museum for months. Wake up!"

At the words "little girl," Jazz had whirled around, advanced on him, and now pushed her face about two inches from his. "Don't you patronize me, you piece of beefcake. I know my father, and I know he's not lying."

Tony slid from the stairs and towered over her, eyes stormy. He'd opened his mouth, doubtless to say something chauvinist and cutting, when a vision in midnight blue strolled through the studio door. A very round vision.

"Officer Eugene Sneller," said the newcomer, snapping the tension. "Just call me Bagel."

Jazz scanned him from head to toe and blinked. No one could have been more aptly named. She raised her brows at the two whole-wheat bagels dangling from Sneller's set of cuffs.

Bagel beamed at her. "Breakfast of champions."

"Whatever happened to doughnuts?"

"So clichéd. Besides, there's no nutritional value in a doughnut, and you get a sugar low only minutes after you eat one. That could be dangerous on the job. Cops have to stay alert."

"I see." Jazz tucked her tongue into her cheek.

Bagel rubbed his pudgy hands together and turned to Sinclair. "How ya doin' there, big hombre?"

"Fine," growled Sinclair.

"And who do we have here, in the bucket?"

"That's your perp. Breaking and entering. I need you to take him downtown."

"Evidence?"

"Handy household crowbar, there in the corner. Boots should match any fiber in the dents on the door, where he and his cohort kicked it in. And there'll be prints, too—never saw any gloves on him."

"B and E, huh." Bagel looked around him with interest. "What was he trying to steal—the dragon? The aliens?"

"A little black book belonging to Myles Taylor, the guy I handed over to you this morning."

"I been held here aginst my will," Bones announced.

Bagel appeared unsympathetic. "Looks to me like a citizen's arrest. You've been detained pending arrival of the police."

"Cain't you get me outta here, now?"

"Yes. Put your hands behind your back." Bagel slipped another set of cuffs out of his pocket and locked them onto Bones's wrists. He turned to Jazz. "What's the best way to get him out?"

"It's just plaster," she told him. "We can lay him on his side and ease off the bucket, then crack the stuff with a hammer. It breaks easily."

Bones suffered the indignity gladly, wriggling his toes with relief when the plaster was off.

Jazz handed him his shoes and socks.

Sinclair glowered at him. "Is there anything else you want to say before Officer Sneller books you on a clear case of B & E? If you share helpful information leading to the arrests of your cohorts, the judge may be inclined to go easier on you."

"Look, I tole you I dunno where the pictures is stored. The only person might know that is a guy by the name of Rico Romanelli, who manages Hot Rockin' Mama's."

"The boys have been there," Jazz nodded. "It's a strip joint."

"The boys?" Sinclair asked.

"The crew that works for me on big projects—like Donovan. And theater sets, things like that."

"You certainly have a wide range of skills."

"It pays to be diverse in a small special-effects market like Atlanta. I do anything I have the skills and the time to do, provided it pays decently."

"I thought you had to be very specialized in FX work."

"In Los Angeles you do, but we've all got to start somewhere. If I can ever get Myles settled and independent, my plan is to move to LA and concentrate on makeup. It's what I most enjoy."

"It's been very interesting to meet you, Ms. Taylor," Bagel said, before guiding his charge outside.

"Ditto." Jazz shook her head as the two left, the whole wheats bouncing against Sneller's thigh.

"I owe you," Tony called after him.

"Yeah. Get me a dozen whole wheats and a six-pack of cream soda, and we'll call it even."

"Done."

Jazz raised her brows.

"Bagel's a good cop," said Sinclair. "He's just got a few idiosyncrasies."

"Sure. Well, I've got work to do. Thanks for coming to help." Jazz tried to look anywhere but at that triangle of male flesh at his collar. She ended up meeting his eyes, and to her surprise they seemed to reflect understanding and even sympathy. It made her as uncomfortable as his anger.

"Look," he said, "I know you'd like to believe your father's retired. I can't blame you for that—"

"He *is* retired, and I'll make you eat crow if it's the last thing I do. I plan to check out this guy at Hot Rockin' Mama's tonight and follow whatever leads he gives me."

As soon as the words were out of her mouth, she knew she'd made a mistake.

Sinclair's brows drew together. "You are *not* going to a strip bar on the southwest side of town at night by yourself."

"Oh, yes I am." She put her hands on her hips.

"Especially not to ask dangerous questions of a mobster's flunky."

"And who are you to give me orders?"

"It's not safe," he said simply.

"I'll be fine. It's a bar full of people, for God's sake."

"Yeah, a bar full of drunken louts in a seedy part of town."

"I can take care of myself."

"Out of the question. I'm coming with you."

"You're not invited."

Tony turned to leave. "I'll tail you there anyway."

"Sinclair, has anyone ever told you you're a real pain in the ass?"

He walked out the door. "I'll take that as a compliment."

Hot Rockin' Mama's sprouted off the highway like a hideous concrete mushroom. It flourished in the dark and fed off the dung of society.

The organic aspects of Mama's stopped there, for everything inside revolved around plastic. The smiles of the waitresses were shiny as plastic; the patrons paid for drinks and table dances with plastic; and the entertainment swelled in all the right places—thanks to the infusion of plastic.

Jazz had never been to a strip bar. While she was prepared to see scantily clad women, she was unprepared for the pulsing, prurient atmosphere. The place exuded a hungry fantasia of male desire, scented with a cacophony of cheap colognes and pure animal musk. And beer.

At her first sight of "the talent," a heavily made-up gyrating trophy, Jazz felt like an ironing board with hair. The woman had buttocks like huge ripe peaches, and cantaloupe breasts with strawberry nipples. When she shook her money-maker, she . . . well, she made money. Wads of it.

The cantaloupes and peaches bounced and shimmied their way over to groups of appreciative men, who decorated them with fringes of green bills.

Jazz studied the female fruit cocktail with a dispassionate eye. The woman had to spend at least six hours out of every twenty-four shaving. She probably dangled like a primate from gym equipment for another four hours each day. That still left her a few hours for washing and ironing that tiny majorette uniform that lay on the floor, touching up her roots, and perfecting her splits. By the time the poor thing got her makeup on and off, she doubtless had no opportunity for sleep.

To her surprise, Tony didn't seem enthralled by the fruit cocktail. When they took seats at a table near the back, he scanned the general layout of the place and the staff behind the bar.

Jazz was free to continue broadening her cultural horizons. The next act was set to "Jungle Boogie" from *Pulp Fiction*'s sound track. A wild-looking redhead emerged at the sound of the Chinese gong, and proceeded to do a number of creative things to the pole at center stage. She slid up it, down it, and twirled around it. She stroked it lewdly and ran her tongue down it. In a particularly dazzling maneuver, Red ripped off her shiny black micromini shorts and pleasured the air with her pelvis.

"Get down, get down," sang the chorus, while the lead vocalist exhorted the audience to "feel the funk now, let it slip low, grrrrrrrrrrrr! Unghh, oohhh, hhhbbbbbrrrrrrrrrggggggg." He made outboard-motor noises with his lips, which excited the crowd no end.

The noises seemed to excite Red, too, for she threw her head back, shaking her wild locks, and ripped open her fuzzy leopard-print vest to bare her magnificence. A table of fraternity guys howled, inciting her to squat in front of them and taunt them with her twin torpedoes. A short blond boy leaped up and honked a hooter. He was summarily removed by a burly bouncer.

The next act featured a pseudoseñorita in a short, flouncy green skirt, white Mexican peasant blouse, and red skyscraper heels. *Pure Velveeta*, Jazz thought. The woman wore a red hibiscus behind one ear and lost little time in shedding everything else. Jazz was filled with admiration for her ability to polish the floor with her derriere.

Though it was barely eight o'clock, at least forty guys sprawled, lounged, or sat bolt upright, riveted by the action. The sprawlers were generally young, early twenties to thirties. They sat with spread legs and downed countless beers. The loungers tended to be middle-aged, crossed an ankle over a knee, and ate vast quantities of phallic finger food. The uprighters were either very young or very old, and leaned forward with elbows on the tables, eyes unblinking, watching the erotic dancers with lascivious concentration.

Jazz found these guys the creepiest.

Tony watched her watch them, an odd expression on his face. "So what do you think?" he asked.

She shrugged. "I can't decide if these women hate or love what they do. Do they feel debased? Or do they get off on the sexual power? Maybe it's a combination of both." She scanned the crowd again. "The men are hard to figure, too. One minute they're loving every skanky inch of flesh, and the next they're treating the girls like trash, as if they themselves are not guilty of being here and watching. There's a really sick atmosphere in here of refractory loathing buttered over with smiling lust."

"That's quite a perceptive assessment."

He looked at her with interest.

"What?" she asked.

He shook his head and ordered two waters for them from the frisky fishnet-draped waitress, whose name was Janet.

"So do you get off on this?" Jazz waved a hand toward the stage.

"Behold me panting and drooling," said Tony dryly. "I can barely contain my wild enthusiasm."

"I can see that."

When Janet returned with their water, he beckoned her closer. "Is Rico here tonight?"

"He won't be in until nine."

Tony nodded his thanks and tipped her. She hovered, apparently taken with his good looks.

"Anything else you need?"

He shook his head.

"Anything else you want?" She scribbled something inside a matchbook and handed it to him.

Jazz didn't have to be psychic to know it was a phone number. She folded her arms.

Janet's gaze slid over her plain white T-shirt, jeans, and work boots, her bland expression signaling that she didn't consider them competition. "Just let me know," she said to Tony.

"Yeah, thanks." When the waitress had moved away, he glanced at Jazz. "You can uncurl your lip now."

"Does that happen often?"

He shrugged.

"Uh-huh. I'm beginning to see that you're quite the chick magnet."

"What, it wasn't obvious at first sight?" he teased.

God, she had to admit she loved that smile of his. It turned his mouth into a woman-vaporizing weapon. She could feel herself getting all tingly and ready to disintegrate under its charm.

That smile was hundred-watt manipulation. Next thing she knew, *she'd* be up on the stage, gyrating and begging him to pluck her fruit.

Jazz could just see herself, shaking her buns inside a pair of completely sheer gauze overalls, prancing in a pair of stilettos. Tony sat in the audience, wolf-whistling and cheering her on. *Yeah, right.*

So why did the image turn her on?

She wasn't going to be some pushover for this beaming beefcake. She felt so strongly about it that she must have muttered the last two words out loud.

"Jazz, that's about the third time you've called me 'beefcake.' It would be insulting, except for what it reveals about you."

"Huh?" She felt her face getting warm.

"You're attracted to me."

Her mouth opened in disbelief. "The hell I am!"

"So you compensate for that by putting me down. If you can reduce me to a hunk of meat with no brain, I'm less threatening. Men do the same thing with women."

"Look, Sinclair. I don't know what kind of psychobabble you've been reading, but you are so wrong. Dead wrong. *Completely* wrong."

"Methinks the lady doth protest too much."

"Not only are you wrong, you're insufferably arrogant."

He opened his mouth to reply, but she cut him off. "As you can see by my attire, I'm no lady. And I haven't even *begun* to protest your obnoxious comment! You have a set of brass b—"

"It's okay, Jazz. I'm attracted to you, too."

"—alls the size of Turner Field, you— What?"

"It's a problem, isn't it? For both of us."

She couldn't seem to look away from those damned eyes, alight with irony. Why the hell would he say something like that?

Suddenly warm, Jazz took a long, cold drink of water. It must be this place. All around them pulsed the suggestion of sex, and though it was theatrical and staged, the spectacle was bound to affect them in some way.

"I've got no problem, Sinclair. So you're not hard to look at. So women throw themselves at you on a daily basis. I'm not impressed, and don't have the slightest urge to join the queue. The only reason I'm sitting here at this table with you is that I want my father out of jail. *Capisce?"*

"I do believe I've been *told,"* Tony murmured, a smile on his face.

"Damn straight you have." Jazz finished her water in one gulp and avoided his gaze. On stage, a dubious schoolgirl was lifting her little plaid skirt to show an insolent set of cheeks to the crowd. *Oh, please.*

She checked her watch and thankfully saw that it was almost nine. Where was this Rico creep?

Chapter 8

*T*HEY SAT IN SILENCE FOR THE NEXT FEW MIN-
utes, and Jazz made a concerted effort to ignore Tony until he leaned over and touched her
shoulder. The warmth of his hand sent pleasure
waves through her, and his breath in her ear
made her shiver. Blast the man!

"That has to be him."

Jazz snapped to attention and followed his
gaze to a heavyset man in his mid-thirties, five-
ten or so, who wore a shiny silk shirt under an
open black sport coat. His curly black hair was a
little long, and he sported a diamond stud in one
ear, a complement to the three gold chains
around his neck. Rico Romanelli vibrated with
self-importance.

He exchanged a few words with the bouncer, then made his way to the bar and ordered a drink. While the bartender got it for him, Rico placed his hamlike hands on his hips and scanned the crowd.

He was soon joined by a burly blond man with a beard, who sat beside him on a barstool. The two men had an intense ten-minute conversation before Blond Beard left the bar.

Rico returned to scanning the crowd, frowning as he locked eyes with Tony.

Jazz realized that she didn't have the slightest idea what to do next. If she'd come alone, she supposed she would have just walked up to the guy and demanded her father's black book. And it was doubtful that he'd have done anything other than laugh in her face. Perhaps it was a good thing the pesky cop had come along. He, at least, had some experience questioning pugnacious lowlifes.

She dug Tony in the ribs. "What's the plan?"

"We go bully the bully." He drained the contents of his glass and rose from the table. "Mind if I do the talking?"

Jazz shrugged. "Whatever."

They approached Romanelli, who watched them cross the room toward him, brow furrowed, arms folded over his chest now.

"Rico Romanelli?"

"Who wants to know?" Dark, deep-set eyes regarded them with suspicion.

"Tony Sinclair, APD." Tony pulled out his badge and flipped it open.

A little "zing" arrowed through Jazz at the macho gesture. She tried to ignore it.

Rico's shoulders stiffened, but his face remained devoid of expression. "Yeah? The club's clean."

"We're not here about the club. I'd like to talk to you about a friend of yours we just booked for breaking and entering. Guy's known by the name of Bones."

"Never heard of him."

"Funny, because he's the one who told us to come talk to you. Said you hired him to break into this lady's studio and remove something belonging to her father, Myles Taylor."

"I don't have a clue what you're talking about."

"You were going to pay him and his partner five hundred bucks apiece for the job, isn't that so?"

"Sorry, you got the wrong guy."

"Oh, I see," purred Tony. "*Two* Ricos manage the club, and I'm talking to the innocent one."

"No—I'm the only Rico that works here. But like I said, I don't know anything about this."

"This your handwriting, pal?" Sinclair reached into his pocket and produced a Ziploc bag containing the address of Jazz's studio written on a scrap of paper.

Rico swallowed, but didn't budge an inch. "Nope."

"Bet it's exactly like the handwriting on your employment application for this joint. And we could find lots of other samples to compare it to."

The manager snorted. "You got nothing on me."

"Bones seems to think you might know something about a warehouse containing some very high-profile stolen art. And by coincidence, your family owns several warehouses in downtown Atlanta."

"I have no idea who this Bones character is, okay? And I got a job to do here, and you're interfering with it."

"I'd be glad to take you downtown and see if your memory clears up in interrogation. How about that?"

"It would be a revolving door, buddy. You got no reason to hold me. I'd be out of there before you asked your third question."

"I'd also be interested in whether your income tax returns declare enough to justify a five-hundred-thousand-dollar house and a Testarossa."

"That would be none of your business. I just got audited last year. You got nothing on me."

"Are you so stupid and small-time that you don't know what you're part of?"

Rico said nothing.

"Cantini needs that black book because it lists contacts for disposing of art stolen from the High Museum. These are paintings from all over the world, so it's not just APD that'll be crawling up your butt. You don't want any part of this, believe me."

"This conversation is over. You need to leave. Now."

"Think about it, Romanelli. Don't be Cantini's scapegoat. We'll be talking in forty-eight hours, one way or another." Tony handed Rico a business card and turned on his heel.

When Jazz looked back at the man, the card was in four pieces and preparing to multiply.

"Well, that went smoothly," Jazz commented. "What do we do, now? Especially since he was so cordial and everything."

"I didn't expect him to invite us to church with him. What we do now is tail him."

Tony and Jazz sat in the darkness of his car and waited for Romanelli to make a move. Not that the Taurus had a chance in hell of keeping up with Rico's Testarossa, if the man caught on they were following.

The expanse of black tarmac that blanketed the lot met the inky dark of the sky and swallowed them up. The club's music was just audible and provided a foil for the night sounds of crickets and tree branches blowing in an asthmatic wind.

Tony was glad to be out of Mama's. Jazz had pinpointed the exact atmosphere of the place: voluptuous desire on the surface and mutual contempt in the undercurrents of the river of money.

Some of the girls were lovely, and almost all of them had extraordinary bodies. But they left Tony cold. He'd passed the age of eighteen long ago, and these days it required subtlety to arouse his interest. He also didn't bother with pointless dating. He was actively searching for the right woman: the future mother of his children. He sure as hell wasn't going to find her on the stage of Hot Rockin' Mama's.

He wasn't going to find her in the person of Jazz Taylor, either, but his body wasn't cooperating with that assessment.

He was aware of each breath she took, each blink of her eyes, each movement of her head—and didn't know why. What in God's name was making him lust after a woman with an attitude that was bigger than her breasts? It was damned inconvenient, and he'd hoped that verbalizing it inside the club would drain its power. No such luck.

He couldn't seem to distract himself from the pale column of her neck in the moonlight, and the way tendrils of her hair fell against it. The same clip gizmo held the mass of silky curls on top of her head; what did she look like with her hair tumbling over her shoulders? Did it fall all the way to that shapely little ass of hers?

Though he'd only seen it covered with denim, careful analysis by a crack detective such as he revealed certain characteristics.

One, it was a perfect upside-down heart, lushly rounded above the thighs, and tapering deliciously where it met her small waist.

Two, it spent its days wrapped in bikini underwear which crept tantalizingly inward and left tiny ridges he could discern through her clothes.

All the evidence pointed to the probability that it was firm and smooth, the perfect size for a man to grip while he—

"Hel—lo! Sinclair?"

"Huh?"

"I asked if you do a lot of stakeouts, and if they're always this boring."

"Yes, and yes." Though *he* hadn't been bored, for once. And the word "stakeout" provided an infinite range of delightful images. But he decided not to thank her; she might not appreciate the movie reel in his head.

The question was, *why* was she in his head? Jazz Taylor was the least suitable woman for him to be having sexual thoughts about. He was thirty-two years old and wanted to find a wife. He had very specific requirements, and Jazz embodied none of them. She had the least childbearing hips he'd ever seen. Her personality wasn't exactly maternal or nurturing. She'd devoted herself to a bizarre career and had every intention of expanding it in LA, a city not known for wholesome family values.

So, he and that uncooperative pal in his pants had better just put her out of his mind. *Got that, Pedro?*

Evidently not. Pedro was long, but not on brains. He twitched impatiently as Jazz stretched her arms behind her back, inadvertently thrusting her breasts forward.

Stop looking! A professional doesn't behave like this.

Pedro swelled lasciviously anyhow, mocking his good intentions.

Look, buddy! Deflate now, or you're going to sport the waffle print of her work boots. She'll grind you flatter than a fruit roll-up.

Pedro, thank God, lost some of his impetuous verve.

"Sinclair, you have a really weird look on your face," said Jazz.

"Do I? Ah, just concentrating."

"On what?"

"On, uh—on the back door, to make sure Rico doesn't slip out unseen."

"Myles used to tell me a watched pot never boils. I'll bet a watched door never opens."

"Ha-ha."

A pause ensued, and Jess began to fidget. "Sinclair, can I ask you a personal question?"

He shrugged. "Sure."

"You told me your father was killed when you were young. But what about your mother?"

The last of Pedro's vitality vanished, to Tony's great relief. "I never knew her. She died giving birth to me."

"So Ellen raised you?"

"Yeah. Since I was eight."

"Wasn't she afraid for you to go into police work, after what happened to your father?"

"In a word, yes. But it's what I've always wanted to do; it's in my blood. The old man would be proud." Well, except for this damned probation. He wasn't eager for Ellen to find out, either.

"What about you, Jazz? How did you get into making monsters?"

Her face became reflective, eyebrows arching a little, angel's mouth pursing in a way that made him want to part it, plunder it, savor those lush lips.

"I suppose it started when I was very young. Myles was still around—probably hadn't been caught yet." Her mouth twisted. "Like a lot of kids, I had fears about the bogeyman under the bed. Mama tried everything to calm me down, with no success. So Myles came to my room one evening with scissors, construction paper, markers, and a big lawn-and-leaf bag. He told me we were going to make a monster that would scare the bogeyman silly, and he'd never bother me again."

She grinned. "We covered a chair with the bag for the body, and gave it paws with old slippers of Mama's. We glued ferocious paper claws onto the slippers. Then we made the meanest, nastiest fanged face to put on the top. But I wasn't afraid of this monster, because I'd made him, so he was my friend."

"Did it work?" Tony asked, fascinated.

"You bet. The bogeyman never *dared* to bother me again." Jazz laughed softly. "After that, I made all kinds of creatures and things. Did art and drama through high school; loved movies. The summer after my freshman year in college, I got an internship at the Smithsonian Museum. There I was able to work on displays—Samurai warriors and their costumes, that kind of thing."

He loved listening to her talk. Loved trying to imagine her as a child, warding off her fears, or as a teenager, exploring her interests.

"I took courses in design, sculpting, painting, theater—all that stuff."

He'd taken business classes, for the most part. Spent a few years mangling the Spanish language. Played baseball. Drank his share of beer. Enjoyed being chased by college women.

He started to ask her when she'd had her first TV and film jobs, when the back door of Mama's opened and their friend Rico Romanelli stepped out, talking on a cell phone and taking quick drags from a cigarette.

Tony briefly imagined mugging him for the rest of the pack. Damn, he wanted one. Just a couple of puffs. Maybe some of the delicious scent of tobacco would waft its way over to them. His tongue just about hung out of his mouth in anticipation.

Rico threw the butt to the tarmac and ground it out with his heel. Still talking on the cell phone, he walked to his shiny red pimpmobile and got in.

Tony let him get all the way out of the lot and turn the corner before starting the Taurus's engine and following at a discreet distance.

Jazz was tense beside him, her arms folded tightly.

They drove in silence, dropping back a few cars when Rico glanced into his rearview mirror. It wasn't hard to keep tabs on a candy-apple red Testarossa, after all. The dark blue Taurus blended into the night traffic seamlessly, not calling attention to them at all.

Rico turned at last into the parking lot of an excellent Italian restaurant, which had almost certainly stopped serving an hour ago, since it was almost midnight.

"*Buona notte*, Salvatore," muttered Tony.

"What did you say?"

"Good evening, Sal—as in Cantini. He owns that place, among others. And what a coincidence—he owns Hot Rockin' Mama's, too."

Chapter 9

*M*YLES FOUND BEING BEHIND BARS IN ATlanta much the same as being behind bars in Boston or Topeka. All in all, it was a miserable and undignified experience, and one he'd sworn not to repeat. Yet here he was, clad in a ghastly orange jumpsuit and deprived of his silk skivvies.

He sat on a bare mattress and stared at the ugly institutional walls, the bare concrete floor, and the naked toilet bowl.

Bollocks. At least the last time he'd been booked, he'd been guilty. This was an outrage, truly it was, and he couldn't even ask Ellen to post his bail. She was undoubtedly sketching the Duomo and nibbling Perugina Baci, her favorite

Italian chocolate. Not that he wanted her to see him in orange, or in this distinctly lowbrow environment. Being in jail played bloody hell with one's appearance.

Myles watched with distaste as his heavyset cellmate dug into his ear with a stubby, hairy-knuckled pinky. He had unimpressive sloped shoulders and a large paunch that bespoke his fondness for beer; a grizzled brown mustache spread from under his nose to bracket his mean little mouth.

"What're *you* lookin' at?" the man said.

Myles raised an eyebrow. "Dross. Detritus. Scurf. Carrion."

His companion drew those mean—quite inadequate, really—lips back into a sneer, exposing bad teeth. "Cain't you even speak English?"

"I speak the King's English, my good man."

"Sounds more like a queen's, if you ask me."

"I didn't."

It took a moment for the Adonis to register the insult. "Shithead."

"Ah," Myles reminisced. "It's been so long since anyone's called me that. I've missed it so."

"Fag."

"I prefer cigars."

The guy rose to his feet and puffed up. "You are one snooty fruit. Come on over here, and I'll pound your face in—make you talk even funnier."

"A delicious invitation, but I'm afraid I must decline." Myles curled his lip.

"You really get on my nerves, man. Swish on over here, why don'tcha? I'll rip off your dick and shove it up your—"

"Very generous of you, old chap, but I shall have to refuse that kind offer as well. I'm saving my pudenda for a certain lady's pleasure."

"Pu-*what*?"

"Genitals. Mighty sword. Manhood. Dick, as you say."

"Oh. So you ain't a homo." The man looked nonplussed. "You got a girl, huh?"

"She's no girl, my boy. She's one hundred percent woman."

"Yeah? She a looker? Stacked?"

Myles eyed the Cro-Magnon across the cell. Why was he even conversing with such offal? Well, perhaps he could teach the man to respect and revere women as he should. His enlightenment would be a trial, but Myles had no doubt that he would persevere in the end. He always did. He was a master.

"Stacked, you ask?" He stroked his chin. "Why, yes. My Ellen is piled high—with admirable qualities."

"I ain't askin' about her *qualities*, man."

"But you would like to, I'm sure, once I lead you out of the philosophical cave and into the light. Plato had this theory, you see—"

"I don't live in no cave. I bought my old lady a mighty fine double-wide."

Myles sighed. Perhaps this was going to take longer than he'd thought. Ah, well. Likely he had several hours before Jazz could post his bail. "Do tell me your name, old chap."

"McGraw. Billy McGraw."

"And I am Sir Myles Taylor. A pleasure to make your acquaintance, dear boy."

McGraw hacked up a loogie and spat onto the concrete floor. "Let's get something straight, Taylor. You ain't callin' me *boy*, and I ain't callin' you *sir*. Got it?"

Myles rather thought he did.

Ellen Whitaker Northrop Banks could find none of the charm Florence had once held for her. It was dreadfully hot. The river stank, there were no bargains to be found, and an impudent boy on a Moped had run over the left toe of her navy Ferragamo sling-backs. She was famished, yet everything was closed for the afternoon, and she might as well admit it—she was worried about Myles.

He's a useless and affected fop, she told herself severely. *He writes execrable verse, and he likes my money far too much.*

Yes, but he makes me laugh, can carry a conversation at a cocktail party or benefit, and he attends to all my womanly needs.

At this last thought, the very proper, pragmatic, Miss Porter's-and-Vassar-educated Ellen felt heat flush her cheeks. Who knew? Who knew that such a . . . such a *slime-trout* as the professionally sincere Myles could command such an under-sheet shimmy?

Ellen didn't precisely know what a slime-trout was, but she'd once heard a fraternity boy say it in reference to a slippery character, and it seemed to fit Myles. He was the sort of man one told oneself *not* to fall for, and then fell for anyway, in full knowledge that one was a fool. How she'd come to be engaged to the man was beyond her, especially when she'd written a check for her own ring.

Ellen blinked her eyes against the sting of pollution and kept walking toward her pensione. How Myles had made that romantic, she didn't quite know. But he'd pulled it off, and she'd been all set to become Ellen Whitaker Northrop Banks Taylor, once she'd put him through a few flaming hoops. The problem was that he hadn't quite made it through one of them: He still hung dangling from it, blazing away.

She arrived at her destination and pulled open one of the huge, heavy wooden doors which sealed the pensione's courtyard from the street. She stalled there, watching the play of the old center fountain, the water spouting from a fish's mouth. The sculpture reminded her of Myles, spouting his usual effluvium.

Her fiancé had sworn to retire from the art-theft business, yet there were dangerous thugs on his trail, and he'd wanted her safe in Italy. Though he claimed innocence from any wrongdoing, could she trust him?

Ellen mounted the stairs, her mouth downturned. What if he'd sent her to Italy just to insulate her behind a wall of ignorance? What if he'd told her a story so she wouldn't catch on to another criminal caper? She tossed her short-sleeved jacket on the end of her bed and sat down at a small mahogany writing desk in her room, fanning herself with a postcard of the Uffizi Gallery.

Her instincts told her to call her nephew Tony, the sweet boy. But she hadn't yet gotten around to introducing him to Myles, or telling him of their engagement. Tony had a guard dog's instincts when it came to her, and she knew he would despise Myles on sight. The thought made her miserable.

Fanning herself with the postcard did little good, so she got up and went to the sink to splash cold water on her face. She even drank some out of her cupped hand, something her mother would never have done.

Ellen patted her face dry with a hand towel and wondered if her panty hose had melted permanently onto her legs. They felt as if they had grafted onto her skin.

Was she mad? What sort of person wore stockings in Italy in July? Only a Whitaker, brought up under the iron rule of Miss Martha. Her mother, deposited in Florence midsummer, would doubtless have worn gloves and a full slip, as well. Ellen could hardly imagine such torture. As it was, she felt like a plate of wilted, steamed spinach, dressed in olive oil.

Miss Martha would have taken one look at Myles Taylor and pronounced him a scalawag. A scoundrel. She would have marched him out of her home by the ear and seen to it that he never darkened her door again. Ellen compressed her lips.

But Miss Martha would have missed out on his engaging grin, and the twinkle in his green rogue's eyes, and the utterly marvelous things he could do with those felonious fingers . . .

Myles had met her by convenient accident, finagled a date, and then stolen a kiss. From there he had burgled her breasts from their terribly proper harness, filched her skirt, and hijacked her body. She still wasn't sure how it had happened, but Myles Taylor had then flown her to a place she'd never been before. He was quite a marvelous outlaw.

Ellen should have felt disgusted with herself, but instead she felt deliciously wicked and decadent. It was the first time she'd ever been *fast*. Whitakers normally courted with all the passion of treacle.

With Myles, sex had sizzled, instead of being a process of dull, mechanical thumping with one of her ex-husbands. She had a feeling it was *because* he was a scalawag that she could relax around him. It had been that way from the moment she met him.

She'd stood that night in the art gallery, pretending to admire some horrid, violent paintings which featured broken china embedded in gloppy swirls of acrylic pigment. She had taken a sip of some pitiful champagne from a plastic cup with a snap-on base. The bubbles were trickling toward her unenthusiastic gullet when a tall, elegant man swept up to her and took her free hand into his possession. Then he kissed it. A sudden surge of electricity shot up to her neck and splashed the bad champagne into her windpipe.

As Ellen choked and coughed, the man took her into his arms, stroking her back with one hand, and thumping it gently with the other. "My dear lady, you may as well sip naptha! Allow me to take you for a proper drink."

Ellen normally didn't enjoy having her personal space invaded: She kept a good fourteen inches between her body and anyone else's. How she'd come to be embracing a man whose name she didn't know escaped her. But she noticed, in the moments before she caught her breath, that he smelled quite wonderful. Like lime sherbet. Lime sherbet and very fine tobacco, laced with a touch of Glenlivet.

His fingers traced down her spine as he released her, which was really quite motley of him. Ill-mannered. And perhaps faintly . . . exciting.

The unknown gentleman emitted vibes that reminded her a bit of the boy in the black-leather jacket who'd tried, in her youth, to take her for a date on the back of his Harley. Miss Martha had chased him away with the fireplace poker, and Ellen had never seen him again. Her next date sported tiny embroidered whales on his belt, and picked her up in a Volvo. She'd been fool enough to marry him.

Ellen looked up at the dubious gentleman. "Thank you for the assistance," she said. "But I don't believe we've met. I couldn't possibly—"

"Sir Myles Taylor."

His voice was so smooth. A larynx brushed with clarified butter, that's what Myles Taylor had. The "sir" was indubitably specious; she didn't believe for an instant he'd been knighted by anyone but himself.

"And you are the lovely and charming Miss Ellen Whitaker Northrop Banks."

She frowned. "How do you know that?"

"That you're lovely and charming? Why, simply by looking at you."

Ellen tilted her chin at him. "How did you know my name, *sir*?" The emphasis she placed on the word was just shy of mocking. Whitakers were never rude.

Taylor's eyes glinted with amusement, as if he didn't mind being doubted. "Our hostess told me. I asked her." He turned toward the gallery owner, who stood perhaps two feet away. "Didn't I, Margaret?"

The woman tsk-tsked. "Be careful, Ellen," she said. "He's got the devil's own charm, and he's after your money."

Ellen turned her gaze back to Myles Taylor, who looked mock-sorrowful.

"Alas, my dear, she's got me pegged. I am a scurrilous character, but not nearly so dastardly as this man who claims to be an artist. Now, how about that drink? You look like a vodka martini sort of girl."

He was right. And it had been a long time since anyone had called her a girl. Besides, she'd never been out with a scurrilous character. It might prove to be fascinating.

The faux knight offered her his arm and a raised eyebrow. She hesitated a moment longer, and then slipped her fingers into the crook of his arm. She'd never left a function with a stranger. Was it safe?

"Margaret," she called over her shoulder, "if I turn up dead in an alley, please notify the authorities." She flashed a lovely smile at Myles Taylor.

"Not to worry," said the gallery owner. "He wants you alive and interest-bearing."

Three hours later, she had violated Miss Martha's social-drinking edicts and accepted a third martini from the man. Feeling deliciously naughty, she *flirted* with him. Agreed to see him again. And after he took her to bed, she resolved never, ever again to date a man with whales on his belt.

Ellen's mind returned to the thugs who were after her fiancé. Myles claimed they were attempting to frame him for the High Museum heist. Even given his background, that was ridiculous. Myles had been asleep in her bed that night.

Unless . . .

The hair on the back of her neck rose. She had awoken during that night, and reached out in bed to find Myles not there. But surely he'd only gone to the kitchen for a drink. Surely he couldn't have slipped out of her house, only to return after the job was done?

She compressed her lips once again, and frowned. She had to be sure that Myles wasn't lying to her. She might be capable of marrying a scalawag, but she *refused* to marry a criminal. Especially not one who had burgled the High Museum. She was a trustee, for God's sake.

Tomorrow she was going to Murano for some

handblown wineglasses. And then she'd go home early to Atlanta. She needed to get to the bottom of this—and perhaps it was time to talk to young Tony.

The white Mercedes wound through hundreds of trees, up the long drive to Ellen's Buckhead home. It was an expansive Georgian of mellow pale brick, with a detached six-car garage in the rear where her driver, Reynaldo, would park the car. For now, he let it idle while he assisted her from the rear seat and removed her baggage from the trunk. Ellen gave a sigh of relief to be home.

The front door opened, and Liddy Hilton, her longtime housekeeper, appeared with a smile of welcome. So did Clover, her five-pound toy poodle. He danced madly around Ellen's legs, yapping for joy. She picked him up and let him destroy her careful makeup with his tongue.

"Yes, my darling! I love you, too, wild thing." She winced as his tiny tongue slurped her ear. More excited yaps let her know he wanted to get down. She set him on the drive, where he did a mad figure eight around her ankles before rushing to assert himself on the Mercedes's front tire.

"*¡Estupido!*" Reynaldo shook his fist at him. "Only the Mercedes, for heem—the Land Rover is not good enough!"

Ellen laughed and mounted the front steps to give Liddy a hug. Only when they released each other did she notice the strain on her housekeeper's face.

"What is it, Liddy?"

"Welcome home, Mrs. Banks. Mr. Tony would like you to call him immediately."

Ellen tensed. "I see. Well, I'll do that."

"And I'm afraid I have some bad news for you, Mrs. Banks."

Liddy followed her inside and waited until Reynaldo had brought in the bags. Then she stood nervously, smoothing her apron, and dropped the bomb that Myles had been taken into police custody.

Ellen stared aghast at her. "What do you mean, he's in jail?" She collapsed inelegantly on her leather carry-all, which sat on the floor of the pale marble foyer. "How long has he been there? Why wasn't I notified?"

Liddy Hilton's normally smooth, placid brow was set into faint lines. "Mr. Taylor insisted that you not be disturbed while you were abroad. He didn't want you to worry."

"But . . . but why hasn't someone posted his bail? His daughter?" She put a hand to her mouth. "Poor child. She probably can't afford it without mortgaging that studio of hers." She bolted upright. "I'll contact my attorneys directly."

Mrs. Hilton hesitated. "Ma'am, it's not my business, but they must have some strong evidence to keep him behind bars. Otherwise, they'd question him and let him go."

"Something tells me, Liddy, that you know what that evidence is. Please share it with me."

Her housekeeper looked at the ground and bent to wipe an invisible smudge from the polished hardwood floor of the hallway. "The papers are saying the police got a search warrant for his apartment, and they found a painting under Mr. Taylor's bed." She ventured to look up, and her eyes were sympathetic. "A Degas, the *Journal-Constitution* said."

When Ellen clutched at the wall for support, Liddy moved forward to give her employer another hug. "I'm so sorry, Mrs. Banks."

Ellen emitted a wild trill of laughter. "Stanley kept a dancer *in* his bed. I thought it couldn't get worse than that. But Myles puts a dancer *under* his bed? It's much, *much* worse. How do I end up with these men, Liddy? No wonder he didn't want to tell me."

Ellen put her hands over her face, the better to avoid the condemning eyes of the eight ancestral oil portraits that hung in the entrance hall. Heaven help her—what would Tony say?

"I'm going to make you some tea." Mrs. Hilton retreated to the kitchen, her ample form exuding a comfort Ellen couldn't accept at the moment.

She opened her eyes to find her great-grandmother looking down her nose at her. "Oh, stop glaring at me, you old bat!" She smacked the frame lightly, knocking the picture askew. "You married an opium addict. All I've done is become engaged to a thief."

But the implications of it appalled her. She was a trustee of the museum, and engaged to marry the man suspected of pillaging the place. It would be all over the papers within a day or two. The scandal would rock Buckhead, and what was left of old Atlanta, to the core.

Suddenly she was furious. Myles had played her for a fool, and she was going to go give the bastard a piece of her mind. Whitakers were never rude, were they? Hah. Times were changing.

"Don't forget to call Mr. Tony," Liddy reminded her.

As if she could. Ellen rubbed at her temples. She felt a migraine coming on.

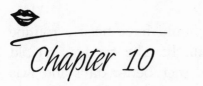

Chapter 10

"*H*OW COULD YOU NOT TELL ME?" TONY struggled to keep his voice modulated. He couldn't shout at Aunt Ellen, no matter what the circumstances. Especially since he knew he was physically intimidating.

That hadn't always been the case. Ellen had come to pick him up that terrible night when he was eight. His father had just been shot, and he remembered clinging to her comforting curves and never wanting to let go. He'd launched all seventy-six pounds of himself at her, and broken a string of very fine pearls, which she'd completely disregarded in order to hold him tight.

They'd lost Sam Sinclair on a bleak, brutal January night, a night filled with icy air that burned the lungs, froze the jaw, and ripped at the ears. Sam didn't usually work the late shift, but had been supplementing his pay to save for Tony's college.

He'd made what should have been a routine stop for a broken taillight. The car was an old Chevy Nova that had seen better days and was riding on a spare. The passengers were youngish, but had done time and didn't want to return to the state pen. The backseat full of stolen valuables wasn't something they wanted Sam Sinclair to see, and blowing a hole in his chest with a silenced .45 seemed the best way to ensure he didn't.

The bastards were still rotting in the very place they'd tried to avoid. That was Tony's only consolation. Since that night, however, he'd been particularly intolerant of thieves.

Which was why he wanted now to shout, despite the fact that it would upset Aunt Ellen. Of all the men in the world to get involved with! Myles Taylor, for God's sake. Not only was the man a thief, he was a leech, an affected pansy, and worse: a *poet*.

Tony wanted to bash the chandelier, knock over tables, and stomp dents in the parquet floors. He'd like to rip the eighteenth-century tapestry of St. George into strips and use the Chinese vases for target practice. But Sam had conveyed to him, even at age eight, that his greatest strength lay in his ability to be gentle; that without control and discipline he was no better than an animal with opposable thumbs. The Police Academy had reinforced this.

"Tony, darling, I know you're angry. I know you're hurt," murmured Aunt Ellen.

"I'm *family*," he said. The word reverberated throughout the room and hung in the air between them. They both knew the significance of that word. Since neither of them possessed a true nuclear family, they'd made one of their own.

And when Tony found the right woman, he'd make a real family with her. Sweet, traditional, blond like Ellen, rounded in all the right places, and a fabulous cook, she'd be a stay-at-home mom, and he'd take a desk job so his children would never go through what he had.

Ellen bowed her ash-blond head. "I'm sorry I never introduced you. I just knew you would hate him."

"For obvious reasons!"

"But you've hated everyone I've even been on a date with, my dear. I realize it only stems from love, but your police training has made you just a little . . . guard-doggish."

Guard-doggish! He was no such thing. "I didn't say a word when you accompanied Oily Oliver to an entire season of the opera."

"That was hair pomade, Tony dear. And you practically *growled* at him."

"And Hideous Henry—the squinty one. I never objected when he took you to the symphony."

"No, you just loomed over him and cracked the bones in his fingers when you shook his hand."

"And Luis the Latin Lover—"

"Tony! A very bad example to bring up. You described in lurid detail how you'd found that Colombian strangled and hung by his own gold chains. I never saw Luis again, and he was a highly respectable businessman from Venezuela, *not* a drug dealer."

He hung his head slightly but jerked it up again at Ellen's next words.

"Darling, I know you intend the very best, but you do tend to be slightly overprotective."

"That's not true!"

"Distressingly macho, in fact."

"What!"

She fixed him with a stern gaze. "Did you, or did you not, follow Marcus Smythe from here to his club and tell him you'd carve new facets in his family jewels if he came near me again?"

Tony opened and then closed his mouth. "How did you find out about—"

"*Did* you, or did you not?"

"The man is pond scum!"

"I think I have my answer. Now, do you wonder that I avoided introducing Myles to you? Has it occurred to you, darling Tony, that perhaps I felt I needed to guard my privacy a little?"

"But you became engaged to the man!"

Ellen had the grace to blush. "Yes. And I should have told you, should have introduced you. I . . . was just putting it off for a bit."

"When would I have found out? After the wedding, for God's sake?"

She shook her head. "No—perhaps after the honeymoon." She attempted a laugh to cut the tension.

He didn't respond with one of his own, but he found that he couldn't stay mad at her either.

"I love you so much, Tony-Bear. I have since the day my sister gave birth to you. But I'm not a Victorian china doll to be locked in a glass case. Nor am I a bone to be guarded and growled over. I'm a woman, with a normal woman's interests and desires and needs for companionship."

Uuuggghhhh. To hear the word "desire" spoken by his Aunt Ellen made his skin crawl. Especially when he thought about Myles Taylor, for Christ's sake. He squeezed his eyes shut. Nope, he was *not* going to go there. He took refuge in self-justification.

"But look what happens when you shut me out, and I don't stand guard over you," he fulminated. "You get tangled up with a character like Myles-the-Master-Thief-Taylor!"

Ellen eyed him sternly, despite the telltale flush of embarrassment on her cheeks. "And that, Tony dear, is my *right*. It was my mistake to make."

He stared at her helplessly, unwilling to admit it. "But—"

"I get lonely in this big house all by myself. You're an adult now; you have your own life. I need one of my own, too."

Later, as Tony walked to his car, he acknowledged that he didn't like the concept of Aunt Ellen having her own life. It practically gave him the hives. She was a sweet older woman with a lot of money and too kind a heart. What would she do without him to look after her? He was *not* overprotective; the idea was ridiculous.

He got into his car, slammed the door, and beat the steering wheel with his fist. He was *not* distressingly macho. It wasn't as if he ambled around in a loincloth and swung on a vine. He didn't pound his chest and yodel. But it *was* a jungle out there. Aunt Ellen had no idea.

He'd just take a quick drive around the back of the house before he left, to make sure all the windows were closed up snug. Oh, and he needed to check with Reynaldo about that malfunctioning spotlight. And remind him to change the security code again.

Like it or not, a link existed between Ellen and Myles Taylor, which meant there was one between her and Sal Cantini. Tony intended to cut that link.

Tony paced up and down his narrow kitchen between sips of coffee, and contemplated stubborn and annoying Jazz Taylor. Though he'd only known her for three days, she wouldn't get out of his head.

He found it intriguing that a woman with her background and interests would hide under overalls and not bother to accentuate her natural beauty. If makeup was her area of interest, then why didn't she wear any herself? Why was she so understated, when she possessed a studio full of costumes and props?

Jazz Taylor was a puzzle. She immersed herself in the elements of make-believe and drama, smoke and mirrors, illusory image. Yet she herself seemed so grounded in reality—defensively so.

He took his coffee outside, and ran his gaze critically over the exterior of his house. The place was a contemporary cedar, with siding that begged to be removed and replaced. Unfortunately, he was fully capable of doing the job himself. He wished he could claim ignorance and hire a contracting crew, but his conscience wouldn't let him do it. Where there was a will and a Home Depot, there was a way.

His house was a marked contrast to Ellen's stately Georgian home, the home he'd never grown used to even though he'd lived there since he was eight. It was simply too large, and too beautifully decorated, and too . . . empty. He'd decided long ago that he never wanted more than four bedrooms in his own home. When he found the perfect woman and got married, he wanted a houseful of kids with all the chaos that entailed. No silent, lovely rooms. He wanted to see Tonka trucks littering the floors, and action figures, and Legos. Barbie shoes and Polly Pockets.

He wanted sturdy, comfortable furniture that nobody was too concerned about. Ellen's antiques were beautiful, but as a boy he'd felt that he was navigating a museum. His favorite play spots had been the attic, the basement, or outdoors.

Liddy was a love, but she'd frisked him daily for contraband after a lizard and several frogs had turned up in her washing machine with his jeans.

Nobody seemed to approve when he'd knocked the nose off of a marble bust of Andrew Jackson with a baseball. They didn't care that it was an accident, and his claim that Jackson looked less snooty without that part of his snoot—well, that hadn't been a wise argument.

Tony had attempted to make reparation by gluing Andrew's nose back on with some contact cement, and then the household *really* went into an uproar.

He'd missed the rough-housing he and his father had done each night. One of his fondest memories was playing cops and robbers before bedtime. Tony, the robber, would sneak around the long mustard gold sofa, dash into the kitchen, and steal an oatmeal-raisin cookie from the ceramic jar on the counter. Sam, hearing the ritual noise, would ambush him on the way out and demand the cookie in the name of the law.

Usually Tony had crammed it into his mouth already, in which case Sam hauled him off over his shoulder to "jail" in the bathroom. There, he was forced to do penance by brushing his teeth before bed.

He grinned at the memory. That was how he wanted his son to be raised. Carefree and giggling, not hemmed in by marble and mahogany. Aunt Ellen, sweetheart that she was, had almost had a coronary when he'd made Silly Putty imprints of her antique Byzantine medallions.

He was content with his nice, normal house and nice, normal furniture. One day he'd have a nice, normal wife, too. He'd been meaning to call Tina Saunders, a woman who worked at the bank branch he frequented. She was cute, feminine, friendly . . .

His unruly thoughts turned instead back to Jazz Taylor's large brown eyes and mass of unruly curls. At first glance, everything about her seemed petite, delicate, fragile. But on closer observation, her biceps under the soft cotton sleeves of her T-shirt were tiny but tough. The pulse beat strong among the sculpted cords of her neck, keeping time to the rhythm of her energy. She radiated competence from the core, a competence that was strangely elegant, given her overalls and work boots. He supposed Myles, the old fraud, had passed that down to his daughter somehow. She had a certain something that came from her bearing and had nothing to do with fashion or money.

Her overalls hid a fierce pride, a spirit that

never crumpled, and an absolute inner courage. What other woman of his acquaintance would have sealed an intruder to the knees in a bucket of plaster, instead of calling 911?

He chuckled, but then frowned. The very qualities he admired could get Jazz into serious trouble.

For Jazz was fully capable of lacing up her work boots and striding right into the lion's den. It was up to him to flatten the lion into a rug before Jazz got herself killed.

Chapter 11

*T*AYLOR FX WAS DARK AND LOCKED, WITH NO sign of Jazz anywhere, and that worried Tony. He'd prowled around the back but seen no sign that anything was amiss. The windows were intact, the garbage cans stood in neat rows, and some geraniums bloomed peacefully in a planter. But this was a Thursday morning. Why wasn't Jazz at work?

With some help from the station, he located her home address and headed over there. She lived in a picturesque little condominium complex where the builders—by some miracle—had left many of the old trees standing. The curved walkway that led to her unit was lined with English ivy, and pots of begonias and impatiens overflowed with colorful blooms. Tony saw no outward signs that a nutty artist type was in residence.

The blinds of her unit were closed, and it seemed dark. Tony looked at his watch. Eleven o'clock. Something *had* to be wrong.

Pictures of Jazz flashed through his mind. The first time he'd met her, with the gooey spatula in her hand. How her big brown eyes had flashed when he'd called her "sweetheart" and asked to see her boss. Her protectiveness of her incorrigible father, and her articulate plea for a week of freedom so that she could prove him innocent.

The muscles in his neck bunched. If he had just thrown her in a cell, she might not be in danger now. This was his fault. If Cantini had gotten to her, hurt her because of his stupidity, he'd never forgive himself.

Tony went around the back of her home, chastising himself. He deserved to be working the parking lot at Bob's Wholesale Club.

He found a tiny back porch which sported a hibachi, a pair of size six running shoes, a pink bandanna, and more well-tended planters. He scooped up the bandanna. It was rolled and knotted, just the right size for Jazz to have worn it as a sweatband while exercising. He could see her in it, her loose curls cascading over her shoulders.

Tony fisted his hand around the pink fabric

and moved to peer into the back door. *If anything had happened to her—*

"Just what do you think you're doing?"

The voice behind him was taut and angry, and it belonged to Jazz. Relief washed over him, leaving him weak. He spun around to find her dressed only in a white T-shirt and blue bikini panties, aiming her trusty nail gun at his heart.

He ignored it for the sight of her beautifully shaped legs. This girl didn't have chicken stems. Her calves flared, smooth as the bowl of a wineglass, to slim again at the ankles and knees. They were built from running, he guessed, and her thighs were a lush, creamy landscape all their own. He traversed it slowly with his eyes, reaching the apex covered by blue silky material.

Tony's mouth went dry, and he forced himself to look at the nail gun. It was braced against her flat stomach, which pulled the simple white T-shirt she wore taut against her breasts. She wore no bra, and the dusky peaks of her nipples rode high, beckoning under the flimsy material. He passed a hand over his mouth and jaw and met her eyes.

They were dark and velvety and furious.

"I asked you a question. What are you doing?" she repeated.

"I was worried about you," he managed.

"Do you always peep into women's windows when you're worried about them?"

"You weren't at the studio. I was afraid Cantini had sent more men after you. I'm sorry."

Jazz lowered the nail gun and tried to tug her shirt down over her panties. "I was up late working on some designs last night, so I slept in. Besides, I'd planned on going down to Little Five Points today, to check out some warehouses for the art."

"You're not going anywhere near there without me."

"I'm not some little cadet that you can order around, Sinclair."

"Jazz, it's dangerous. Can't you see that I'm only concerned for you?"

She sighed. "Come inside and let's argue about it over a cup of coffee." She led the way back to the front of the apartment, still tugging her shirt down self-consciously.

She should have thrown on a robe before dashing outside to catch the intruder.

He followed her in and looked around the place while she disappeared into the bedroom. While all the trim was painted high gloss white, Jazz had done every wall in a different color. Soft purple set off lemon yellow, which glowed against periwinkle blue, to contrast with deep apricot.

Her furniture was simple and neutral: a futon, a basket chair, a modern kidney-shaped coffee table. She'd scattered bright, woven rag rugs on the gleaming hardwood floors, and plants flourished everywhere.

Tony was surprised to find that he liked it—in fact, he liked it a lot. It was colorful and cheerful.

Jazz returned, wearing baggy jeans, and moved around her small kitchen efficiently. She spooned dark roast into a filter, filled the coffeemaker with water, then produced sugar, a couple of spoons, two mugs, and some milk. The coffeemaker gurgled as she went to the sink, turned on the water, and flipped the disposal switch. A horrible noise ensued. Jazz flipped the switch back off. "There's more than coffee grounds in there," she sighed, and stuck her left hand down the hole.

"Be careful," Tony warned. "Why don't you let me do that?"

"It's okay."

He watched her face as she groped fearlessly. Most women he knew would explore a disposal only with a knife and a flashlight. But Jazz was unique.

"Feels like it used to be a spoon," she muttered. "And it's good and stuck. I'll have to get some pliers." She tugged hard, and then stood still. She tugged again. "Um, I seem to be stuck myself."

"What?"

"My watch somehow got caught on the spoon, and now I can't get my hand out."

"You're kidding." Tony walked over and stood close to her, looking into the sink. "I'll get you out," he said with all the confidence of a man in a uniform. "No problem." He maneuvered closer, standing directly behind her. The top of her head barely reached his shoulders, and he could smell her shampoo—that sweet woodsy scent he'd noticed the first time he'd met her in the studio. He could also smell warm, still-rumpled-from-bed woman. It was a dusky, sensual scent, and something primal in him wanted to taste it. Something primal in him wanted to do a lot more than that.

Tony tried to ignore the urge and eased his right hand down the disposal, which meant that he was now shoulder to shoulder, arm to arm against Jazz. It was a good thing that her hands were so small. Even so, it was a tight fit. His fingers slid down her inner wrist to her palm, and he felt a tremor go through her body. Tony inched closer to her, and made contact with her firm little bottom. He took a deep breath.

"Don't think I'm getting fresh here—it's unavoidable."

"I realize that. Don't worry about it."

She felt warm and lush and soft against him, and he wished fiercely that they were both naked. But that was a dangerous train of thought, one that needed to be derailed from his one-track mind immediately—before his engine filled with steam.

Tony wiggled his fingers around and encountered a metal object. "Yeah, it's a spoon, all right." The handle was bent almost in half, and the loose woven band of Jazz's watch was hooked on it.

She turned her head toward his, and he did the same. Now he was staring down at the tip of her nose, which seemed to point the way to her full, angelic mouth. Her tongue darted out nervously and flicked at her upper lip. "Do you feel it?"

"Oh, yeah," Tony said. "I feel it."

She stared up at him, her eyes huge. He noticed that there were tiny gold-and-green flecks in them. Her eyelashes were so thick and dark, and as long as he'd ever seen. She blinked, and he transferred his attention back to that angel's mouth of hers. Inside the disposal his fingers traced her palm again, and without thinking, he lowered his head.

Jazz felt the kiss right down to her toes. Tony's lips brushed hers lightly, and then again in a more demanding way. His mouth was hard on hers, hot, and elicited sensations she'd never felt before. It was like pouring a soda over ice—every nerve in her body popped and fizzed, and rose foaming to the occasion.

His tongue teased the roof of her mouth, and then came dancing down to meet hers, to flick and tease and plunder. His chest was hard against her back, and he smelled like fresh soap and musky man. She wanted to turn to face him, but the disposal situation made that impossible.

Disposal. She was stuck in a garbage disposal, sucking face with a horny cop. What was wrong with her? Even a lunatic shouldn't find this situation arousing.

She pulled away from Tony as far as she could, given the circumstances.

"I'm sorry," he gasped, sounding strained. "That was hardly professional."

Jazz was too embarrassed to say anything. She'd egged him on, after all.

She felt his hand turning, fingers scrabbling in the hole, and then a pressure on her wrist. He tugged.

"Ow."

"Sorry, but I'm trying to slide your watch band off the spoon." A few more uncomfortable tugs, and he said, "There!" He removed his coffee-ground-encrusted hand from the hole, and she was able to do the same.

"Soap's under the sink," she told him, trying to avoid his eyes.

"Thanks."

"No, thank *you*. I had visions of spending the rest of my life here." She laughed lightly, to take the tension out of the air. Too bad it wouldn't leave her body. "How about that coffee now?"

"Great."

She poured two cups, trying to ignore the mocking mantra inside her head. *You kissed a cop. Kissed-a-cop, kissed-a-cop, kissed-a-cop.*

"Sugar? One spoonful?"

"A little more."

More, more, more, the voice in her head sang. *You want more. More than a kiss, much more.*

"Cream?" He was looking at her breasts, dammit. They tingled in response.

"Please." Tony averted his eyes and paced to the window.

Jazz stirred cream into both cups. She grasped one to hand it to him, and the heat burned her skin. *Hot, hot, hot.* Like the blasted cop in her kitchen. Of all the men in the world, she had to lust after a cop who believed her father was guilty of robbing another museum.

Jazz wished she could find something despicable about him, something to stop this attraction cold. He'd been worried about her this morning. He'd given her cab fare to get home from the station. He even said "thank you" when she gave him the coffee. Jazz frowned. She'd find something wrong with Tony Sinclair if it killed her.

She took a gulp from her cup. "Sit down," she told him. "Let's talk about these warehouses downtown. I'm going to check them for the missing paintings whether you like it or not, because the only way to prove Myles innocent is to track down the real thieves."

Tony folded his big frame into one of her kitchen chairs and set his mug on the table with a determined *clunk*.

She sighed. "And I don't want you with me when I go. Even out of uniform, you have COP written all over you, like a banner. Any prayer of seeing these guys goes up in smoke if you're there."

"You're not going alone. Do you know how easy it is to dispose of an inconvenient woman?"

"Not any easier than disposing of an inconvenient man," Jazz returned.

"There's about a hundred pounds of difference. And civilians shouldn't get involved in police work."

"Sorry—I'm a civilian on a mission."

They stared at each other, arms folded, across the table. Tony's eyes were serious, determined. His jaw jutted forward, and his mouth was set in an uncompromising line.

"Before you go stirring up any hornets' nests," he said, "we need more information. My gut tells me that someone working for the High Museum helped out, but I can't prove that without getting inside."

"You're a cop; they have to let you in, don't they?"

"Not exactly."

"Why not? Flex your pecs, flash your badge, look beefy. Say you're there in the name of the law."

"Jazz, it doesn't work that way, particularly not with the international nature of this case. I'd have to be officially assigned, and I haven't been.

"But I need to get inside the museum, even though the place is crawling with GBI and FBI and cops and insurance examiners, and none of them can recognize me. If word got back to my captain, I'd be dog meat."

Jazz lounged back in her chair and crossed her

legs at the ankles. "I might be able to help you," she said. "If you agree to keep an open mind and help me."

She looked so ridiculously young and vulnerable, despite her cocky attitude and smart mouth. He spied the pale skin of her ankles just above her rolled socks, where her jeans had ridden up. His *wrists* were bigger than those little ankles.

"What, you're offering to dress me as a woman?"

"Nope. I'm thinking you'd make a helluva doddering old collector, though."

"*Doddering?*"

"Yep. Not to mention decrepit and half-blind."

"Me."

"Uh-huh. You."

Tony shook his head and grinned. "You're not *that* good."

She stiffened. "I'll bet you any amount of money—no, let's make that my father's freedom—that I am."

"Jazz, you know I can't get him released at this point—not that I would."

"Then let's bet your commitment to proving his innocence."

"Forget it."

"If I can get you into that museum so you can investigate undetected, you'll owe me at least impartiality where my father's concerned."

Tony eyed her thoughtfully. "All right."

She uncrossed her legs and stood up. "Let's go get started, then."

Chapter 12

*F*IVE HOURS LATER, TONY WAS AN OLD-TIMER. Using a skillful combination of heavy makeup and appliances, Jazz accentuated and built up every line in his forehead, and somehow deepened his faint crow's-feet until they almost swallowed his eyes.

In the FX industry, Jazz explained, appliances were not washers, dryers, or microwaves, but very delicate foam-latex facial parts. She fitted him with extensions for his nose and chin, blending the lines into his overall age makeup. She attached bushier gray eyebrows to his own, and even lengthened his earlobes, caking them with age. She yellowed his teeth.

Her fingers were gentle and competent, the

nails short and bare of any polish. She had beautiful hands, artist's hands. The tiny pores and
ridges and crisscrosses etched there were a map
of vitality: strong and sensual, the skin taut, as if
barely able to contain their talent and energy.

Her wrists were twice as delicate as her ankles,
and Tony was continually amazed that they
didn't simply snap when she picked up something heavy in the studio.

Her nearness was unsettling, to say the least.
He could smell her woodsy shampoo, and the
dense, sweet scent of her scalp. She used the same
laundry detergent he did, he was sure of it.

She had exactly thirty-eight perfect lashes on
her left lid, and forty-three on her right. When she
concentrated hard, she poked the tip of her small
tongue out and held it prisoner between her
teeth, pulling it back inside when her task was
complete.

Tony knew she wasn't doing any of this inten-
tionally to torture him. But she was driving him
insane without a word.

It somehow made it worse that he was simply
a job to her, another challenge to meet with her
tackle box of makeup. She wasn't thinking of him
as a man—he was an armature for her sculpting
skills.

Every time her fingers touched his face, his

neck, his ears, she sent tingles and chills and spurts of electricity rippling through him. He vibrated like the plucked string of a guitar.

The oddest questions popped into his mind. How did she sleep? On her stomach? Her side? Her back? Did she curl a hand under her cheek? Was she a blanket hog? Did she sleep with that angel's mouth parted, breathing through her mouth, or did those soft lips cradle each other all night?

Jazz smoothed back his hair with some gel, and pleasure arced through him at the feel of her fingers on his scalp. She had magical hands . . . he closed his eyes. She set something—he supposed it was a wig—on his head, and tugged it into place while he inhaled her scent all over again.

Tony opened his eyes to find her face mere inches from his, her eyes intent on blending the edges of the wig into the heavy makeup on his forehead. Up close, her irises weren't truly brown, but an unusual mix of cognac and deep green. Her breath was sweet in his nostrils, and held the freshness of new apples.

He didn't consciously decide to kiss her again. He just leaned in, man to woman, until their mouths almost touched. Her hands froze in place, and her pupils dilated, but she didn't back away immediately.

Then her laughter broke the sexual spell. "Hey Chick Magnet," she said. "You look too old for even Granny Clampett."

Heat flashed to his face under the makeup. He turned to behold a stranger in the mirror: a wizened old man with a pate gleaming under the long gray strands of a hideous comb-over.

His skin was ashen and sagging, and his earlobes drooped like raw chicken on a fishhook. His eyebrows resembled fluffy rodents.

Any woman he knew would rather eat the contents of an ashtray than kiss him. And even a dump truck full of Viagra wouldn't get this old geezer laid.

He'd tried to kiss Jazz Taylor, looking like this?

Are you out of your mind, Sinclair? What in the hell is wrong with you?

Not that he should be angling to kiss Jazz Taylor even looking like a *GQ* ad. Certain behavior was just not professional.

Jazz excused herself to wash her hands of hair gel and makeup. She twisted the faucet and stuck her fingers under the tap, annoyed that they were trembling.

Tony Sinclair had almost kissed her again out there. Worse, she'd wanted him to, even looking like Methuselah. What was it about him that drew her? She didn't *like* muscular, square-jawed men who looked as though they belonged in comic books about saving the world from evil megalomaniacs.

Sinclair, under normal circumstances, was a . . . a *caricature* of a jock. You just knew by looking at him that he'd been captain of his high-school football team, and had held the head cheerleader enslaved for years just with a dimple. The sun always shone on golden boys like Sinclair. Even if it rained cats and dogs in one area of town, the clouds parted over *him* to rain naked women.

Yep, thought Jazz, scrubbing her nails furiously with a little brush. *Torrents and monsoons of naked chicks, hurtling onto his roof, rattling his windows, blowing in gusts onto his front porch.*

And she was damned if she'd be one of them. She had her pride, after all.

She gazed at her reflection in the mirror without illusion. The desilvered spots in its surface became metaphors for her cynicism, which had rusted through her shiny dreams about what life would be like when she grew up.

As a young girl, stuck in Grandmother Sophronia's fiercely clean home, she'd imagined that one day a white knight would gallop up the weedless front walk on a noble steed. He'd sweep her up before him, and with his lance, pin Grandmother to the wall by her topknot so she couldn't follow.

Jazz and her handsome knight rode off into the sunset, kissing, and she never had to smell disinfectant again.

Her mouth twisted. She'd given up waiting for a white knight long ago. Nobody was going to rescue her from life and assume all her burdens upon his broad shoulders—especially not some useless oaf of a man.

No, men simply added burdens. Her boyfriend Evan had wanted her to do his laundry. His predecessor had asked her to write his college papers. And Myles?

Myles had taught her how irresponsible men were, how shifty and unreliable the critters could be.

She didn't even trust men to be competent. What made her think that Sinclair would investigate thoroughly enough on his own? She frowned.

The more she thought about it, the more convinced she became that she needed to get inside the museum herself.

Jazz turned off the water and dried her hands on a threadbare old towel. Since she'd made Sinclair a geriatric collector, what better cover for her than his traveling nurse?

In the meantime, however, she had to confront Sinclair's disturbing machismo yet again. She had a few more details to see to, such as his posture and eyesight.

He complained bitterly at the senior fashions she made him don, and protested even more when she knotted a cord around his neck, attached the other end to his belt, and pulled it tight so that he couldn't straighten to his full height. She buttoned his collar completely to hide the rope. An old pair of prescription eyeglasses saw to it that his vision truly was impaired. He couldn't even walk straight.

Sinclair with slumped shoulders and a hunch was much less threatening to her peace of mind. A moss green cardigan was the final *pièce de résistance*. She'd transformed Sinclair into a certified, droopy-drawered old fart.

"Think this'll really work?" he asked.

"Look in the mirror."

He tottered over to see himself in all his glory, and simply stared. "Hello, Handsome."

Jazz laughed.

"You did everything except put tufts of hair in my ears," marveled Tony.

"Hey, we can fix that."

"No, no. That won't be necessary."

"Pull your pants up even more," she told him.

"They're already up to my chin!"

"Not quite. Anyway—make yourself comfortable. It's my turn to get ready now."

Sinclair fixed her with a beady-eyed stare. "What do you mean? You're not coming."

"Yes, I am. I'm your traveling nurse. You couldn't possibly have flown here all the way from, say, Berlin, at your age without an attendant."

"No." Tony glowered at her.

"You know, I really don't remember asking your permission." Jazz walked to one of the large wardrobes and flung it open, ignoring him. She selected a dowdy old knee-length tweed skirt in brown and retrieved its matching jacket.

"Jazz, I can't be worrying about a civilian. It's out of the question."

She grabbed the exhibition catalogue for the Impressionism show, and scanned the acknowledgments page quickly. "You are Baron von Appen, wheelchair-bound because of arthritis, and terribly upset over the burglary. You've come to see the premises, to make sure no stone is left unturned in the investigation. As a major collector and victim of the heist, you demand to see all the documentation on the case—"

"I am not taking you," growled Tony.

"You speak English with a heavy Teutonic accent, and I must occasionally interpret for you, as well as push your wheelchair and ensure that you take your medication."

Jazz was now sorting through a box of accessories, from which she pulled some sturdy leather pumps, a pair of ocher tights, and a serviceable old handbag. "I am Fraulein Schneidelhopf, a distant unmarried cousin of yours. I put up with your crotchety personality only because I am paid to . . . and I am so sorry we arrived unannounced, but you insisted."

"Forget it."

"Sinclair, you're being unreasonable."

"No, I'm not. I'll do this alone, or not at all."

"I guess that means you won't do it, then. So I'll just have to be Frau von Appen. My husband's too ill to travel, and—"

"No! Jazz, I swear if you try to go in alone, I'll call the museum and alert them."

She came toe to toe with him, and met him glare for glare. "Then I'll be forced to do the same to you, won't I?"

Tony swore under his breath and hitched up his plaid pants.

"Besides," she reminded him, "you can't go in there without my help, and I just spent five hours on your disguise. Doesn't that count for anything?"

He just muttered something—all she caught were the words "women" and "early grave"— and began to pace unsteadily, hampered by the spectacles and the cord pulling his head down.

Chapter 13

*T*HE HOLDING CELL WAS REALLY BEYOND VILE, Myles ruminated. He ran his fingers up and down the heavy metal bars that caged him and McGraw like animals, and amused himself by deciding which species each of them would be. McGraw would be something unpleasant—perhaps a hybrid of hyena and walrus, covered in reptilian scales. He, Sir Myles, had more style. He rather thought he'd be a sleek panther, or a large, well-muscled antelope, endowed with a noble, liquid gaze and graceful curving horns.

The bars left a nasty, flaky residue on his hands, and he brushed them together. Why did they paint them black? And all these shades of gray and putrid green—they were enough to make *anyone* commit an act of violence. It was sadly apparent that the arts education of those in law enforcement had been neglected. He'd speak to Ellen about it; the public schools were in dire need of arts funding.

McGraw made a foul noise in the back of his throat which involved clearing his nasal passages. "Damn, but I'm horny," he declared. "I even miss the old lady."

Myles raised his brows. "It's hardly romantic to refer to your wife as 'the old lady.' "

"Ex-wife. Anyways, she don't care."

"I doubt it causes her to blush with pleasure, either."

"I got other ways to give 'er pleasure."

"You are truly unenlightened. Women are more than an instrument for sex."

"How do you figure?"

"They are fair blossoms in the sunshine of the world," exclaimed Myles.

McGraw stared at him as if he'd lost his mind. Then he guffawed.

"A lady is a fine porcelain vessel, upon whose fair surface glorious features have been bestowed by the heavens."

His words were drowned out by his companion's chortling.

"You're not listening!" Myles thundered. "Woman is like a fine wine, an exquisitely crafted poem, a masterpiece of spun sugar. I, Sir Myles Taylor, will teach you this."

"Is that so." McGraw gazed insolently at him.

Myles strode across the cell and came to stand in front of McGraw. He drew himself up into his loftiest poetic stance, then he cast a dramatic arm out. "Woman," he exclaimed in a majestic tone. "What enters your mind when I conjure the term?"

McGraw shrugged. "Hooters. Snatch."

Myles's arm wilted. "No, no, no, no, no."

"Hey, Fruit, this is *my* mind, and you asked me what I thought about when you said 'woman.' That's what I think about."

"Work with me, here!" commanded Myles. "You are quagmired in the vortex of the vulgarian. You must rise above the vileness of the Visigoth!"

McGraw blinked.

Myles sent him a pitying glance. "You employ hideous terms to describe what it is for which you truly search: the nectar, the essence of femininity."

McGraw shook his head and opened his mouth.

"Stop! Close your eyes, and focus upon the concept of woman. The grace and dignity of the ages. The curve of humanity. The gentle breath of kindness."

McGraw's sketchy eyelashes brushed the puffy pouches beneath his eyes, and his mouth, under the scraggly mustache, hung open in concentration.

"Now, come again. Wooh-muhn," Myles said patiently. "What do you think of?"

"Pasties and a G-string."

Myles rolled his eyes heavenward. "Let's try again. Woman is swaying before you, awakening all your ideological notions. She is complex, she is layered with emotions, she is the soul of music and story . . . she is Mother Earth."

As he continued along these lines, McGraw began to take deep breaths, and Myles was encouraged. "Woman," he repeated. "The nectar and essence of woman. Now what do you think of?" He leaned forward, holding his breath.

His pupil's brow furrowed, and his small lips stretched to reveal those disgusting gray-brown teeth. "Ohhhmmmm."

Myles knew, deep down inside, that he was a great educator. Perhaps Ellen would finance a Poetical College for him. He would illuminate lives, and be recognized for the great man that he was.

He put aside the pleasant vision, and turned his

attention back to his pupil. "Well? I pose the question once again. The essence of woman is . . . ?"

"Poontang," said McGraw.

"I *beg* your pardon?" Ellen Whitaker Northrop Banks could scarcely believe her ears—or her eyes. She was in a squalid, beastly jail, for God's sake, and there was Myles, parading around in an orange jumpsuit, exchanging conversation with an odious man who said things like—well, she couldn't possibly repeat it. Really, a lady shouldn't even know the meaning of the word.

"Ellen, my love!" said Myles, jumping back against the wall. "What are you doing in this place? You shouldn't have come. Why aren't you still abroad?"

"Looks like a broad to me," declared the horrid, flabby man who shared his cell. "A mighty swank one." His eyes gleamed, and he sucked on his teeth.

Ellen repressed a shudder. "I decided to return early, Myles. I came home to discover that you're in jail. How could you not have told me?"

"Didn't want you to worry, my love," he said sheepishly. "But I forget my manners. Mrs. Ellen Whitaker Northrop Banks, may I present Mr.—ah,

William McGraw. We didn't hear you approach."

His horrid cellmate made a guttural noise deep in his throat, looked her up and down from head to toe, and smacked his lips.

Ellen stood riveted in horror. She clutched her Dior handbag to her chest, and pressed her legs tightly together. In spite of the humid July heat, a shiver ran down her spine. Even though she was enraged with Myles, she couldn't bear to see him in a place like this. Her sweet scalawag, deprived of his handmade Egyptian cotton shirt, cuff links, and ascot. Her darling, wearing cheap shower thongs instead of his polished Gucci loafers. This was awful.

His hand crept up to brush his hair back, and he turned away from her slightly. "Afraid I'm not looking my best, m'dear. Frightful shade of tangerine, isn't it? And what's worse, it's a *polyester blend.*" His voice crept down to a whisper on the last words; he was deeply mortified. His eyes met hers, only to skitter away.

"Myles—" her voice broke. "I don't care about that! But a Degas, under your bed! How could you? You promised me—"

"It was a plant. Ellen, dearest Ellen, you've got to believe me. I've been framed!"

"Where did you go, that night?"

"What night, my love?"

"I woke up, and you weren't there. *Where were you?*"

McGraw made a noise akin to a toilet plunger's suction. "Ooooh—eeeee, Mr. Slick is up a crick!" He shoved his right hand deep into the pocket of his coveralls. "Don't you worry, hot mama, Billy here'll take care o' you."

Both she and Myles ignored him.

"I couldn't sleep. I got on the Internet and checked out the polo schedules."

"Myles, my security system was off in the morning." Her voice trembled, but she stood firm. Where was the righteous anger that had propelled her over here? She needed it, but it had deserted her.

"I went out to the patio for a smoke! You've got to believe me . . ."

"I never gave you my personal code."

He shrugged uncomfortably. "Ellen, it's child's play to disarm a system such as yours."

"The shit has hit the fan, Sir Swishy! Heh, heh, heh."

"McGraw—"

"Child's play. I see." She felt herself begin to hyperventilate. "And was it child's play to disarm the High Museum's security system, too?"

"No! I told you—"

"Myles, surely you don't expect me to believe

that these alleged people who framed you would leave an original Degas oil under your bed, when they could sell it on the black market for millions?"

"Yes, I do expect you to believe me. Think about it: the Degas dancer series is far too well known and cataloged to fence easily. It's the mark of an amateur to take something so high-profile, Ellen, not the mark of a professional. I was one of the best! Why would I take the Degas, when there were less well known paintings available? Several Pissarros, and Braquemonds, and an Eva Gonzalez."

"Simple, Myles. The Degas is worth more."

"You're not listening to me, Ellen. In order to resell that painting, I'd have to vault it for years and years, then handle it with the utmost discretion and privacy. Only a very special buyer will take the risk. To find that buyer can take decades."

He sounded so sincere. Looked the picture of orange-clad innocence. But too many things weren't adding up, and it gave her the creeps that he'd been able to disarm her alarm system so easily. Normal people, honest people, didn't come by that sort of knowledge, much less act upon it.

Ellen shook her head. "Look me in the eye,

Myles, and tell me that there's nothing you're keeping from me."

He threw up his hands and gazed at her quickly, but his eyes shifted, and she noticed a tiny, wry twist to the left side of his mouth.

He was omitting something. Something big. She knew it deep down inside, and the hurt which had been like a dull, muscular ache burst forth with all the agony of a kidney stone. She had once again been made a fool of by a man. Stanley Northrop had had his mistresses, Morton Banks a fondness for Chivas and bookies. Of *course* Myles had a bad habit, too. Skunks couldn't hide their stripes, and neither could men. She was just so tired of being used by them.

She looked at the face she'd grown so fond of: the green eyes flashing in that thin, but vitally masculine visage with an angular jaw. Here was her self-proclaimed "scurrilous character," who'd repaired her childhood dollhouse, and served up a divine veal marsala, and made her feel like an exquisite fairy princess in bed.

Ellen closed her eyes. She didn't ask for love in a marriage—she knew that love was a pretty word, and a pipe dream. But his tenderness and affection had brought tears to her eyes; his outrageous opinions had made her laugh; his style had

taken her breath away. Myles Taylor the lover
could almost make her overlook Myles Taylor, the
thief. She longed, right this moment, for his fingers to caress her cheek . . .

McGraw began to make guttural noises from
the corner of the cell. He was hunched over, with
his hand still deep in his pocket. Dear God, surely
he wasn't—? No!

Myles's eyes, wide and sincere, narrowed at
the foul sounds. "Excuse me," he said, his face
reddening.

She turned away quickly and forced herself not
to run. Behind her came the sickening thud of a
fist hitting flesh and bone, and then a body collapsed to the floor. "You bloody pervert!" Myles
shouted. "Behave yourself."

"I'm breaking our engagement." The words
came out of her mouth in a forced whisper, punc-
tuated by a most unwelcome sob.

"Ellen, no! Don't do this—"

"I can't trust you. And where there is no trust,
there's no relationship. It's as simple as that."

"Ellen, stop—"

"Good-bye, Myles."

"Damn it all to hell, woman! Whatever you
think of me, get yourself back out of the country—it's not safe for you here!"

"Thank you for your concern. Perhaps you

should have thought about me *before* you became involved in all of this."

Miss Martha had always told her to carry a clean handkerchief in her purse. Why hadn't she remembered? Ellen wiped the tears off her cheeks with her fingers as she walked away.

Chapter 14

*T*HE HIGH MUSEUM ROSE LIKE A GREAT, WHITE modern molar in the afternoon sunlight. Designed by famous architect Richard Meier, the building had opened its doors in 1983 and been declared a sculpture in itself. Slabs of pristine white concrete wrapped the steel armature of the structure, true to the South's penchant for veneers.

Tony and Jazz had rented a wheelchair for his Baron von Appen performance. Their plan was to do reconnaissance and get some idea of the museum's security. They would also try to identify any possible inside players in the heist.

They parked in a nearby hourly garage, dug the wheelchair out of the Taurus's trunk, and Tony clambered into it, grumbling. Hunched over, with his knees drawn up, he looked even more ancient and pathetic.

Jazz dusted him with a last-minute storm of powder and laughed, but the joke was soon on her, since she had to push Sinclair down the couple of blocks to the museum, and then up the steep ramp that gave access to it.

Sinclair weighed a good two hundred pounds to her one hundred, and she was hampered by skirt, stockings, and pumps. She began to curse as she panted and pushed.

"Eh?" said Tony, cupping a hand to his ear. "Schpeak up, then, Fraulein! Can't hear."

Jazz leaned close in her tortoiseshell glasses and told him he was one heavy bastard.

"Schimpfen verboten, Fraulein! To speak to your employer so!"

She made a face at him.

"Make it schnappy, now. Hup, two, three, four! We barely inch forward—you are like ein schnail with lobotomy!"

"Sinclair, I'm starting to take a real dislike to you. Keep in mind that I can always—" she heaved a breath—"step out of the way and let you roll back down this ramp."

By the time they reached the front entrance, Jazz was completely winded and drenched in perspiration. Her makeup was in danger of sliding right off her face in a puddle.

An automatic door swung open to allow them inside, and she leaned on the back of the chair as she wheeled Tony the last few feet.

A young man behind the ticket desk shot her a look of sympathy.

"I vant to see Herr Director!" Tony declared in a crotchety, quavering voice.

"Beg pardon, sir?"

"I am Baron von Appen, and I demand to see Herr Director immediately."

"Mr. Phillips is unavailable. I regret to inform you that he's out of town."

Which they already knew.

"I haf travelt great distance to schpeak mit museum management, youngk man. You will fetch one directly!"

"One what, sir?"

"A manager, please." Jazz laid a soothing hand on the baron's shoulder. "Baron von Appen is terribly upset at the recent news of the burglary. He has a vast collection of Chinese bronzes that he was planning to leave to the High, since his daughter lives here in Atlanta. But he'd like to speak with someone about security measures here at the museum. You understand his concern, I'm sure."

The baron made a snorting noise in his throat and clenched the arms of his wheelchair. He glowered at the poor attendant, who promptly picked up the phone. No museum employee would risk offending a potential donor.

A Miss Genet, assistant to the director, appeared promptly to fawn over the Baron. She took his large, trembling, wizened hand in her own, batted her big blue Southern eyes, and told him how pleased she was to meet him. "Chahmed," she said. "Delahted."

For Jazz, she had a pleasant smile and a nod that said it all: She had dismissed her as the lowly paid companion. That suited Jazz just fine; she'd be able to slip away more easily, unnoticed.

"*Wie gehts*," replied Tony-the-Baron, using up what were probably the last two words he knew in German.

Jazz was examining Miss Genet's perfectly proportioned legs and svelte feet, encased in Ferragamo pumps, when to her horror the woman spouted a string of perfectly pronounced German to Tony.

While Jazz almost had a heart attack, Tony didn't even blink before beaming her a dazzling geezer smile. "Your German, my dear, it is wunderbar! Many compliments. Baht I must ask you to indulge me: Here, I practice my Enklish, yah?"

Miss Genet's ample bosom swelled with pride and Southern grace as she agreed, while Jazz let out the breath she was unaware she held. She reminded herself that one should never, ever underestimate a Southern woman. The glaze of cosmetics and charm often hid a fine education and great intelligence.

Jazz herself was neither Southern nor Northern. She'd become a hybrid, moving all over the country because of Myles and his antics. Though Atlanta had been her home for some years, she'd never fully assimilated the city's original Deep South ways. And for the last decade or two, it had become a city of corporate transients, who brought with them their own attitudes and customs.

Miss Genet, by the look of her, had been born and bred in Atlanta. Carefully blond, with flawlessly buffed nails, skin, and manners, she appeared to have stepped out of a gift-wrapped Rich's box.

Jazz neither liked her nor disliked her. She was too smooth, too flawless to create any such response. Annoyance rose inside her that the woman displayed no warp or woof of personality: She was simply a well-oiled hospitality machine.

Tony's eyes, behind the age makeup, seemed all too appreciative of Miss Genet's curves, but Jazz scoffed at the tendril of jealousy that curled around her heart. For once, the Chick Magnet possessed no magnetism. Greasepaint, plaid pants, and bad posture hid his muscles, his dimples, and that raw edge of physicality.

They followed the director's assistant on a personal tour, starting at the stunning quarter-circle atrium, lit by sunshine through wedge-shaped skylights.

The place was beautiful, but blindingly white. Jazz imagined the janitorial staff just pressure-washing the whole interior with bleach and water.

From the atrium they took an elevator to the fourth floor, which housed the current exhibit, and then wound down through the permanent collection. The High's design paid tribute to the Guggenheim in New York, featuring an open-ramp walkway that wrapped around the interior space like a ribbon. Jazz fantasized briefly about roller-blading all the way down it, before turning her attention back to the business at hand.

Tony actually had Miss Genet giggling at his octogenarian compliments. The dog.

"Fraulein, you glow with ze soft rhadiance of zat Whistler portrait."

"You're too kind, Baron."

She pronounced it "kahnd." The words in her

mouth were butterscotch, and she drew out and savored each one.

The tour continued. "And here is a lyrical little Rousseau landscape, one we're particularly proud to have."

"Aach," said Tony, "to be lost in zose woods with a luffly lady like yourself . . . one would not desire a compass."

Jazz fell into a fit of coughing, and, unaccountably, her knee jerked up and hit the Baron in his noble Teutonic arse.

"Ooof."

"I'm so sorry, Herr von Appen! An unfortunate accident."

"Clumsy! Very clumsy of you," growled Tony, twisting around and knitting his fuzzy gray eyebrows at her. Unfortunately, the hellish humidity of their walk outside had caused one of them to peel up at the outside corner, and his nose was in danger, too. Damn this Atlanta heat!

Miss Genet, busy with her tour and her vowels, hadn't noticed yet, but it was only a matter of time. "Downstayahs," she told them, "we ah proud to display ahtifacts from Papua New Guinea. Come this way . . ."

They followed the genteel wiggle of her hips down the ramp and into yet another gallery, while Jazz looked frantically around for rest rooms. In the meantime, she reached her hand around Tony's head and pressed her index finger firmly against his eyebrow.

"Miss Schneidelhopf!" he protested, not understanding. "I can't see. You are eempairing mine vision."

Jazz ignored him and pressed now on the left side of his nose.

"Aaach! Take off your hands from me!"

"Shut up," hissed Jazz.

Miss Genet stopped in the middle of her speech about the donor of a Papuan mask, and raised an eyebrow.

"So sorry," Jazz said. "It's all terribly interesting, but it's time for the baron's medication. Can you direct us to the WC?

"Rest rooms," she clarified, at the woman's blank expression.

Miss Genet wiggled them down to the facilities.

Tony frowned. Jazz was behaving very oddly . . . not that anything about this charade could be considered normal. What did she mean, it was time for his medication?

To his horror, Jazz wheeled him toward the ladies' room. Miss Genet coughed, and he felt himself redden with embarrassment. "Nein, Miss Schneidelhopf!"

"Huh?" Jazz pulled open the door.

He was damned if she was going to force him into the powder room! "I go to ze other rest room, *bitte.*"

Jazz shrugged, let the door close, and wheeled him to the door marked MEN. She tugged on its handle.

Tony cleared his throat. "*Alone*, Miss Schneidelhopf."

Her eyes flashed with exasperation behind her horn-rims. Then she said the unspeakable. "Now, Baron, you know you need help—you can't do your business by yourself."

Miss Genet pretended to examine a nearby bulletin board. "How about some coffee?" she asked in bright tones, and backed away. "Ah'll be right back."

Tony drew his breath in with a hiss, and made no further protest as Jazz wheeled him into the men's room. "Was that necessary?" he bit out between clenched teeth.

"Yes, it was." She pulled a small tube of something from her handbag, ignoring a scandalized glance from a gentleman who'd just turned away from one of the urinals.

She pushed Tony's chair to one of the stalls, while the gentleman knit his brows and washed his hands.

Tony closed his eyes. "What the hell are you up to?" he whispered fiercely, once they were inside.

"Your eyebrow and nose are peeling off."

Tony put his hand up to his nose.

"Don't touch it! You'll smear the makeup or tear the foam rubber."

The hand-washing gentleman's feet turned toward them as he extracted a couple of paper towels from a dispenser. Then his loafers walked slowly to the door and left Tony and Jazz alone.

She sat gingerly upon the toilet rim and opened the tube of adhesive, squeezing a little out onto her finger. Then she bent toward him, peeled up his bushy false eyebrow, and dabbed at the skin under it. She added a little more to the back of the brow itself, and then blew gently before sticking it once more to his skin.

Gray fuzzy hair, brown lipstick, horn-rims and all, her breath on his skin excited him, raising geezer goose bumps. Tony wanted to pull her onto his lap and have his way with her until the wheels of the chair spun and smoked. Hubba, hubba, he'd show her what a senior citizen in plaid pants could do. He'd invent a new meaning for AARP: Always at the Ready for Pleasure. Yeah, baby!

Jazz leaned forward and poked at his nose, while he thought about poking her with his tongue. And with other things. Those soft lips of hers beckoned him, and he leaned into them without further ado.

God, the taste of her! She was a heady combination of fresh apple and mint . . . and then that sweet skin of hers, a scent impossible to describe, the signature of Jazz and Jazz alone.

Her arms crept around his neck, and she kissed him back with fervor. His tongue slipped into the wet warmth of her mouth and engaged in a sultry tango with hers. Pressed together intimately, sliding in rhythm across the dance floor of their joined mouths, they teased, rubbed, flicked—broke apart only to seek each other once again.

Their tongues were naughty coquettes, impudent with desire, seeking forbidden pleasure. They longed to escape the chaperoning presence of lips and go further astray.

Tony's hands crept up under her shirtwaist to encounter warm, creamy fragrant skin. Yum. He splayed his fingers over her waist, pleasantly surprised again by the firm muscles at her stomach and diaphragm.

When he tried to undo buttons, she stopped him, which left him no choice but to move lower, cupping her bottom, and then lower still, to ruck up that bothersome skirt of hers. His hands crept up her thighs, slowly, and then—he couldn't help it, honestly!—his unruly fingers crept between her legs.

Jazz gasped, sagged against him for a moment, and then jerked back.

Off-balance, he slid again into the wheelchair, banging it against the stall door.

Jazz, arms flailing, fell into the open toilet.

With a splash.

It wasn't funny. It wasn't funny at all—but the expression on her face was priceless.

Tony's self-control lost the battle to a belly laugh, even though now they were really in trouble. How could they explain to Miss Genet how Fraulein Schneidelhopf had fallen into the commode?

Tony strong-armed her out of the toilet, and they avoided looking at each other while they exited the stall in search of paper towels. Luckily, since Tony had obligingly rucked up her skirt, only Jazz's underwear and stockings were wet.

When he attempted to help Jazz dry her derriere, she burst out laughing. "Get away from me, you pervert! This is all your fault."

He grinned. "I'm just trying to help."

"Help yourself, you mean." Jazz scrubbed at her stockings and bit her lip.

Tony didn't deny it. "Looks hopeless," he said, waggling his brows. "The only thing to do is to take *everything* off and hold it under the hand dryer."

"Nice try. Back off, or I'll wipe the gleam out of your eye with this fine recycled paper."

"I don't know what you mean." He pulled his most innocent face.

"Hah. Though that's not a bad idea about the hand dryer." Skirt still up around her waist, she walked over to the machine, punched its round steel button, and bent over in front of it, pointing her nether parts toward the warm draft.

Tony focused on the ridiculously sexy image she made, and the wet outline of her bikini panties under the ugly stockings. Getting to see the contours of her legs again was no punishment, either.

But his gaze returned to the panties, and the way the damp fabric clung to her tantalizing mons, dipping inward at the forbidden cleft.

"I'd be happy to blow on your front side," he offered. "Purely in the name of efficiency, of course."

Color rushed into her face. "That's big of you." *But I think we both know that would only increase the dampness.* Her voice gruff with embarrassment, she waved a hand at him. "Get over here—your makeup is all messed up again."

Once she'd repaired his mouth, she cast a glance into the mirror to fix her own.

"Do you know how *weird* this is?" she choked. "How absolutely *bizarre*? You could cut the hormones in here with a knife, yet you look like you just stepped off the set of *Cocoon*, while I have a dryer up my butt!"

Tony threw back his head in a guffaw, but was nearly guillotined by the cord she'd used to create his feeble posture. He was clawing at it, and Jazz had turned around to blow-dry her front, when the men's room door swung open again.

Tony got a quick glimpse of Miss Genet standing in the hallway with a tray of coffee cups, before his view was blocked by a large, bearded blond man—the very man Rico had been chatting with at Hot Rockin' Mama's.

Chapter 15

*I*T WASN'T EVERY DAY THAT JAZZ WAS CAUGHT blow-drying her crotch in a men's room.

Blond Beard blinked and let the door swing closed behind him.

Tony fell into a coughing fit.

Jazz pulled her skirt down to her knees again, patted at her gray hair, and pushed her horn-rims up to the bridge of her nose. "Good afternoon," she managed.

The blond guy just eyeballed her, his face devoid of expression. He wore a walkie-talkie on his belt, and a blue museum name tag that identified him as B. Trenton, Security. "You may have noticed the sign on the door," he said to Jazz. "A common three-letter word excluding your gender."

"Oh, dear. Beg pardon. But my employer, Herr von Appen, does need a little help doing his business, you see."

Tony had assumed a helpless, pathetic slouch once again, and now affected a Parkinson's-like head tremor.

B. Trenton didn't respond, but she could see the cogs turning behind those flat gray eyes. He probably wondered how long it had been since she'd had a date.

After a moment, he gestured toward the urinals in the back of the room. "Yeah, well, if it's all the same to you, I'd like to do *my* business."

"Of course. We were just leaving." Jazz aimed a flustered smile at him and grasped the handles of the baron's wheelchair. They exited the men's room.

Well, well, well, Mr. Trenton. Lucky for us you needed to drain your main vein.

Ms. Genet beamed at them as they reconnected, and proffered the coffee. "If you'd like, we can sit down in one of the museum education rooms, and I'll tell you all about the children's programs while we drink up."

Tony-the-Baron grunted and shook his head. Jazz took that as her cue to make their excuses.

"I'm so sorry, Miss Genet. You've been wonderful to take us on such an informative tour, but the baron isn't feeling well after the long flight yesterday. Perhaps you could just quickly tell us about museum security and the measures taken to improve it since the . . . ah, unfortunate incident with the Impressionist paintings." She took a cup of coffee from the tray so as not to be rude, and sipped it.

Miss Genet put the tray down on the information kiosk, took a cup herself after Tony shook his head, and smoothed her skirt. "It's not museum policy to share specific details about our security system. I'm sure you understand. I can tell you that we meet all requirements for our insurance policy, and that there's a combination of alarms, motion detectors, pressure plates, and surveillance cameras." She smiled. "Of course, we also have guards in the galleries who are alert and attentive at all times."

"Hmmmmpphh," grumbled the baron. "Zis system, it would seem zere are flaws. How else would ze rhobbery haf taken place?"

Miss Genet's lips tightened. "I'm not at liberty to discuss any aspect of the investigation, Herr von Appen."

"Zen I cannot be rheassured of ze safety of my Chinese bronzes, eh?"

"On the contrary. The lapse in security has been repaired and reinforced, and the person responsible for the lapse is no longer on staff. We have a new head of security now—as a matter of fact, there he is." She gestured toward B. Trenton, who had just emerged from the men's room. He headed in the opposite direction, toward some offices.

"Bruce is just wonderful," Miss Genet enthused. "He has a background in criminology, and has made all kinds of improvements since his appointment."

I'll just bet he has, thought Jazz. Why was he still here? Was he planning an even bigger heist for Cantini?

They thanked Miss Genet for her tour and information, giving her a bogus address and telephone number for her files. She assured them that the director would be most interested in talking to the Baron about his collection, and they parted ways.

Tony was sad to see the wheelchair returned to the rental place, his fantasies for it unfulfilled. He found himself looking speculatively at the monkey bars and the slide in a playground as he drove back to Jazz's studio. He knew he needed professional help when he saw an ice-cream vendor's truck cruise by, and imagined the things he and Jazz could do naked with a Dove bar.

The seam of his plaid pants dug into his balls

as they turned into the warehouse parking lot. He'd be glad to ditch the geezer garb and take a nice cold shower before he went barking mad.

They'd made a huge breakthrough in identifying Trenton today, and he should be concentrating on that, not his prong.

Jazz was quiet beside him, thinking her own thoughts. "Why did you kiss me in the men's room stall?" she asked suddenly.

Why? Why did acorns fall off trees? Why did the wind blow? Why did men have nipples? Tony racked his brain for something logical or suave to explain his behavior. "I dunno," he said.

"We were on a reconnaissance mission," she stated. "A job. A matter of urgency. It was highly inappropriate."

He knew that. He didn't require that it be spelled out to him. "Yeah."

"So, why?"

"Hell if I know." Why was she putting him on the spot like this? "Look, sweetheart, you didn't exactly protest."

Her eyes narrowed at him, but she said nothing for a long moment. "I don't think we can work together."

Tony let out a long, exasperated breath. "Look, this is something we can control. We are two mature adults. Whatever this thing is between us, it's temporary. It'll work its way out. I mean, it's not like we have an iota of anything in common.

"I'm a regular guy, with regular goals in life. I want my aunt safe. I want my job back. I want to side my house. I want to meet a nice Southern girl and have a houseful of kids."

Jazz stiffened. "And I'm a freak who makes monsters. A chick who plays with power tools. I'm different, I'm dangerous, and my closest relative's in jail." She opened the passenger door and climbed out. "Better stay away from me, Sinclair." She slammed the door, and leaned into the open window. "And don't kiss me again."

She was unaccountably upset. Jazz shoved the hair out of her face and clomped in Fraulein Schneidelhopf's serviceable shoes through the hallways, digging into her bag for her keys.

I'm a regular guy.

What did that make her, an irregular girl? A substandard woman? A freakin' cyborg? Well, that was just fine.

She liked her independence, and had no need for a relationship with a man. She'd decided long ago never to marry. Men just got in the way or took credit for your work. She gritted her teeth, remembering an unfortunate "collaboration" with Dane, a fellow special-effects artist.

Dane had used her body, her studio, and her talent—only to forget about all of them when he was offered a major Hollywood contract.

She slammed her studio door behind her. Donovan the dragon greeted her as always, and she gave his lower leg a maternal pat as she passed under him. Her creatures were better than any guy, "regular" or otherwise.

Regular guy, her ass. Sinclair didn't kiss like a regular guy. She would never have sucked face with a regular guy in a bathroom stall, jeopardizing a five-hour makeup job. Regular guys didn't attract her with the force of an industrial electromagnet. She'd sometimes wondered what was wrong with her, because she'd never been overwhelmed by a rush of hormones for anyone in particular.

With Tony Sinclair, the hormones stacked up in six-lane freeways running to every nerve in her body. They honked and swore at each other, trying to get to their destinations. They shimmered in the heat, and gunned their motors. Keeping the brakes on all those damn hormones was exhausting.

Jazz slowly mounted the stairs to her office and

glared at her desk, which was covered with bills and project descriptions and due dates, written in red on her calendar.

The answering machine light flashed at her, informing her that several people wanted to talk to her. She was too tired to talk to anyone, and she still had work to do. She shot the bird at the answering machine and slumped into her chair.

She thought about the information they'd acquired at the museum and put it together with what they already knew. Cantini was the driving force behind the heist. Bruce Trenton, the inside man, had provided a lapse in security and set his former boss up to take the rap, by the sound of it. Rico Romanelli knew where to hide things and was paid quite well to do it.

She curled her hands into fists. These three men, and probably others, were now scarfing down linguine, following baseball, and dreaming up more sleazy activities while her father languished in jail. That was completely unacceptable.

Equally unacceptable was that instead of concentrating on solving the case, Jazz was panting and drooling over the cop who'd arrested Myles. All those honking hormones needed to be driven into a dark parking garage and left to cool down.

Jazz grimaced and reached for the stack of bills with one hand and her checkbook with the other.

She stuck her tongue out at the bill from the electric company. She barely controlled the urge to spit on the one for her mortgage, knowing that about three dollars went to her principal, and all the rest was interest. She accidentally spilled two-day-old coffee on the check for her quarterly taxes, and hoped it smelled nice when the IRS cashed it.

The rest of the bills weren't too bad, and at least she didn't need to wire money to Myles's bank account this month, since he was an honored guest of the state. She sealed the last envelope, added stamps and return address labels to them all, then finally turned to the answering machine, pen poised.

"Hi, I'm John with CitiSlick Financial," said a prerecorded voice like caramel. "Are you aware that you qualify for a home equity loan of up to thirty thousand dollars? That's right, I said thirty thousand dollars! Think what you could do with that money . . ."

Uh, huh—pay it back at only 29 percent interest. Jazz hit the DELETE button.

"Hello, dear, this is your neighbor, Thelma Sue Treadwell, reminding you that Congressman Barney Fiddle needs your support."

Poor Thelma Sue obviously hadn't heard that her candidate had a predilection for white powder and other congressmen's wives. Jazz deleted that message, too.

The next message was obviously from a cell phone. Hiss, crackle, pttfh. "Jazz Taylor. Lon Adams, here. Howar'ya, babe?"

She wrinkled her nose. She really, really hated being called "babe." It ranked right up there with being pinched on the butt and getting paid half what a man did for the same job.

"Listen—we gotta speed things up a little. We're gonna start production three weeks earlier than scheduled—another project got canned. So I need your stuff like *pronto*. I also need a full-body *male* plaster cast, if you can whip one up for me. Plan on shipping in forty-eight hours, okay, babe? Bill our account number." Click.

Click? Freakin' *click?* No apology, not even a mollifying "if you can" clause? Jazz stared at the machine wrathfully. Aaaarrggghhh!

How dare he call her up and demand this from her in two days? She indulged in a brief fantasy of calling him back. "Lon Adams. Jazz Taylor, here. Howar'ya, ya wrinkled little cocktail wee-nie? Listen—I'm kinda busy here, with all my work for Spielberg. So you can just take your two-day turnaround and shove it."

Ooooh, it was so tempting. Her palm itched to pick up the cordless phone and leave the message.

But working remote from Atlanta, she was lucky if she got considered for jobs in LA, and Lon knew that. He also knew she'd break her neck to get it done for him by deadline, and charge him less to boot, just because she needed the business and the contacts. But the steam curling out of her ears could set off a fire alarm.

She was so angry, she missed the beginning of the last message. But the end of it wasn't very promising.

". . . *capisce*? Or you'll end up one dead bunny," rasped a gravelly, adenoidal voice.

Huh? She hit the REPEAT button.

"Stop asking questions. Stop snooping around. Back off, *capisce*? Or you'll end up one dead bunny."

Great. Today had been just great. She'd fallen in a toilet, been forced to write an obscene check to the IRS, and had Lon holding her feet to the fire. Now she was receiving death threats. Could a Tuesday get any worse?

A knock on her studio door told her that it could. She opened it to discover the last person she wanted to see: Tony Sinclair.

Chapter 16

"DIDN'T I JUST GET RID OF YOU?" JAZZ ASKED.
He'd showered and dressed in blue
jeans, a fresh white T-shirt, and his own nose. He
grinned, flashing her those dastardly dimples,
and handed her the neatly folded plaid pants,
moss green cardigan, and other senior accessories. "Yeah, but I think we need to talk."

"Why?" she asked baldly.

"Don't be difficult."

"I'm good at being difficult. It's one of my best
personality traits."

"I can think of other, more intriguing ones."

"Like what?"

Tony's grin faded, and his blue eyes deepened.

"Like your loyalty to your father. Your guts. Your creativity. Your total inability to ask for help when you need it the most, and your lack of grace in accepting it."

"Hey!"

"Are you really going to argue those last two points?" The corners of his mouth turned up again.

All right, so she'd been told often that she was cussedly stubborn and obnoxiously independent. Better that than to be an idiot Daddy's girl who couldn't put gas in her own car and cried when she broke a nail.

"I don't like asking for help," she admitted.

"Me neither," said Tony. "But like it or not, we're going to have to help each other out. We've got three guys to watch, and we also need to find those paintings. I think I can put the squeeze on my friend Bagel to help, but we'll still have our hands full."

"Meanwhile, I've got a tight deadline to meet on the Lon Adams stuff."

Tony knit his brows.

"Remember Alicia? The model for my Venus de Milo?"

"Oh, yes. How could I forget?"

"I have to do a male statue, too. High classical, on a two-day turnaround. The plaster inside the cast won't even be fully dry by then. I'm more or less screwed." She stuck the tip of her tongue out and touched her upper lip, thinking. "Unless . . ."

"Unless what?"

"Unless I do something I hate to do, and ask for your help." She looked at him speculatively. "You'd actually be perfect."

"Perfect for what?"

"As a model. Proportionally."

"Don't even think about it!"

Jazz walked a slow circle around him, evaluating his long legs, nicely muscular buttocks, and the way his waist segued into those gorgeous broad shoulders. He had great arms, too—not overly bulky, not too lean. Why hadn't she thought of it before? Tony the Chick Magnet was the perfect Greek God! All she needed to do was duplicate him in plaster. If she started tonight, and stalled Lon for twenty-four hours, she could do it.

"Forget it," said her chosen model.

"But you're right here, in my studio."

He shook his head.

"We both want to pursue this case, but neither of us can watch three guys at once. So you need my help."

He folded his arms across his chest.

"And in return, I'm asking for yours."

"No."

"Why not? Didn't we just have a discussion about how hard it was for me to ask for help? You're not exactly encouraging me."

"You are *not* glopping stuff all over my nude body."

"I'll make a plaster cast first, and pour more plaster into that. I'd normally use a dental algi-nate, and pour it on you, but that takes a team of two or three people. Since I'm alone, and the fin-ished product is supposed to look like aged mar-ble, I can just use plaster bandages—though it'll take longer."

"You are *not* going to mummify me."

"Please, Sinclair?" She widened her eyes and tried to look as cute and feminine as she could.

He glowered at her, but she had a hunch he was wavering.

"Hah. A big macho guy like you, afraid to be a model," she teased. "Why so self-conscious?"

He shrugged.

Deciding that the end justified the means, Jazz let an evil chuckle escape. "Ohhhhhhh. *I* get it."

"You get what?" demanded Tony.

"You're embarrassed because . . . well, never mind. Don't worry about it."

"What? Why am I embarrassed?"

"God, do I have to say it out loud? I'm trying to spare you mortification."

His eyes narrowed.

"Really, it's a shame. For a guy to have an Olympic athlete's body like yours, and a tiny . . . you-know-what."

He drew in his breath with a hiss.

She cleared her throat. "It happens to a lot of guys who take steroids. Were you a high-school athlete?"

Tony now looked downright dangerous. "Are you implying," he said in thunderous tones, "that I don't want to take my clothes off because I'm *inadequate*?"

"You know what, Sinclair, size really doesn't matter—"

"That is *not* the problem!"

"Don't get all defensive about it, okay?" The man was truly magnificent when pissed off. It was almost fun to goad him.

"There *is* no problem," he declared. "I'll do it."

Jazz swallowed a smirk. "You will?"

His shirt had already hit the wall, and was soon followed by his shoes and socks. The buckle on his pants jingled, and Jazz stood riveted. Then they, too, hit the floor, and Tony Sinclair stood before her in his quite magnificent altogether.

"Oh my," said Jazz. Her smugness at how easy he was to manipulate disappeared, replaced by simple awe. The cop had a nightstick to rival all nightsticks. She swallowed.

"Well, are you going to do me, or not?"

Do him. "Um, yeah. Let me get my supplies. You can lie on that long table over there. But before we apply the plaster bandages, you'll want to, er, use this."

She disappeared behind the plastic curtain that housed the changing room and shower. When she emerged again, she handed him a pink plastic disposable razor.

Sinclair put his hands on his hips and looked from the razor to her. "Oh, that's funny. But the joke's over. Let's get started."

Jazz cleared her throat. "It's really not a joke. If you don't shave, it'll be very painful when I take the plaster off."

Sinclair's face darkened. He asked suspiciously, "Exactly which areas do I need to shave?"

"All of 'em."

He stared at her. "*All* of them?"

She nodded.

"My chest?"

She nodded again.

"My arms and legs?"

"Uh-huh."

"Even . . . Mr. Happy and his two best pals?"

"Yep." She refused to look him in the eye.

He threw the Daisy shaver at her and headed toward his clothes.

"Please!" She ran after him. "It's summer! You don't need that hair to keep you warm, or anything."

"It's a man thing, Jazz. We like our monkey fuzz."

"Nobody else will know! Just do it as a favor to me. I'm really screwed, here. I don't have another model lined up."

He shook his head and jumped into his pants. She almost envied them as they slid up his tight butt. She touched Sinclair's arm in appeal, and he froze instantly, looking down at her. God, she wanted to eat those dimples with a spoon.

"The hair will grow back," she whispered.

Tony cast his blue eyes heavenward, and groaned. "Aw, Jesus. I must have the letters 's-c-h-m-u-c-k' engraved on my forehead." When he looked back down at her, she still wore her pleading expression.

"All right. But if I'm going to play a modern Samson to your Delilah, we're going to a pharmacy and getting some Nair. I'll cut myself to ribbons with that pink thing."

* * *

Rubbing Vaseline all over Sinclair's naked chest to protect it from the plaster was a real chore. It was probably because it was so large, and so warm, and so *sculptural* that she was breathing hard. Really, it was a lot of work. But she couldn't look a gift model in the mouth. So instead she looked at his—no, no, no, that was an inappropriate place.

She gazed at his toes. They were very attractive toes—long and shapely, pointed erect at the ceiling.

Well, of course they are, stupid! Whoever heard of limp toes, dangling toward the floor? She was going to have to look at something else, something shaped quite differently.

Her hands swept over Tony's nipples, which hardened instantly at the contact. Then she was at his ribs, briskly rubbing, and soon down to his taut, flat muscular stomach. Gulp.

"Uhhhhhh . . . here you go, Sinclair!" She forced her voice to be sunny. "You can do the next part."

But the "part" had awoken, and stared shamelessly at her with one eye.

Tony's face flushed a deep crimson. "Uh, it appears introductions are in order. Jazz, meet Pedro."

"Excuse me?"

"Spanish for Peter."

"No shit?" Jazz hid her embarrassment under sarcasm. She'd seen a lot of naked people in the course of her work, but she'd never encountered *this* particular situation.

"As you can see, he's not shy."

"Um, no. He seems pretty full of himself." Pedro looked like a freakin' Tomahawk missile.

"The thing is, Sinclair, that I can't, ah, apply the plaster bandages to him while he's . . . acting up, so to speak. The statue has to be high classical, which is to say, Pedro should be . . . off duty."

"Jazz, you're adorable when you blush."

"I'm not blushing!"

"Yes you are."

"Well, you have to make him stop!"

Tony began to laugh. "He's got a mind of his own, and he likes you. That's the problem."

Her face felt like it was being flambéd. "Sinclair!" she hissed. "This isn't funny. Tell him *not* to like me. Tell him I'm really mean and I bite!"

"Look at that, Pedro. The unflappable Jazz Taylor is in a flap—and all because of you, my bald, one-eyed friend."

Jazz narrowed her eyes. "You seem to enjoy exposing yourself an awful lot. Do you lurk in city parks wearing nothing but a raincoat?"

"No, I'm very selective about whom I expose myself to."

"Well, we've got a job to do here, so explain to your special friend that what he's doing is inappropriate, okay?"

"That could be a problem," Sinclair told her, his eyes very blue. "You see, Pedro doesn't speak the same language as you and I."

"Oh?" Jazz folded her arms and waited.

"Nope. He only understands an ancient, highly respected oral tradition called . . . cockamamie."

Her lips twitched in spite of herself. As she walked around the table to Sinclair's feet she studiously avoided Pedro, but he seemed to follow her with his one eye. "Oh, for God's sake! Can't you cover him with something?" She threw a hand towel at him.

"You're hurting his feelings, Jazz."

"Just cover him—it!—up, okay?" Why did men behave as if their penises were ventriloquist's dummies? Women never felt compelled to name their privates. Men were such bizarre creatures!

Jazz started on his feet with the Vaseline and worked up toward his thighs, leaving about eight inches of safety between her and the towel-swathed Pedro. "Okay, you do that area. I'm going to start soaking the bandages."

As Tony began to do the job Jazz tried, honestly tried, not to watch. But she couldn't look away. He had marvelous, beautiful strong hands, and covered his thighs rapidly. Then, with a wicked glance in her direction, he moved his fingers under the towel to coat the rascal.

Her breath caught in her throat and beat feeble wings there, trying to reach her lungs.

He grinned at her and wiped his hands on the towel. "That didn't take long, seeing as how he's so tiny and inadequate."

Jazz swallowed. "Please stand up so I can pose you correctly."

She worked quickly to mummify Sinclair, doing her best to ignore the little zips and flashes igniting inside her body. She had to run her fingers over every hard inch of him. She was so close to him she could smell the clean scent of his skin, feel the heat he gave off. He was a heady combination of rough and smooth; he intoxicated her like a shot of neat whiskey.

It was a damn good thing that she was wrapping him from head to toe. The man was a dangerous temptation, and needed to be sealed off from the female populace. She should leave him mummified for all time, lock him in a crypt so she couldn't lose all self-respect and jump his bones.

Jazz took a deep breath as she reached that marvelous tight butt of his. Lurking on the other side, as they both knew, was Pedro. She hadn't looked in a while, but she had a bad feeling he was still ready to play. She reached over for more bandages and checked.

Pedro indeed stood at attention, poised to bat a homer in the game called lust.

Jazz closed her eyes. This was it. She was going to have to cop a feel of the cop's billy club. She'd have to somehow subdue it and wrap it up with the rest of him. Jayzus! She'd never been more embarrassed in her life.

She opened her eyes to find Sinclair grinning at her, eyes alight with devilment. He was enjoying this, the bastard!

Hell—she was no 1950s miss in a poodle skirt; why shouldn't she enjoy it, too? She locked her gaze with his, then took Pedro into her hand, and gave him a healthy squeeze. Tony's eyebrows shot up. "Hi, there, big boy. How's it hangin'?"

Pedro jerked and quivered.

Jazz wound the first of several snug plaster-soaked bandages around his root. She wrapped until the rascal was entirely covered and then taped him flat.

"Ow!" Tony complained.

She ignored him, continuing to work until he was completely mummified. Then she stood back, gazed at him with a critical eye, and swallowed a giggle. The cop was much less threatening to her peace of mind this way.

Tony simply glared at her.

In classic Myles fashion, she placed a hand over her heart and heaved her bosom dramatically. "My hero," she sighed.

His only reply was a deep, wordless growl.

Chapter 17

*E*LLEN WHITAKER NORTHROP BANKS SIGHED as she donned her slip. She then added creamy fourteen-millimeter matched pearls, a tasteful mauve lipstick, and translucent powder to dim her swollen, red nose. She stepped into her Stuart Weitzman pumps and then dropped her St. John knit over her head, easing it down over the silk and lace of the slip. In spite of the air-conditioning, the horrid stockings were already sticking to her legs. Atlanta was as bad as Florence in summer, but Miss Martha would spin in her mahogany coffin were her daughter to dispense with her underthings.

Ellen gazed at the silver-framed photograph of her mother, who wore a wide-brimmed hat, a dress with large printed magnolias, and a prim smile for the camera. Ellen chewed at her lip, unconsciously destroying her lipstick. Miss Martha hadn't drunk alcohol, hadn't sworn, hadn't danced. She had simply disapproved.

Following her mother's rules had never gotten Ellen anywhere that she particularly wanted to be. What was the purpose of such edicts as "a lady always wears a slip"? Why, pray tell, couldn't a *lady's* breasts or bottom be discernible under her skirt just like those of a mere *woman*?

It was very simple: A lady was squished and squeezed into thirty layers of nylon and tricot because she wasn't allowed any sexuality. In order to reach her exalted status, a lady not only had to perspire and hyperventilate, but also give up orgasms.

As one who had discovered them late in life, Ellen didn't think that was a fair trade-off. She stared at Miss Martha's portrait once more.

Ellen felt a rivulet of perspiration roll from between her shoulder blades down into the small of her back. The misery and stress and guilt of the last few days helped her make up her mind.

Then she kicked off the designer pumps, hiked her dress back over her head, and whipped off the slip. She peeled the despicable panty hose off her grateful hips and down her gasping thighs; past her damp calves and ankles. She pulled the horrid nylon off one foot and stepped on it. For good measure, she ground it into the carpet while freeing her other foot. She balled the dreadful things into a missile in the palm of her hand. Then, Ellen Whitaker Northrop Banks slam-dunked her stockings into the wastebasket.

Myles gazed blankly at the cracks in the plaster wall of his cell. He embraced Hell with no enthusiasm, kissed its grubby, pock-marked cheek with reluctance, knelt before it in shabby humility. He, Sir Myles Taylor, was down-at-heart, defeated, and in short, despondent. His heart had been trampled by Satan's own snorting steeds. It lay squashed flat and bleeding.

He couldn't get Ellen's distressed face out of his mind. He was used to his daughter's disapproval, but his darling Ellen—he'd always made her laugh, not cry.

His cellmate grunted and flushed the toilet. Myles found the sound a metaphor for his future without his fiancée. How could he convince her of the truth? How could he convince her of his love? He longed to caress the silver-blond tendrils of her hair, to smooth the worry lines from her brow, massage the tension and unhappiness from her posture.

He turned a fierce gaze upon McGraw, who now sat upon his bed, digging with renewed vigor into his ear. Speaking of metaphors! The man was a plague. A peasant. No, a dumb ox, yoked to vulgarity.

McGraw had not responded to his reasoning or philosophy. No, the only thing he'd paid attention to was brute force: Myles had informed him, with his hands around the sod's neck, that if he ever insulted his fiancée again, he would pound him into a bloody pulp.

It irked him that McGraw had been impressed only by the warrior, and not the poet, in him. He still considered the man a challenge. If he could succeed in wooing McGraw from the dark side, then surely he could succeed in wooing back Ellen.

Myles lay back on his bed, arms folded under his head, and stared at his bony, double-jointed toes while contemplating strategy.

He was gazing through the gap between his big toe and its first mate when he saw her legs. Surely they didn't belong to his darling Ellen . . . though they were the same delicious shape, long and succulent. Yet these beauteous calves didn't hide behind the shimmery haze, the virtuous veil, of hosiery. They approached him, brazenly bare and flaunting their muscle. They were silky-smooth highways for a willing tongue.

Myles allowed his gaze to roam upward, past her still-modest skirt to the waist that begged for his hands to span it. Above that, a slight climb up the sensual ladder of her ribs, were the glorious rounded twins he had christened Dom and Cristal.

She wore dark glasses, and he noticed that her gently aristocratic nose was red. He jumped to his feet just as McGraw began to pant behind him. Before he could whirl on his cellmate and threaten him, Ellen took charge.

"Mr. McGraw," she said imperiously, "I would like to speak to Myles as privately as possible, and without any hoots, catcalls, or *strumming* of your *instrument*. Do I make myself clear?"

McGraw stared at her sullenly.

"I'm willing to make it worth your while."

He brightened. "Yeah?"

"Yeah," she repeated dryly. "I'll offer you a choice of toy surprises, if you'll go to the far corner and not interrupt." She opened her polished calf Dior handbag.

McGraw's eyes glistened, while Myles looked on in curiosity.

Ellen withdrew two plastic packages. "Pork rinds or beef jerky?"

"I like both," angled Billy.

"Choose one for now. You may have the other when I leave—if you keep your word."

He chose the beef jerky and retired to his corner, gnawing like a beast.

Ellen reclasped her Dior, and gave her fiancé a small smile.

"My love," said Myles, grasping the bars in his fists. "My darling, my sweet. You have returned! You have not forsaken me!"

She took a step closer, and a tear rolled slowly from under the frames of her dark glasses. She looked tragic and mysterious. He should compose an ode to her, entitled "Glamour on the Rocks." Oh, yes—he envisioned the first lines already: *Cruel Sun, he beat upon her brow, and Wind tormented her locks. Cross-legged, bowed with sorrow she, was Glamour on the Rocks . . .*

"Myles, why do you look as if you have a bad case of gas?"

"Beg pardon, my love, I was composing verse. In your honor, I should add."

Ellen looked unimpressed. She took a deep breath, which brought Dom and Cristal to his attention once again. If he could but see their naked glory! Regale himself upon their effervescence, nuzzle between their sweet slopes!

"Myles, please look at my face and not my breasts. I do believe your cellmate is having a bad influence on you."

He tried desperately not to think about her naked, but it was extraordinarily difficult, with her dress hugging her curves in that sexy way, and no stockings, and a delicate sheen of perspiration beckoning the light. If he didn't know better, he'd swear she wasn't wearing a slip.

"Yes, my dear," he said obediently.

"I need to know the truth," Ellen said quietly. "When we met at the art opening eighteen months ago, did you seek me out because I was a trustee of the High Museum? Did you choose me deliberately so that you could pump me for information that would help you in the burglary?"

"Confound it, Ellen! How many times must I tell you that I didn't do it?"

"As many times as it takes. Did you seek me out deliberately?"

He was silent.

"I want the truth, however ugly it is."

He gazed at her helplessly. "I love you."

She folded her arms.

"God help me, I love you!" He turned and

paced away from her, then wheeled and came back. He admitted, "I sought you out deliberately, but not because of your position as a trustee. I wanted to meet you because you were unmarried, attractive, and . . . with means."

The line of her lips grew flat.

"It sounds horrible, I know. But we each must face certain truths about ourselves, my dear. I realized long ago that I'd make a fabulous house-husband and had little desire to do anything other than make a woman happy. I make marvelous small talk; love to do lunch; keep a beautiful house. Those talents leave me two choices: I can become either a butler or a husband. I believe we can agree that I would be a sorry bastard of a butler."

A corner of his lovely Ellen's mouth lifted—but only for an infinitesimal moment. "I knew you were interested in my assets, Myles." She sighed. "My ex-husbands were, too. At least you didn't lie about it at the beginning of things. So don't start now, just to save your investment."

"I'm telling the truth! I *do* love you!"

Her rounded lips quivered, and her chin dimpled with emotion. "*Don't* say that again. I'm so tired of men and their lies. Tell me, Myles, when you kissed me, were you kissing dollar bills? Were you dipping your wick into the treasury?"

She stood rigid with pain. "I fell for you, and it makes me ill to think of it. But do you know what makes me even sicker? Fool that I am, I can't just leave you here to rot."

Ellen opened her handbag once again, and extracted a small rectangle of paper. Her hand shook as she let it flutter to his feet behind the bars. It was a check.

"Give this to your daughter. It's enough to cover your bail. Just don't ever, *ever* contact me again."

Ellen turned and walked away, ignoring the rude comments and whistles that came from other cells. Myles watched her go with mounting hurt and rage. His love didn't believe him, had thrown money in his face, and never wished to speak to him again. All this, and he was innocent! Myles bent to pick up the check. It was the last time he would stoop so low. He ripped it once in half, and then again, until 1.2 million dollars of confetti littered the floor of the cell.

"Hey!" yelled McGraw. "What about them pork rinds?"

"So kin you teach me how to bag a dame like that? A real classy one, like to make you wanna roll over 'n' howl?"

Myles asked morosely, "A woman like Ellen? All honey gold hair and supple hips and musical laughter?"

"Uh . . . yeah. Like Miz Class Act what just she-bopped in here."

"Mmmmmmm. It *was* a bit of a she-bop, was it not?" Myles scrutinized his cellmate. "Although 'bop' conveys an upbeat mood. Now, she didn't *slink*, exactly. But neither did she *forge ahead*. It was somewhere in between. She *undulated*—yes, that's it. Tragic undulation. No, *calamitous gyration*. Yes! Ah, it's coming to me . . ."

"What I wanna know is, what was she doing with *you*?"

"She blessed the threshold with her presence, her luminosity," launched Myles. *"But then she cursed the man within, became his own calamity."*

"Aw, don't start with that shit again," begged McGraw. He covered his ears.

Myles returned from the lofty clouds of inspiration to the mundane reality of jail. "What's that you say, McGraw? You are at last begging me for the secrets of beauteous-babe-bagging?"

"Yep."

"And are you willing to be a most devoted student?"

"If'n it'll get me into some righteous hot pants." McGraw nodded.

"To learn each lesson I impart to you with reverence and great study?"

"Well, I dunno about reverence."

"Reverence!" Myles demanded. "Or I teach you nothing."

A long pause ensued. "Okay, okay."

They shook on it, and then Myles stood back, arms folded across his chest. "Then, my good man, down on the floor and give me twenty. To begin with, we must rid you of that dreadful paunch."

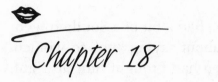

Chapter 18

*T*O ALLOW A WOMAN TO CUT ONE OUT OF A plaster body cast required a certain amount of trust.

Tony stood, jaw locked, hoping Jazz's sharp knife wouldn't slip while she freed him.

It was horrifying that he trusted the offspring of a thief. Not just any thief, either. No, he had to go and trust the *Old Master's* daughter.

When had his brains been boiled into a mess of limp collard greens? Whipped into a banana cream pie?

It could all be traced back to when he, Tony-the-Chump Sinclair, had agreed to give Jazz a week to try and prove her father innocent.

And why did you do that, you knothead?

Well, first of all, there were her eyes. And then, the successful collar of Myles had made booking his daughter on an iffy charge unimportant.

And?

And obviously he had a bit of a Southern gentleman's complex about saying "no" to women. So sue him. So Ellen had brought him up right. He knew how to open a door for a woman, and pull out a chair . . . and countless other ways to be of excellent, ahem, *service*.

With a last cut by Jazz, Tony was able to step out of the plaster mold, naked and still greased with Vaseline.

Jazz held the plaster skin, but her glazed eyes were fixated upon his nudity.

His lips twitched. So did Pedro.

Her eyes widened. "How do you make it move like that?"

"Special secret power surge." Tony grinned.

"No, really."

He shrugged. "The same way you, as a woman, can tighten your . . . magic muscles."

"My magic muscles," she repeated. As if in slow motion, she placed the plaster mold on her worktable, never taking her eyes off him.

Tony knew, with a man's inner instinct, that they were finally, at last, against all better judgment, going to make wild monkey love. If he'd had a long, prehensile tail, he would have used it to swing from the rafters in jubilation, whooping and beating on his hairy chest.

He opted for a smoother initiative. "I'm thinking that with my special secret power surges, and your magic muscles, we could have a pretty spectacular time together."

"I know," said Jazz, advancing upon him, "*exactly* what you mean."

Their kiss was hungry and explosive, a tangle of pent-up sexual energy, wild curiosity, and gentle humor. He closed his teeth around her lower lip, tugging it. She nipped at his tongue, sending a sharp arrow of lust arcing through his body, skittering clear down to his toes. He wanted to devour her and take command of all her nerve endings until they waved a million little white flags of surrender. But before he could do that, he had to get her naked.

Since it was extraordinarily difficult to play masterful tongue hockey while pulling a woman's T-shirt off, Tony took two fistfuls of it and tore it right down the center of the V at Jazz's neckline. Then he pulled it from under the loose straps of her overalls and tossed it behind him.

As he continued to make love to her willing mouth, more sparks and shocks ignited all over his body, electrifying a furious desire. He grasped the denim straps at her shoulders and pulled her hard against him. She inhaled on a squeak as he then pulled the bib of her overalls down, wedging it under her pert, perfect, naked breasts.

Pink nipples—he gazed at the perfect buds framed by cream and denim, just waiting, aching for his mouth. God, they looked as they had in his fantasy, that first day after he'd seen her in the studio.

The vision carried a heated sense of déjà vu, a rush of nameless emotion. His mouth had been made to suck those nipples, to lave and tease them.

As he cradled Jazz against his arm and bent his head to possess her flesh, a wave of unfamiliar tenderness crested in him. Lips met breast. His grip on her tightened as she keened helplessly.

Jazz heard her own voice as if from a distance, making sounds that would have embarrassed the hell out of her under normal circumstances. But the feel of Tony's mouth on her aching, wanting, on-the-verge-of-screaming flesh wasn't normal. It was beyond exquisite.

His tongue and lips solicited alternately hot, sizzling stimuli and icy, shivery sensations. They collided and spun into a vortex, a tornado of aphrodisia.

Her hands slid up and down his slick back, re-visiting each knot of muscle, each ridge of bone, each dip and swell of his skin. He was heated, his breathing rough, his mouth urgent to pleasure her.

His lips moved up to her throat, the bristle on his chin and cheeks abrading the delicate skin, making her want the same roughness scraping her inner thighs.

Sinclair's big hands unfastened the clasps on her overall straps, and they slid to the ground. She stood nearly naked before him, in a puddle of denim.

"Tulips," he murmured, with a devastating, crooked smile.

She had flowers blooming on her cotton bikini panties. She'd forgotten.

"Mind if I tiptoe through them?" He helped her step out of the overalls.

"Not at all." She now wore nothing but tulips and work boots. Jazz bit her lip, frowning down at them. Not the sexiest footwear.

He knelt at her feet and began to unlace them with strong, sure fingers. "One day, sweetheart, I'm going to make love to you in nothing but your Timberlands. But for now, we can dispense with them." He pulled them off and tossed them, along with her socks, into a corner. "Now, where were we?" He looked up at her.

Jazz gazed down at him, paralyzed by the sheer male beauty of his face. "I'm—I'm not sure," she whispered.

He grinned, then lunged without warning.

With a shriek, she found her thighs on his shoulders, her calves hanging down his back, her tulips against his mouth, and his big hands clasping her bottom. Then they rose into the air.

Jazz beat her heels against his back, grabbed his ears, and shrieked again. "Put me down!"

"I don't think so," he said against her tulips.

She stopped making a fuss immediately. His words were warm, and moist, and felt unbelievably delicious. *Never* had there been a better time to argue with a man.

But her brain refused to come up with any intelligent sallies, especially when he ran his tongue in a slow circle around the most sensitive part of her. "Does that feel good?"

"What?" she gasped. "It's hard to understand you."

"Well, my voice is a little *muf*fled at the moment."

"Ohmigod. Could you repeat that, please?" Her insides were melting into warm baby oil.

"Which part?"

"Aaahhhhh . . ."

"The noun? The verb? The modifier? Or the prepositional phrase, sweetheart?"

"Aiiieeeee," said Jazz.

"Perhaps it was the punctuation you particularly admired."

"Ohhhhhhh!"

"I really love exclamation points, myself."

"Ahhhhhh! TonyTonyTonyTonyTonyTonyTony!"

Several sublime female moments passed before he declared, "Off with the tulips!" and lowered the two of them to a convenient table.

Jazz vaguely noticed her flower-dotted undies flying through the air. A moment later, a foil package followed, and Tony eased his arms lovingly under her back, pulling her to his broad chest. "Can I come inside?" he whispered.

In answer, she grabbed his buns and pulled.

Nothing standard-issue about this cop's weapon. Slick and hard like the rest of his body, Pedro entered her, needing no fumbling guidance, no direction. He pulsed against her inner walls, massaging zones she'd never been aware she had. She tightened on him with those magic muscles, and he answered with even deeper thrusts. Smooth, so smooth. So fine. So rhythmic.

His big hands kneaded the flesh of her bottom, spread her open for his sensual siege. She gave herself up to the vulnerability of the position, allowing herself to go lax again, to enjoy this strange, foreign power sliding within her.

Her breasts rubbed against his slick chest as he drove deep, pushing and pulling and kneading a buried tension.

She felt a bone-deep liquification of all her organs as she responded to Tony thrust for thrust. Then that liquid seemed to spin and swirl, as if inside some sort of cosmic beaker. With a cry, she morphed into the female equivalent of a very dry martini: thoroughly shaken.

Chapter 19

SHE'D GOTTEN NAKED WITH THE COP. SHE still couldn't believe it. She'd known the man less than a *week*. What had possessed her? How had she lost control so utterly, and allowed her studio to be turned into a . . . a den of iniquity?

She might have been able to live with herself if they had only done it once. She could have chalked it up to human weakness. Written it off to circumstances: nude man steps out of plaster cast and woman-who-has-been-celibate-for-over-a-year jumps his bones.

But they'd done it twice. And then thrice. In the shower. On the stairs. And *then* he'd done that thing with the arches of her feet.

Normal women did not reach orgasm during a foot rub. How was that possible?

Tony was dangerous. He menaced her self-control. Jeopardized her self-respect, threatened her peace of mind. So she'd thrown herself back into work, finishing the projects for Lon Adams and another director, and then starting the design and bid for Izzy Hampton's new production.

Now she stood back, gazing with a critical but satisfied eye at her work. What she really needed was to get to LA and join forces with someone who had a digital-animation and computer-graphics background, but for now, what she'd done by hand was damned good.

The script called for the FX team to create a huge mechanical baby doll. While Jazz loathed the story, the film would probably be a box office hit and garner her more work if she got the contract. Hampton was willing to look at bids from outside California, hoping to save money.

She reread the synopsis of the script and tried not to gag.

In Come to Papa, *a baby doll is brought to life accidentally by a teenage boy. The horny adolescent can't get any girls to go out with him, so he employs the aid of a magic spell to bring his sister's Barbie doll to life.*

Unfortunately, the love spell is cast upon the wrong doll, and the teenager finds himself saddled with an enormous, adoring toddler who needs canvas drop cloths for diapers, and who can't be left alone.

Jazz put her head down on her arms. Who came up with these ideas? If the movie was done well, it could be funny; if not, it would be an indescribable debacle. The huge toddler would probably chase her in her nightmares, especially since she'd used one of Myles's baby pictures to create the face. It had seemed appropriate, given the reversal of their parent-child relationship.

Jazz sighed. She really should go and visit him while she was still capable of standing. Then she'd come home and have a long snooze.

The Fulton County Jail was a cesspool of humanity, and that was putting it nicely.

She found Myles in a cell with a nasty, flabby little man who snored at twenty decibels. Her father's face looked gray and drawn, and his benign superciliousness seemed frayed at the edges.

Jazz found it in her heart to feel a tiny bit sorry for him, locked up in this awful place. But though she normally didn't care about money and gave it to him freely, she wasn't about to mortgage her studio or borrow from a loan shark to get him out on bond. Enough was enough, and God knew she'd warned him until she was blue in the face. Until Ellen returned from Italy, he was stuck there.

"Buck up, Myles," she said. "If you really didn't do it, they can't convict you. I'm working on tracking down the stolen art, and I've sent a message to Ellen through her housekeeper. She'll have you out of here soon."

He eyed her, the picture of gloom. "I'm afraid she won't. You see, she's ended things with me. She came here yesterday."

"Ellen broke it off with you?" Jazz stared bleakly at her father. "I'm so sorry." That was an understatement. She was devastated—and so were her plans to move to LA and open a larger studio. Myles ran through money like a bum through Mad Dog 20/20. There was no saving, with him around. Ellen had gotten him off her hands for a while—and made him happy.

"She thinks I'm involved with this confounded burglary!" His voice strangled on outrage.

"I can't imagine why." Jazz's tone was bone-dry. "It was only a *small* Degas they found under your bed."

"They planted that!"

"So you say."

Myles clapped a hand over his heart, and staggered with drama. *"Et tu, Brute? It's true!"*

"I'll give you the benefit of the doubt, Myles. But you can't blame others if they don't."

"Ellen should not qualify as Other. We were going to be married!"

"Oh, Myles. You didn't tell me that she's a trustee of the High Museum. Isn't that a little suspicious?"

"Pure coincidence, I tell you!"

Jazz wondered. His beloved, if amoral, features vibrated sincerity, and she wanted to believe him, but he'd always been a hell of an actor. Time for tough love.

"Sorry, Papacito. Perhaps you're starting to learn that there are consequences to your actions. It's a tragedy that I was never able to ground you, or make you stand in the corner."

"Superiority is very unbecoming, my love," chastised Myles.

Of all the gall! "So is felony, not to mention grandiosity and general irresponsibility."

"Children! How they disrespect their elders!"

Jazz folded her arms and faced him down. "Only when there's cause."

"Do lighten up a bit, dearest Jazz. Your outlook is frightfully dour and verges on the cynical. A young girl like you should be out flitting from beau to beau. Giggling, cavorting, and, not least, shopping."

Jazz snorted. "I don't *flit*. I need beaux like I need a hole in the head. And you have the market cornered on shopping yourself."

"Really, my love, how crotchety. And have you considered what Freud would say about your constructing monsters in a garret all day?"

"No. And I believe his name has been misspelled all these years: it was really F-R-A-U-D. He knew *jack* about women. The very idea of penis envy is laughable."

"It isn't healthy, what you do! And it's not feminine."

"It's far healthier for me to build my monsters out in the open, rather than have demons chasing me in my subconscious."

Myles sighed. He sidled up to the bars and gazed winningly at her. "Not to change the subject, love, but when are you going to get me out of here?"

Jazz swallowed and gave him a long, level stare. "I'm not."

Her father blinked his eyes rapidly, and then cupped a hand behind his ear. "My hearing, you understand . . . I grow elderly and feeble. What was that you said?"

"You heard me," she said evenly. "Your bond is posted at 1.2 million dollars, and I couldn't raise that without going to a loan shark and mortgaging my studio. I refuse to do that. I'm not sure you're worth the interest, and I don't need broken kneecaps when you flee the country, either."

"You cut me to the quick! I would never—"

But they both knew he would. It took all the nerve she had to simply stand there in silence.

After a long moment, Myles seemed to realize that there was nothing more to say. His shoulders drooped inside the orange jumpsuit, and she hated the slump of them. She hated the necessity of walking away and leaving her own father in jail. She almost hated herself.

"Talk to me, Myles. If you're innocent, we'll get you out of here. I'm on the trail of the art. I know about Cantini. If he asked you to consult on this, why haven't you told the police? Why aren't you helping yourself?"

"My hands are tied. I can't talk to the police. Cantini has threatened both Ellen and you if I do so. You must promise me that you will stay out of it, Jazz. Don't search for the missing paintings. It's dangerous, and will do me no good if they are found."

"What? Myles, you've gone around the bend. We've *got* to find them!"

"I have a plan, dearest Jazz," he said mysteriously. "Can you doubt it? I, the Old Master, have a master plan. You must be patient."

She threw up her hands. "What kind of plan?"

"I'm not at liberty to share it."

"You're not at liberty, period. Let me help you, for God's sake."

"Out of the question. Too dangerous."

"I won't do anything stupid."

"No, because I won't give you the rope to hang yourself."

Jazz lost her temper. "Oh, now's a fine time to play the concerned daddy!"

He winced and turned away.

"Look, Myles! Your rotten thugs have already been to my studio, okay? They think I know something, so you might as well tell me."

"They came for the black book."

"Yes. And unfortunately, they got it."

"Ah, good."

"Good? Are you crazy? That means they'll use your contacts to unload the art, and we'll never be able to prove your innocence!"

He ignored this. "Jazz, I want you to be extremely careful. Don't go anywhere by yourself. And get that cop to keep an eye on you."

"Tony Sinclair? Forget it." She didn't see any

need to mention that he'd had not only his eyes, but also his hands on her recently.

"You cannot handle this alone," her father said. "Do you understand?"

"I've been handling things alone my whole life, Myles. Why should this be any different?"

"I suppose I deserve that, but you listen to me this time, Jasmine: You and I are both in over our heads here. This," intoned her father, "could mean your life."

Chapter 20

*B*AGEL SNELLER WAS NOT ENJOYING HIS AF-
ternoon. Heat spiraled up off the tarmac in
brutal waves, soaking his dark blue uniform. His
hat was an instrument of torture. He couldn't decide whether or not to fling it to the ground, since
it served both to make his head sweat and to
shade his face from the sun. He was out of his favorite food. Worst of all, the police captain had
just called to demand that he tell him what he
knew of Sinclair's activities.

"Activities, sir?"

"Sneller, don't screw with me."

"Never, sir."

"I know he's messing around with this Old
Master case."

"Really, sir?"

"If you're helping him in any way, you're in deep shit. Got it? So if you're covering for that worthless s.o.b., you'd better come clean right now."

Bagel had swallowed. "I don't know what you mean, sir."

"You didn't make those collars on your own, Sneller. It's too coincidental. And it's not *your* aunt who's mixed up in this."

"Oh, no, sir. I don't even have an aunt."

The captain had snorted and hung up.

Bagel wiped the sweat from his brow once again. His stomach grumbled, and he fingered his empty set of cuffs. It didn't feel right, not having the weight of a few whole wheats dangling there.

He sighed. He'd better give Sinclair a call and let him know the chief was on the warpath.

Jazz put the finishing touches on a "zoo" of Muppet-like hand puppets she was donating to a school for hearing-impaired children, as Tony watched.

She added bright magenta lipstick to Bridget-the-Boa, combed and teased Lionel-the-Lion's mane, and adjusted the swank bow tie on Pauly-the-Penguin. "There," she said to Pauly. "You look ready to present the Oscars."

Sinclair chuckled. "You're like a mother hen with her chicks."

"I am not!" Jazz was horrified. But when she thought Tony wasn't looking, she dropped a kiss on Pauly-the-Penguin's orange beak.

"I saw that," said Sinclair.

"Huh. You have no witnesses."

"Bridget-the-Boa would testify."

"I'd tie her cute little forked tongue into a knot so she couldn't say a word."

"Witness intimidation!"

Jazz put her hands on her hips. "Sinclair, don't you have better things to do than hang around my studio on a Saturday morning?"

"I have a feeling you're gonna be up to no good. You're *not* going to check out the Romanelli warehouses by yourself."

Jazz tried to look innocent.

"Widening your eyes and cocking your head to the side isn't going to snow me, darlin'," drawled Sinclair. "What are you up to?"

She gave up the pretense. "Look, just because we've slept together does not make me your property, okay? Back off!"

He ground his teeth. "I have never considered

any woman my property. I'm simply interested in keeping you alive, all right?" He stared her down.

She looked away. Okay, so maybe she'd been unfair. But Sinclair, with his square good looks, would ruin everything. The warehouses were around the Little Five Points area, a very funky part of town.

"Tony, I can blend into Little Five Points. You can't. You're not exactly the . . . *hippest* guy around." He was too built to be hip. And he never wore black.

"We police officers *do* go undercover, you know. And I happen to know a special-effects artist."

She groaned. "Not this again."

"What, I haven't helped *you* out? Where's the problem?"

You're the problem, she thought silently. *You're always in my head. You're distracting me, making me behave like some adolescent girl. I'm writing your name, over and over again, on my notepads. My own behavior is making me nuts.*

But she knew she wasn't going to win this argument.

"You're a pain in the ass," she said.

He grinned.

"Sit in the pink salon chair."

"Do I get to take off my clothes again?"

Her lips twitched. "Now, why would you want to get naked in my pink chair?"

"Well," Tony confessed, "I noticed that it rocks *and* spins."

"Is that right?"

"Yep. It's also got real nice cushy springs, and rolling wheels."

"So you were hoping to . . . rock 'n' roll?"

Tony grinned. "With a little Jazz thrown in."

She groaned. "Why can't I ever have the last line around you?"

She began going through disguise possibilities, and was bending over a box of uniforms when a pair of strong arms wrapped around her, and Sinclair's husky voice murmured, "Gotcha!"

"Tony!"

"Hey, you *did* call me a Cro-Magnon." His big hands slid under her overalls to cup her breasts through her T-shirt, and his fingers teased circles around her nipples. "You want to see my wall etchings of pterodactyls?" he murmured suggestively.

She'd never kissed a man while laughing. "I'd rather see your woolly mammoth."

"The mammoth is no longer woolly, thanks to your Nair." But it strained against his jeans and pressed into her midsection.

"Then I guess I'll settle for your club." She ran

her tongue lightly over his lips and down the cleft of his chin. Then she bit it.

"Ouch!" Tony's hands encircled her rib cage, and his mouth covered her own, hard and demanding. His palms moved up to cup her breasts and caressed them lightly through the soft cotton. She moaned as he played with her nipples.

Tony kissed well and thoroughly. His tongue was a finely honed instrument, awakening nerves and sensations in every nook and crevice of her mouth. She wanted his tongue everywhere on her body.

Tony dispensed with their clothes and obliged her, scraping lightly with his teeth down the sensitive column of her throat, tickling and lapping the hollow, nibbling and teasing into the cleft between her breasts. They ached for his fingers again, taut and begging for attention.

He drew one peak into his hot, seeking lips and her legs collapsed. It didn't matter, since one of his arms held her clasped hard against him at the small of her back. His other hand gripped the flesh of her bottom, kneading and rolling it.

He bit her nipple lightly as his fingers slipped between her legs and toyed with her. Jazz bucked against him, swept down a raging river of sensation.

Tony pulled her onto his lap in the chair, and

entered her in one strong, sure stroke. Closing her eyes, she threw her head and shoulders back, relishing the full, slick heat of him. She sank even farther onto him, sending him deep within her, and heard him groan.

She leaned into him, rocking the chair back, and rubbed her cheek against his rough jaw. Then she slowly slid up a few inches, tightening around him.

"Jesus . . ." he pulled her back down.

She shimmied up again.

Hands on her hips, he took her back.

The age-old dance between them became symbolic: Jazz wriggling away, Tony tugging her back. A metaphor for their relationship, it also created a mad, spiraling tension between them.

She began to rotate her bottom, caught in the sexual rhythm and helpless to break it. Tony plunged within her, and the force and friction spun her into a weightless, pulsing heat.

When he shuddered and pulsed within her, she echoed each spasm, falling against his chest. His arms wrapped around her as if he'd never let her go, and she lost herself to bliss. It was a long time before either of them moved.

* * *

Jazz showered quickly, unable to believe she'd played hide-the-salami with the blasted cop *again*. In her workplace! How did he get past her defenses? This had to stop.

But when she emerged in a towel, Sinclair wolf-whistled at her.

"Stop it. You come near me again, and I'll hold you off with my nail gun. Got it?"

"I love it when you talk tough, baby," he growled. But to her relief, he disappeared for his turn in the shower.

After both were clothed once again, Jazz began going through costume possibilities. Sinclair would fool nobody dressed as a woman. With his muscular neck and shoulders, narrow, flat waist and long legs, he was one hundred percent man.

He was too athletic-looking to make a convincing street person. His demeanor would give away that he was no college student. Hmmmm. Maybe she would make him an appliance repair man.

Her gaze lit upon a couple of wigs she hadn't used in years, and Jazz chuckled. She picked one up and turned to scan Tony's face. It would be a challenge, but she could do it. She was good.

Jazz walked toward him with the wig, and watched his mouth drop open.

"No way. Not even a chance!" He rolled backwards in the salon chair, away from her.

Jazz shook the long, woolly dreadlocks of the wig until they fell naturally into place, their orange, green, and yellow beads anchoring them at the bottom. "Peace, mon."

"I don't *think* so. Back off, woman."

"But Tony, the only other option is for you to be an appliance repair guy, and you'd still have that square cop look about you."

"And you think I'll look less uptight with an oversize tarantula on my head? Nope. Take it away!"

Jazz put it back on the shelf. Well, damn. She'd had such a great excuse to rub self-tan lotion all over his naked body. But then they'd *never* get out of here.

Well, they definitely had to cover that Republican hair. Last time she'd used a bald pate and a comb-over. This time . . . ah-ha! This time, she'd make it simple on herself.

She rummaged through a few plastic bins while he looked on suspiciously. "Close your eyes," she commanded. "I'm going to transform you, and you're going to *like* it. Okay? No more complaining."

Tony shifted and twitched, but refrained from mouthing off while she gunked up his hair with gel, dotted his face with pasty makeup and fake acne, and added a broader, flatter nose with a stud in it. She tied a purple bandanna onto his head, then she added a hemp necklace and a beaded bracelet for good measure.

A tie-dyed T-shirt over a little belly padding softened his jock's build. She added a silver ear cuff and shower thongs, and then looked him over again.

Something was still missing. She took a nail scissors and ripped his jeans over one knee.

"Hey!" yelped Tony. "Those were perfectly good Levi's!"

"Not anymore," said Jazz, making another cut below the knee. Then she sliced at the fabric in between the cuts. "Okay, now take 'em off. Time for the oscillating sander, to age them."

"*What*? Forget it!"

"And practice slouching and saying, 'dude' in a moronic tone of voice. You're now Tony the Dead-head."

Jazz walked over to a machine at the far wall, turned it on, and began to attack his jeans with a construction-grade sanding belt.

"You're a *most* unusual woman," he said, when she gave them back, shredded and frayed. "And you owe me a pair of 501s."

A couple of hours later, Jazz and Tony were ambling down Moreland Street in Little Five Points, past a ghoulish restaurant-bar called the Vortex. The facade of the building was a mammoth replica of a human skull, with blood red eyes glowing out of deep hollowed sockets on the second level. The ground-floor entrance was the skull's mouth. The bar's creepiness fit in perfectly with the surrounding shops, which hawked everything from tattoos to shiny vinyl pants and sex toys.

One window sported a leopard-clad mannequin in a spiked dog collar and five-inch heels. She reclined provocatively in a neon pink plastic chair shaped like a hand.

Tony kept a lookout for the first warehouse they needed to check out. By the address, it should be just on the other side of the tattoo parlor. Tony kept his walk to a slow, rolling gait—so casual it almost hurt.

Jazz, beside him, exuded sultry attitude from under a pair of tiny, wire-framed sunglasses. She'd painted her lips a nasty gray-purple color that made her skin appear cadaver white in the strong sunlight. Under the glasses, her eyes were rimmed with black lines, shadowed with the same purple-gray, and surrounded by spiky false eyelashes.

She looked as if she'd risen from an open casket at a funeral. Tony wanted to find a water pump and scrub all the gunk off her face.

He averted his eyes from her and checked the address on the next building. This was it. The brick walls were at least forty years old, and jagged glass hung in the windows. Weeds grew willy-nilly over the ground.

"This the place?" Jazz asked.

"Yeah. Let's go around back and see if there's a less conspicuous entrance."

"Don't bother. This isn't it."

"How do you know?"

"It's not climate-controlled. Look at the broken windows. They wouldn't risk it."

"Climate-controlled?"

Jazz nodded. "These are valuable paintings, and most of them are over a hundred years old. You have to keep them at a steady temperature and humidity level to avoid damage."

"Would these clowns know that?"

"I'd think so. They're in this for profit, so they'd want to protect their stock."

"Let's check it out anyway." Tony strode through the weeds and broken glass to the rear of the building. The rusty padlock on the door had long since been broken, and they found only signs that street people had been sleeping there. A couple of old blankets lay limply on the dusty concrete floor, with the squat stub of a candle and an empty bottle of Boone's Farm still in a crumpled paper bag.

"One down, two to go," muttered Jazz.

They exited the building and headed toward North Highland Street. The next warehouse was also a disappointment. Jazz and Tony headed toward the last address, which was nearly a mile down the road.

Tony brightened when he saw a pharmacy in the next block. He could finally fill his prescription for Nicorette! The craving for a cigarette was driving him slowly mad.

Inside the pharmacy, the air was cool and dry, and Tony sighed with relief, dragging out a handkerchief to mop at his forehead.

"What are you doing?" Jazz hissed, grabbing it. She pointed to the tan smudge on the white fabric. "You're wiping off your face!"

"Ooops." He bent his head while she used her fingers to blend the makeup again. A stockboy glanced at them curiously, then went back to unloading a crate of women's deodorant. They brushed past him and headed down the aisle to the back of the pharmacy, where Tony spotted the prescription counter.

"Stay in character," Jazz whispered.

Tony nodded, and dug the prescription out of

his wallet. He passed it to the young clerk behind the counter, and cleared his throat. "Duuuuuu-ude," he said. "I need some of this Nicorette stuff."

The clerk's eyebrows rose. He looked from the paper to Tony and back again.

Belatedly, Tony remembered that he sported a five-leafed plant on his T-shirt, with a message reading, "Legalize It!" in big white letters.

The clerk tucked his tongue into his cheek. "Sure, man. Let me check to see if we have it in stock."

He disappeared into the back, and hope leaped within Tony's chest. It had now been twenty-eight days, five hours, and thirteen minutes since he'd had a cigarette. The only craving-free sec-onds of that time had been when he'd had Jazz naked, and his thoughts were otherwise occu-pied. He needed some relief.

But Murphy's Law had the clerk popping out of the back empty-handed. "Sorry, duuuuude," he said insolently. "But we're all out."

Tony glared at the kid, and Jazz put a soothing hand on his shoulder.

"Come on," she said. "We'll check another pharmacy later. For now, why don't we cut through Piedmont Park to get to the third place?

There's some kind of festival going on there; it'll be fun."

To distract himself from one craving, Tony treated himself to another: He admired Jazz's ass as she led the way out of the pharmacy.

Sensing his gaze, she turned to face him once they were on the street again. "Enjoying the view?"

All right, so he was a goat.

The sunglasses had slipped down her nose, and he was treated to her smoky-plum shadowed eyes. With all the makeup, they looked huge in her pale face.

Tony found both of his hands on her shoulders, unconsciously pulling her toward him. He lowered his head. Grayish purple lipstick and faux nose ring notwithstanding, he wanted to kiss her.

"Stop right there, Dead-head. We can't mess up the Gen X Rock 'n' Roll Slut lips."

Jazz had placed her small hands against his chest, but she wasn't exactly pushing him away. It was one of those frozen moments in which the attraction between them hovered like a tangible thing.

Tony was the one to break it, albeit reluctantly. "We'd better get going."

* * *

Jazz leaned against the trunk of a large tree in Piedmont Park and laughed. They'd found the festival, all right—but it probably wasn't doing Tony's craving any good. A huge canvas banner hung over the back entrance of the park, sporting the words, "Citywide Smoke-In. Legalize It!"

Various booths dotted the well-kept grass, offering T-shirts and information from different groups lobbying for government acceptance of marijuana. Jazz was interested to see that many of them were medical and religious in nature. Pot was supposed to help glaucoma? Arthritis? Counter the ill effects of chemo? Cure a hangover? Bring you closer to your Maker? Heal the chasm between body and mind? Who knew?

The crowd ran the gamut from small children to wizened old couples, from Anglo to Asian, Hispanic and Afro, from tie-dye to coat and tie. Jazz enjoyed people-watching, and made lots of mental notes on individual styles.

She and Tony signed fictitious names to a petition making the rounds. She peered over his shoulder as he scrawled on the line. "Reef R. Tokin? Nice, Sinclair," she whispered as they walked away.

"Huh—you signed as Brownie Alahash!"

She grinned. "I didn't think you saw."

Jazz noticed a couple of tattooed louts giving

her a lazy once-over. She ignored them, but Tony grabbed her hand, baring his teeth in their direction. His own hand was large and slightly callused, dwarfing her own. A tingle ran up her arm and danced from there into her stomach. Her hand felt good in his; it felt . . . right. Uncomfortable with the thought, she put it out of her mind.

Jazz caught a waft of pot smoke as she and Tony sat on a bench and watched the crowd. To the left, a Willie Nelson wanna-be held the hand of his girlfriend, a Crystal Gayle clone.

To their right, a man with a mop of dyed platinum hair in a black suit argued philosophy with a ponytailed guy in cutoffs.

A couple of college kids sauntered by. "I'm tellin' you, man," one said to the other, "if he talks to my sister again, I'll rip off his arm and beat him with the bloody stump."

Jazz blinked. She hoped he was exaggerating. The smell of marijuana was growing stronger around them, and it worried her. Behind them, she heard raucous laughter and the music of Peter Tosh. A large group of Jamaicans were passing something around, and she didn't need an encyclopedia to figure out what it was.

Tony stood up and pulled her to her feet. "I think it's time we got out of—"

"Hey, Sinclair! Geez, man, is that you? Haven't

seen you since high school! You sure have changed."

Tony cursed under his breath. "Turbo. How are ya?"

Turbo? Sinclair knew a guy named Turbo? Jazz tried not to giggle. The old high-school friend was a wormy little guy with long, unkempt yellow hair and enough body piercings to set off a metal detector.

As Tony talked with Turbo, Jazz concentrated on the muscles that jumped in his jaw and neck as he spoke, and her eyes traced his muscular shoulders and chest once again. He was a beautiful man, no question about it. She remembered pleasurably what his warm skin had felt like when they'd made love, and reached out to run her hand over his biceps and down his forearm.

He turned his head to look at her, and his eyes grew dark and intense.

"You look sexy with a nose stud," she teased.

He turned to say good-bye to Turbo, and someone put a doobie into her hand. As she turned to look for the culprit, smoke from the damn thing curled into funny little fingers and rose up into the trees. Suddenly she heard shouts and the crowd scattered around her, chased by men in police uniforms. It all seemed to happen in slow motion.

Tony whirled and saw what she was holding. "Christ!" He ripped the joint out of her hand, threw it into some bushes, then grabbed her by the arm.

"Hands up!" a police officer with a crew cut roared at them.

Tony cursed.

"It wasn't mine!" Jazz said. "Somebody just stuck it into my hand."

"Tell me another one," said Officer Skin-Head.

"I'm APD, undercover," Tony said. "You can check my ID in my back right pocket."

The cop patted down his pockets and produced Tony's badge. After inspecting it to see that it was genuine, he handed it back. "Fine, you can go. But I'm taking her in."

"No," Tony growled, "you're not."

"What, you're gonna tell me she's APD, too?"

"No. But she's with me."

"Not anymore, buddy. She was toking it up on municipal property!"

"No, she wasn't. She explained what happened, and you won't find any marijuana in her system."

"I don't need it in her system; it was in her *hand*."

Tony loomed over him. "You arrest her, you'll have to arrest me, too."

"But I don't have any charges against you."

"We can fix that," Sinclair said angrily. "First, I'm calling you a dumb-ass rookie. Second, I'm telling you to release her. Third . . ." he drew back a fist, and stood protectively in front of Jazz.

"Tony, stop it!" she exclaimed. "I don't want to get you in trouble. Come on, what's the penalty? A fine, for a first-time offender? I'll just pay it."

"No." He said it through gritted teeth. "You don't want an arrest record, period."

"Okay, asshole. Have it your way: I'll take you both in and write you up for obstruction of justice. You can have a nice little chat with not only your captain, but Internal Affairs."

Next thing Jazz knew, they were locked in a big van with a steel grid across the windows, and Tony was cursing a blue streak.

She went to him and put her arms around him. "I'm so sorry I got you into this."

"You didn't. It was just plain bad luck."

"I'm the one who suggested we cut through the park. I'm the one who wanted to people-watch."

"Jazz, what's done is done. There's no point in worrying about it now." But his face reflected lines of strain: lips flat, nostrils flared, jaw set pugnaciously.

Jazz rubbed her cheek against his shoulder, then kissed his neck. His expression softened a little, and a corner of his mouth lifted. He touched her hair tenderly, fingering a lock she'd streaked purple for their foray into funkytown.

"You slay me, woman. Even dressed as an old nurse, or smeared with purple-gray cosmetics, you're sexy. You're beautiful, did you know that?"

Heat rose to her cheeks. "Stop it, Sinclair."

"Stop what? Telling the truth?"

"Huh. You obviously inhaled too much of the funny smoke out there."

Tony brushed her mouth with his. "Can't take a compliment to save your life, can you?"

She opened her mouth to protest, but he drove the words out of her head with a skillful, tender kiss. Jazz angled her head to taste more of him, and released her breath in a half sigh, half moan. The things this man could make her feel were nameless and dangerous.

Their kiss deepened, blocking out all worry for long, delicious moments.

Suddenly the back doors of the van flew open. "Sinclair!" thundered Captain Rathburn. "What in the hell has gotten into you?"

Chapter 21

*J*AZZ CHEWED NERVOUSLY AT THE INSIDE OF HER cheek. She hoped Tony wasn't having too bad a time. The captain had finally allowed her to go, dropping the charges after Tony's explanation.

Tony had put her in a cab home, but he himself hadn't fared as well. The last she'd seen of him, he was sitting in the passenger seat of the captain's car, purple bandanna in one hand and fake nose in the other.

His first concern had been for her. She still couldn't believe it. There he was, caught fooling around with a suspect in the back of a police van, and his focus had been on protecting *her*.

Jazz found herself gazing dreamily at nothing and thinking about Tony's bare chest as she drove to the last address they'd planned to check out. As she reached the building, she remembered the feel of his lips on hers, the way his arms had held her. She'd actually been tempted to get naked right there in the van. How did he do that to her?

Tony's intensity, his tenderness, was the key. He somehow made sex a gift—a gift of pleasure. Whereas other men had been selfish, and taken from her, Sinclair . . . *made love* to her. That was the difference.

She'd always thought the term was merely a verbal whitewash for sex, but Tony had taught her otherwise.

Then Jazz frowned. She was thinking about boinking—*again*—the man responsible for throwing her father in jail. Never mind that these were boinks of epic proportions, boinks that rattled her brains and shook her world. She had to think of Myles.

He may have once been a thief; he might be the bane of her existence. She occasionally wanted to shake him, but he was still her father. He deserved her loyalty. He needed her help.

And what was she doing? Letting him rot behind bars while she thought about rolling in the hay with the arresting officer. Nice.

Frowning, Jazz focused on the old yellow-brick warehouse in front of her. Its windows were intact, and a light glowed from somewhere within. She crept around the back, keeping flat against the wall. A big loading door stood open, and three men were stocking a green rental van with large, flat, bubble-wrapped packages.

Adrenaline surged through her body.

She recognized one of the men as Pug, the escapee from her studio. The one who seemed to be in charge was tall and thin. He barked orders to Pug and the third man, a youth with a buzz cut whose biceps were the size of Thanksgiving turkeys.

She'd found the right warehouse, all right. The problem was that the goods were about to travel.

Turkey Boy and friends were about to take off with four bubble-wrapped Monets, two Renoirs, several Pissarros, a few Sisleys, and a Seurat, leaving the blame for their theft on her father. That, she simply would not tolerate. But how could she stop them? What could she do?

The only "weapon" she had on her was a ballpoint pen. She wished she had a gun, and a couple of boys in blue. But even if she called, they wouldn't take her seriously. She could see it in her mind's eye.

"Yes, this is Jazz Taylor, the woman found sucking face with Tony Sinclair in the police van?

I'd like another officer, please, a Biggie, with fries."

So here she was, with no backup. Tony would be trying to explain both his costume and his behavior to his police captain until a white Christmas dawned in hell.

Well, she'd just have to follow these men wherever they were going. She crept back around the building and climbed into Floozie, the yellow 1973 Volkswagen bus in which she sputtered and lurched around Atlanta.

Floozie had given up her backseats long ago to make way for Jazz's equipment and creations. She was a paint-spattered, lovably battered old gal, and though she wasn't welcomed at the city's tonier addresses, Jazz didn't care.

She opened Floozie's door, vaulted into the driver's seat, and turned the key in the ignition. She drove slowly around to a side street and waited for the green truck to emerge, wishing that Floozie's engine was a little more subtle. It sounded like a lawn mower spitting gravel. She shrugged. So stealth wouldn't be her strong point. Camouflage reigned. The crooks would never expect to be tailed by a Gen-X Rock 'n' Roll Slut fueled by flower power.

The truck pulled out with Pug at the wheel, and Jazz followed. She knew a moment's panic at the thought he might recognize her, but decided the chances were slim. Her hair had been pulled up the day he and Bones had rifled through her studio, and she'd worn no cosmetics.

Today her brown curls flowed freely around her shoulders. Her lipstick garishly suggested that she'd sucked the chrome off many a bumper, and her eye makeup would have done a Hong Kong hooker proud. Jazz relaxed, and put the pedal to the metal as they all got on the highway.

"Captain Rathburn, it's not what you think." Tony sat in a hard plastic chair with his purple bandanna in one hand and his studded rubber nose in the other. "I was pursuing a lead on a case."

"Really." The police captain leaned back in his chair, looking like an angry bulldog. The pouches under his small, puffy eyes shook with each word he spat. "Seems to me you were pursuing some tail. At this point, I wouldn't even trust you to round up shopping carts in the parking lot of a Bob's Wholesale Club."

Tony held on to his temper. "From your perspective, sir, I know it looks very bad."

"Can you tell me how it looks any better from yours? You've proven yourself untrustworthy, irresponsible, and perverted."

Tony ground his teeth.

"And what the hell is this"—Rathburn threw his hand out scathingly—"this costume?"

"I was undercover," Tony said.

"That's one way to put it. Have you lost your marbles, Sinclair? You used to be one of my best officers. I was friends with your father, God rest his soul. Now you're hanging out at pot parties and molesting women at every opportunity."

At that, Tony almost came out of his chair. Only sheer willpower forced him to stay silent.

"My daughter," Rathburn bit out, "my baby girl, is so infatuated with your low-down, sorry ass that she tried to tell me what happened wasn't your fault. That makes me want to puke, Sinclair."

Tony clenched his jaw and looked Rathburn right in the eye.

The chief dodged his gaze, looking away. It was a telltale sign: the captain had his doubts, but couldn't admit them. He couldn't really blame the poor bastard. What man wanted to grapple with the fact that his daughter was a wanna-be slut?

He resigned himself to a serious ass-chewing, and—if the captain wanted to play hardball—a suspension. At least he'd managed to get Jazz out of trouble.

Sweet, sexy, incredible Jazz. She was a force of nature, a gorgeous little volcano. He semihardened again just thinking about her, as the captain droned on and on. Tony was glad he had the bandanna to cover himself.

He folded his arms, reliving the scene in the van. He could have taken her right there, and he hadn't had backseat sex since high school. Not exactly debonair, but Jazz made him forget all the rules.

With difficulty, he brought himself back to the unpleasant present. As soon as he got out of here, he needed to find her.

"... I suggest you get some psychiatric counseling, young man," the captain was saying. "You need help. You're suspended from duty, pending an ethics hearing—"

Tony could no longer contain himself. "Damn it, Rathburn! I'm as sane as you are, and I'm dressed like this only so I could investigate in Little Five Points without calling attention to myself. You can do a drug test on me right now—I'm clean."

"What the hell did you need to investigate in Five Points?"

"I've linked the head of security at the High Museum to the manager of a strip club—"

"*Strip club?* So when you're not frequenting

smoke-ins, you're getting your jollies at strip clubs?"

"—whose family, name of Romanelli, owns a string of warehouses. The club Romanelli manages is owned by *Sal Cantini.*"

Rathburn was suddenly silent. He steepled his fingers together and pursed his mouth. "Go on."

"I've got a strong hunch it's Cantini, not the Old Master, who's behind the Impressionist heist at the museum—"

Tony's cell phone pealed, and he looked down at the ID window. "Taylor, J." flashed from the small screen. "I'm sorry, sir, but I *have* to take this."

Rathburn looked thunderous, but Tony ignored him and hit the TALK button. "Sinclair," he said into the phone.

"Tony! Are you okay?"

"Jazz. Where are you?"

"I've got the crooks!" Her voice shook with excitement. "Looks like we're headed to the coast, possibly Savannah. I'm tailing three guys, who are driving the paintings in a moving van."

Tony swore. Adrenaline shot through his blood, chased by fear that shattered his nerve endings like skeets in the air. "Jazz, I can't believe you took off alone! If these guys catch you—" She was in unimaginable danger. Not only were millions of dollars at stake, but the thieves wouldn't give up their identities—or their freedom—without a fight.

"They won't catch me," she assured him. "I'll be careful."

Dread cannonballed into the pool of acid in his stomach. He knew what her definition of "careful" was.

"Jazz," he said, his voice tight, "you don't go anywhere near them. Do you hear me?"

"I'm not going to confront them, Tony." She exhaled audibly. "I'll just follow them at a distance." She gave him the truck's license-plate number.

He scribbled it down. "Keep me updated," he demanded. "I'm going to get on the road now. I'll be there as soon as I can." He hit the END button and met Rathburn's furious gaze.

"That was—is—an emergency, sir. I've got an unarmed civilian, Myles Taylor's daughter, following these art thieves on her own." He leaned forward, gaze intense and serious. "Her *life* is at stake.

"I have never asked for special treatment from you before, Captain, but I'm asking you now to let me go. If you feel you still have grounds to suspend me after I wrap up this case and make sure she's safe, then fine."

They stared at each other for a good ten seconds. Finally, Rathburn growled, "Get out of here. Take backup. But I want you to report for drug testing first thing in the morning, Sinclair. And keep me updated."

Tony nodded. He tore out of the captain's office, past the surreptitious glances of other officers and their smothered guffaws at his appearance. All he could think about was Jazz.

Chapter 22

*F*LOOZIE SPUTTERED ALONG, ROCKING A LITTLE in the south Georgia wind. Streamlined she was not, but she had character. Jazz settled back against the seat she had reupholstered in zebra-print velvet, and popped a Natalie Merchant tape into the cassette player.

Her thoughts turned unbidden to Tony Sinclair. Her heart ached for him: the poor guy was probably rolled up in a pink slip so large he could use it as a bedsheet.

The police captain hadn't looked like he was a nice man under the best of circumstances—he reminded her of nothing so much as the mascot for the Georgia Bulldogs, pointed teeth, squashed nose, and all. His expression had been black, and she was willing to bet he had seen red.

In all honesty, she couldn't have expected the man to scatter rose petals and blessings upon them. While *she* thought Tony's service exceptional, the captain probably didn't.

She kept her eyes on the green moving truck in front of her. Green for "go." Green for cash. Green for the grass on the other side of the law. She wasn't going to let these pissants get away with this. She refused to see her father rot away his twilight years in jail, even if he hadn't reported their scheme.

The thought crossed her mind that keeping her father in jail would be much less expensive for her. He'd wear that orange jumpsuit instead of Savile Row suits and silk ascots. He'd eat cheap slop from a tin plate, not filet mignon and truffles. And polo was surely not on the list of prison recreational activities.

Jazz was immediately ashamed of herself. What a terrible daughter she was! She stepped on the gas.

She had listened to Natalie Merchant, The Black Crowes, and most of a B-52's album before the green truck exited I-75. The thieves were making a pit stop at a gas station.

Jazz realized that now was the time to ditch

Floozie. She might go unnoticed several cars back on the interstate, but Cantini's men would definitely spot her if she tried to follow them into the heart of Savannah.

Since there were no handy rental-car businesses located next to the Jiffy-Mart, she made a snap decision, one that Sinclair would not approve of. She whipped Floozie behind the car wash and climbed out, grabbing her nail gun from the back and wrapping it in a jacket.

She had to move fast, while all three of the jerks were occupied.

A quick look inside the Jiffy Mart confirmed that they were. Pug was purchasing a foot-long weenie with sauerkraut and extra relish, a package of beef jerky, and one of those nasty fried pies in a bag. As he thumbed through the cash in his snakeskin wallet, he added a package of antacids to boot. She applauded his foresight.

The youth with the turkey-sized biceps stood in line behind him, buying some kind of Power-Shake and a container of sunflower seeds. The thin, well-dressed man had finished with the fuel pump and was helping himself to an instant latte.

Jazz darted around the back of their van, worked the latch open, and raised the door about a foot. She belly-crawled into the dusty darkness, then pulled the door down behind her.

It rolled shut with a squeal and a thunk, a horrible sound like the gate of a dungeon. God, what had she just done? Crawling in here was the single most reckless thing she'd ever done in her life.

What if the thieves had seen her? What if they came out to check on their cargo before making the final leg of their journey? Acid churned in her stomach, and she rolled back a little farther, until she bumped into something wrapped in plastic.

It had to be a painting. There were quite a few of them, most still in their frames. They'd provide the perfect cover if she got behind them.

It was pitch-black inside the truck. The floor was gritty with dust and dirt, and the air was stifling hot. Jazz crawled on her hands and knees to the far right side of the vehicle, and then felt around. The crooks had leaned a large wrapped painting against the wall, and she turned onto her side and slipped behind it. Farther back, she had to shimmy behind a couple of boxes, and finally seemed to reach the wall that backed up to the cab.

At the sound of footsteps and voices outside she froze, her heart trying to gallop out of her chest.

Doors slammed and the truck's engine grumbled to life.

Thank God! She was safe for now.

Jazz felt around some more and discovered a

pile of moving blankets. It was too stifling to crawl under them, but she could pull them over her when they got to their destination, which was almost certainly Savannah. That made the most sense: It was a port town where they could start the paintings on a journey overseas.

Jazz decided it was time to update Tony again on their whereabouts. She pulled her cell phone from her pocket and dialed his number slowly, by feel.

"You did what!" he raged, when she filled him in. "Tell me you're kidding. Tell me you're not such a goddamned stupid little fool!"

Jazz winced and held the phone away from her ear.

"I'm gonna wring your neck! I'm gonna—"

"Tony, it was the only way. They would have spotted me otherwise. I'm well hidden. I'll call you as soon as we stop, and I promise I'll get out of here, okay?"

"Don't make promises you may not be able to goddammned keep! Jesus Christ, I don't believe this . . ." he sounded frantic. "Sneller, notify Savannah PD, *now!*"

"Good-bye, Tony. I'll talk to you soon."

"Jazz—"

She pressed the OFF button, feeling guilty that she'd worried him so much. For the next couple of hours, Jazz sat in the back of the truck, unable to do anything but sweat copiously and pray.

They finally exited the highway, and their speed for the next five minutes was slower. They made lots of turns. At last they pulled to a stop, and Jazz secreted herself under the moving blankets, rolling as far back against the wall as she could.

She heard the cab doors open, and the men got out. Her heart began to race, hurling itself against her ribs.

But the thieves didn't approach the back of the truck at all. Their footsteps and voices faded; she heard a door open and close, and they were gone.

Her breathing slowed bit by bit, and she decided to risk looking around. She waited a minute or two longer, then crawled out of the blankets and across the truck floor. She raised the door a couple of inches.

Below her were the unmistakable cobbled stones of historic Savannah, and she could smell the brackish water, indeed, *hear* it slapping up against the docks. She waited a few moments to see if the noise of the door had attracted any attention, and then eased it up far enough to roll out.

She landed unsteadily on the uneven stones and moved quickly away from the truck. They were parked in an alley outside a dilapidated wood-

and-stone building. Though its sign read, CLEGG & SONS, MACHINE PARTS, it was so faded and peeling that she felt sure the place was abandoned.

Bobbing in the reddish brown water behind the old machine shop was a forty- to fifty-foot trawling boat.

Jazz found cover behind a Dumpster and hunkered down next to one of the old stone walls that characterized this part of Savannah. The rocks were reputed to be ballast, tossed off eighteenth- and nineteenth-century ships that had docked in the port.

She pulled out her cell phone again and called Sinclair. "I'm out," she said to him when he answered. "They don't have a clue I'm here."

Tony was vocal in his relief. She gave him the address and cross streets of the place, then hung up.

About twenty minutes passed—long enough to give her a leg cramp—before Pug ambled out of the machine shop and sat on a wooden bench outside to enjoy a cigar. She wrinkled her nose as the strong scent wafted her way. It was a brand, she felt sure, far inferior to the one Myles smoked.

Presently he was joined by the tall, thin man in the good clothes, who carried some sort of rolled catalogue in one hand. He inhaled a snootful of air, shot Pug a look of distaste, and walked with his catalogue to the edge of the water. When he unrolled it, Jazz saw that it was a Sotheby's art auction booklet. He was undoubtedly checking comparable sale prices for the paintings they'd stolen. She narrowed her eyes.

The back door of the place opened once again, and Turkey Boy appeared to round out the trio. He did a few contortionist leg stretches, then dropped to give them all forty push-ups over a copy of *Strut* magazine. Jazz was alarmed to see his biceps inflate even more. Surely they would explode if he raised himself even one more time.

As she watched from her hiding place, though, it appeared that reading his body-building rag was straining him more than the physical exercise. She shook her head. How on earth had these three found each other? The criminal element was fascinating.

They all appeared to be killing time, waiting for some signal to go ahead and unload the goods onto the boat. Or perhaps this wasn't the final destination?

Jazz frowned. All she could do was wait and see. She folded her arms across her chest and remained in position behind the wall, trying to ignore the persistent mosquitoes that were dining off her bare arms. A slap at one had caused the thin man to turn his head in her direction, so from then on she rubbed surreptitiously.

Jazz had been lurking unnoticed for the better part of an hour when her cell phone vibrated, startling her. She jumped and squealed, then clapped her hand over her mouth in horror. All three men turned in her direction, and the thin man gestured to Turkey Boy.

Abandoning her hiding place, Jazz wheeled and ran. Panic surged through her veins, but though she jogged two miles every morning, she was no match for the mass of muscle pounding behind her. Turkey Boy caught her around the waist and pulled.

She found herself bent over his arm, legs still pumping, like a cartoon character. "Let me go!" she panted.

His only response was a grunt as he hoisted her higher, his monstrous biceps bulging. His hand, which gripped three of her ribs at once, was the size of a ham.

"Who is she?" demanded the thin man.

Turkey Boy shrugged, jolting Jazz up with his shoulders. She'd never hated being small more; she felt like a toddler scooped out of a sandbox. Oh, for the nail gun in the back of the truck!

"Who are you?" the thin man demanded.

She simply stared at him, her face set. Fear twined around her like kudzu, but she refused to display it.

Turkey Boy shook her until she rattled. Jazz was sure that it was only the hookerish clumps of sticky mascara that kept her eyeballs from falling out of their sockets.

Pug chose that moment to approach and peer at her. His breath was befouled with greasy pork, beef jerky, refined sugar, and his horrific cigar. Jazz gagged as he pushed her hair out of her face and stared down at her.

"Why, this little slut is Myles Taylor's daughter," he declared. "She got 'er face gooped up, and she got purple hair, but it's her, all right."

"Well, now. This presents us with a small problem, doesn't it?" the thin man mused. "For she knows exactly what's going on, and we can't have that."

"You ask me, we oughta string her up by that nasty nose ring o' hers." Pug leered.

Jazz shivered and thanked God that her nose ring was a fake.

"Lemme have her." Pug's pouchy little eyes gleamed.

"No. We don't have time for any of your games," said the thin man. "Sal will be here any minute."

Jazz couldn't help herself. "Sal Cantini?"

He whirled to face her, eyes narrowed. "What do you know about Cantini?"

"Enough," she spat. "I know he tried to set my father up to take the rap for your burglary. I know he's a no-good, murdering son of a bi—" Turkey Boy dug his free thumb and index finger into both of her cheeks, impeding her speech and forcing her to make a fish face. "Aawggh!"

"Don't you talk about my Uncle Sal that way, girlie!" The big lug was enraged. "And don't you call my grannie a dog, either."

"I never meant to call your grannie a dog," Jazz said, once he'd removed his digits from her face. "But your uncle does murder people."

"I don't see it that way," Turkey Boy argued, "and neither does he."

"Oh?" Her tone was scathing. "Then how do you see it?"

"He just gives certain people the business, that's all."

"You make it sound like a capitalistic virtue."

"Huh?"

"Never mind. I'd just prefer not to get your uncle's business, that's all."

"Well, by showing up here, you've asked for it," the thin man said sharply.

"Isn't it a woman's prerogative to change her mind?" Jazz asked hopefully.

He ignored her. "Does anyone know you're here?"

She immediately nodded. "The entire Atlanta Police Department, the Navy, and the Marines, too."

"Yeah, right. Who was trying to call you?"

"*Inside Edition.* They'll be here any moment with their camera crew, so you'd better not hurt me. Tell me, who's buying your hot paintings?"

"You'd better keep your mouth shut if you want to live an extra two minutes, Sweetness."

Fear kept her talking. "Myles knows who you guys are, you know. He told me you asked him to consult on the job."

"Myles, my dear, is in jail." The thin man was unconcerned. "He's got a record as long as a football field, no alibi, and a tendency toward dandyism that any hardworking jury will despise."

She ground her teeth. "You've got it all worked out, don't you?"

"Why, yes. Thank you for noticing." He smiled, displaying teeth that were long and pointed. Then he glanced at his watch. "Get rid of her now, before Sal comes. I don't want to have to explain this to him."

Jazz choked on her own breath. *I don't want to die. I want to live, create . . . Make love to Tony Sinclair one more time.* She turned her gasp into a sob, and hung limp over Turkey Boy's arm. "Don't hurt me," she pleaded, in her best *Perils of Pauline* imitation. "Please."

Turkey Boy scuffed his feet and cleared his throat.

She degenerated into crocodile tears.

His voice miserable, her captor said, "Aw, don't do that." His grip on her relaxed slightly as he turned in the thin man's direction. "I hate it when they—"

Jazz drew her leg forward and kicked back with every ounce of her 103 pounds, straight down into Turkey Boy's giblets.

"Aaaaaarrrrrrghhhhhh!" He let her go to clutch himself, rock back and forth, and drop to his knees.

Jazz shot away faster than a greased watermelon and hurtled toward freedom. She ran to the cobblestoned street, hopped over a low post-and-rope fence, and barreled straight into a black merino wool sweater that covered the substantial girth of a man.

"*Cristaccio!*" he swore, his accent heavily Italian.

Jazz looked up for a split second, and recognized his face from news photos. She realized, before a paralyzing clonk to her temple, that she'd just collided with Sal Cantini.

Chapter 23

TWENTY-EIGHT DAYS, ELEVEN HOURS, AND twenty-three minutes since he'd last had a ciga-rette. And he'd never needed one more. Tony wished that he had a couple of Marines with him for backup, instead of a bagelophile and a cross-dressing art thief. The latter was wedged unceremoniously into the MR-2's poor excuse for a backseat, crouched like a preying mantis in his Gucci loafers and an ascot. Secure in the knowledge that Myles wasn't guilty, Tony had sprung him to pump him for more information and to ID the thieves.

Bagel rode shotgun, chewing phlegmatically on his comfort food. Tony gritted his teeth and drove. His longing for a cigarette had become an acute pain that wracked his body almost as much as the urgent need to know Jazz was safe.

Her father appeared unconcerned. "I know my girl," he declared. "She'll either keep her distance, or have these people trussed up and awaiting our arrival."

"Clue in," Tony said, behind clenched teeth. "She *isn't* keeping her distance. She weighs 103 pounds. She has no experience with violent criminals. Your daughter, *sir*"—he spat the word—"is in extreme danger." In the rearview mirror, he watched Myles blink at his scathing tone.

The gentleman cleared his throat. "You may be correct in that assumption, young man, but until we arrive at our thieves' *pied à terre*, we can do nothing but speculate. We rush to the rescue, do we not? Three musketeers in a Toyota . . ."

Tony aimed for a large pothole in the road, wondering if perhaps he could dislodge the horror in his backseat. Why had they brought him? Birds of Myles's feather should be taken out and shot together.

The abominable man launched, in a fine singsong baritone, into an ode.

"Danger," he intoned. "Danger sets us all ashiver, causing heart and mind to quiver . . ."

Bagel shot Tony an alarmed glance.

Tony kept driving.

"Just when we most wish to squall, we set our backs against the wall . . ."

Bagel swallowed hard.

"We peer into the inky night, invoking courage—poised to fight!"

Tony felt his face congeal into disgust.

Myles was on a roll, now. "With Truth and Goodness on our side, we worry not about our hides . . . We lift a noble firearm—"

"And blast you to the funny farm," Tony finished, unable to stop himself.

"You're as unsympathetic regarding my Art as my dearest Jazz," Myles mourned. "The young have no appreciation for the finer things in life. It will be just my luck to have one of your ilk as a son-in-law."

Tony's foot slipped off the accelerator for a moment. *Myles for a father-in-law?* It was a concept so ghastly that his mind refused to bend around it.

Yet a vision flashed into his mind. Jazz walked down a red-carpeted aisle toward him, wearing a lovely white gown, her curly hair piled high on her head under a veil of white netting. In her arms, she lovingly cradled not a bridal bouquet, but her nail gun.

To his surprise, he didn't recoil from the idea. He let the vision continue to unfold in his head. Her face was lovely and fresh, filled with a glow of love for him, her teasing smile tender and warm. He took her hand, kissed it, then pulled her into his arms, devouring her tempting little mouth.

"You may not yet kiss the bride!" thundered the priest. "Can we not uphold at least the *semblance* of chastity?"

They pulled apart reluctantly.

His daydream was interrupted when Bagel dug him in the ribs. "Sinclair, why are you grinning like a moron at the pigeon poop on the windshield? Pay attention to the road."

Tony blinked, and returned his concentration to the endless stretch of tarmac ahead. The landscape was beginning to change as they drove farther south, and the air smelled heavier, with a tinge of brine. They would be in Savannah within the hour.

Bagel began to amuse himself by using his thumbs to squeeze the cream cheese from one end of a silver packet to the other, and Tony was free to return to his thoughts. He now pictured Jazz standing outside a suburban home, watching fondly as four small children wreaked havoc in a grassy yard behind a picket fence.

What, are you crazy? Your kids would probably have all the criminal tendencies of their grandfather.

Now Tony watched as two of his four children

played bank robber with water guns—one of them driving the Big Wheel getaway car with the crown jewels in the plastic back hatch.

The other two, toddlers, displayed just as much criminal career promise: one of them played computer hacker with a Fisher-Price plastic machine. The other carried large amounts of Monopoly money and wore a diaper emblazoned with the words, "Trust Me" on the seat.

Tony frowned. He couldn't possibly marry a woman like Jazz Taylor. She wasn't blond. She wasn't sweet. She probably couldn't boil an egg. She'd wreak havoc in his life. And yet . . .

Huh-uh, no way! Tony *refused* to let Cupid shoot him in the heart with a nail gun.

Jazz awoke to darkness and a horrific pounding in her head. For a moment she lay disoriented, unable to remember where she was or what had happened. Slowly it came back to her. Someone had hit her on the head—Sal Cantini, and she was now truly scared.

She couldn't move. She was bound hand and foot, blindfolded, and gagged. Tight, itchy rope cut off her circulation at the wrists, and her hands had gone numb. All the moisture in her mouth had been sucked out by the disgusting cloth they'd jammed between her teeth. Jazz concentrated on not hyperventilating with fear. She tried to inhale and release long, slow breaths through her nose.

Where was Tony? *Please*, she prayed, *let him come soon.* Those strong fingers and those muscular arms would have her out of here within ten seconds.

Tears welled in her eyes, shocking her into disgust. Here she was, a capable woman of the millennium, blubbering for a knight in shining armor. She could take care of *herself*.

Yeah, said a small inner voice, *but maybe it's not so wrong to wish for a little help here and there.*

Jazz heard sounds of a heavy engine rumbling to life, and her heart hammered. She felt the vibrations and realized that they were under her. They had thrown her back in the green truck, with the stolen paintings.

Where were they planning to dispose of her? And how? A variety of gruesome possibilities assaulted her mind. Would they cut her into little Woman McNuggets and feed her to the sharks?

One look at Cantini's ugly mug had left her in no doubt as to his cruelty. Brute violence simmered under that greasy comb-over.

Jazz's Mighty Woman of the Millennium attitude crumbled entirely. She was terrified. Fear shook her like a rag doll and melted her backbone.

"Please, Tony," she whispered. "Please get here soon. You were right, I shouldn't have come alone. Maybe I can't always handle everything by myself."

A silent sob, then another and another, shook her body. She hadn't cried since that awful childhood night the police had dropped her off at Grandmother Sophronia's house, and it was painful.

She wept out of fear, out of helplessness. She wept because she was so tired of doing everything alone. She was tired of battling chauvinist studio execs and pompous directors. She was tired of parenting Myles while he played. She was exhausted by the effort it took to carry the world on her own small shoulders.

She *needed* a man's strength now, and not just any man's strength. She wanted Tony Sinclair with an ache that filled her entire body.

Chapter 24

*T*ONY CAME DAMN CLOSE TO FLATTENING A horse and buggy on the streets of historic Savannah, as he flew around a corner and hit a big pothole near Mercer House. One of Myles's Gucci loafers went flying onto the square, and Bagel wound up with cream cheese on his glasses.

Tony recovered, gunned his motor and drove on, ignoring Myles's repeated requests for his shoe.

They arrived at the correct street just as a large green moving truck pulled out from behind the address Jazz had given him. No doubt about it: It was the truck Jazz had described. Tony knew an impulse to chase wildly after it with his gun, pull it over, and apprehend the criminals. He'd be an international hero, thanked by museums all over the world for restoring their property. He'd probably get his job back and be assigned other important cases.

But there was Jazz to think about. She'd sworn she'd gotten out of the truck, and he had to make sure she was safe and unharmed. No amount of ambition was worth a human life, and especially not the life of Jazz Taylor.

Savannah PD would tail the truck, just as he'd requested. Tony darted down a side street and waited until the moving van turned out into traffic.

Then Tony put the MR2 into reverse and squealed backward to the street where Clegg and Sons was located, parked, and gestured to his partner to follow him. If Jazz was hidden, they had to find her. He prayed that the worst hadn't happened.

"Myles," he barked, "stay in the car until we get back, or your life won't be worth salvaging."

The old bird managed to look both elegant and resentful at the same time, but with a sniff did as he was told. He'd probably compose Act I of an opera while they were searching for his daughter. Tony had never met a man as useless as Myles Taylor.

Jazz was not anywhere in the vicinity, inside or out. After a thorough search through the premises, Tony headed outdoors and hunted again for clues. His heart stopped when he found her smashed cellular phone. The battery had been ripped out, and the phone had been tossed onto the cobbles and stepped upon.

Breathe, he told himself. *Just breathe, damn it.* "Sneller!" he shouted. "Sneller, we've gotta hustle. They have her. Let's go!"

He ran like hell for the MR2 and leaped in. Bagel tried the same thing on the passenger side, but only succeeded in hurting himself. Tony tried to contain his impatience while his partner opened the door, and squealed off as he shut it.

"Well?" asked Myles.

"You'd better snap out of your upper-crust complacency, Taylor, because Cantini's hired guns have got your daughter, and he's one nasty customer."

The florid countenance above the silk ascot turned gray. "Bloody *hell*," said Jazz's dear old dad.

Tony wondered cynically if his concern was for his little girl or for his monthly allowance. "This is your fault, old man," he said through gritted teeth. "If you hadn't gotten involved in these shenanigans, she wouldn't be in danger. So you'd better make yourself useful."

Myles was silent.

"Talk to me!" Tony shouted.

"I don't know what to say," Taylor admitted. "I never meant for her to become involved. My former career was never dangerous in this manner. There were always the law and security companies to deal with, but Cantini is out of my depth. I'm no effing James Bond. I hoped to dodge Cantini, and that was all."

"What's your part in all this?"

"He asked me to serve as a consultant for the robbery at the High Museum. This is a new area for him, and he needed guidance. I turned him down, and he began to threaten me and Ellen. Fearing for her safety, I popped her onto a plane out of the country. Then I simply disappeared. I never dreamt, at that point, that he'd hurt Jazz. How he found out I even had a daughter is beyond me."

"Cantini's whole business is based on knowing everything about everyone. He gathered intelligence on you, Taylor, or he had you followed. It's not hard, believe me. Now, where's he going with the paintings?"

"The water. He must get them out of the States, and then he can smuggle them to outside contacts. If he's down here, his first destination is probably South America, possibly Caracas or Rio de Janeiro."

"I'm thinking they'll head for Tybee Island—

it's the closest. Bagel, call the local cops and get the truck's location. Hurry!"

Bagel did as instructed. "Savannah PD reports them going over the causeway, Sinclair."

"Good." Tony drove even faster. "Now," he said to Myles, "don't lie to me: Cantini wanted you for contacts, not just consulting. Isn't that right?"

"Yes, that's true."

"Did you provide him with any names?"

Myles hesitated.

"Taylor, we know one of Cantini's men got away from Jazz's studio with your little black address book! Did it contain names of your contacts?"

"Indeed it did."

"So you've paved the way for them."

"I suppose you could say that."

Tony looked disgusted.

Myles's expression was bland.

In minutes, they were crossing the bridge over the saltwater marshes to Tybee Island. They were ten minutes behind Cantini & Co. Every additional minute that passed meant sixty seconds during which Jazz could be terrified, hurt, or in the process of losing her life.

Jazz felt her rolling prison lurch to a stop. Perspiration trickled down every inch of her, from forehead to toes, and she scented her own fear. She'd heard it said that death had a smell, but she'd never known that terror had its own as well. *Fearomones*, she thought, and giggled, near hysteria.

She heard the slamming of doors, and her captors got out of the truck, talking among themselves.

"If the girl recovers consciousness," said the thin man, "we'll just hit her again, and pitch her overboard when we get to open water. No one will ever be the wiser."

"She was kinda cute," mourned Turkey Boy. "I wish Uncle Sal hadn'ta had to give her the business."

Pug snorted. "She deserved it."

She heard another car pull up, and guessed this was Uncle Sal. His voice carried over the others. "Come on, ya dumb lugs. Don't just stand around; let's get movin'—we got a cargo to unload, already! Geez, what do I pay you for?"

Turkey Boy cleared his throat. "About getting paid, Uncle Sal—"

"Not you, you're family," his uncle interrupted.

"Ain't you s'posed to treat family better, not worse?"

"Who keeps your mutha a bleach blonde? Who coughs up for your fancy gym, knucklehead? Who cosigned on your wheels? Huh?"

"The wheels are just a '73 Impala," muttered Turkey Boy.

"Shut the hell up and show me some gratitude. I coulda sent you off to college, you know."

His nephew drew in a hiss of breath at that gruesome possibility. "All right, all right."

Somebody unlocked and opened the back door of the truck, and Jazz froze. *Please let them think I'm dead*, she prayed.

"Leave Miss Thing there, until the last load. We'll get rid of her later."

Rustling began around her, and Jazz lay as still as possible. So as not to panic, she forced herself to think again of Tony, who would be there any minute.

As her captors continued to unload the truck around her, she fought off her growing panic. Too soon, she felt herself being lifted, and deliberately stayed limp. So this was it. They would just throw her overboard, alive. Jazz gave up all hope and prepared for the worst.

But as her captors trudged toward the water with her, she heard squealing tires and shouts behind them.

"Stop! Hands up! Police!"

The words gave her the incentive to struggle like a mad thing. Though she couldn't kick or hit, she wriggled like a demented worm. Surprised,

Turkey Boy dropped her, and she rolled downhill. She picked up momentum, then bounced off of something that stopped her.

Since she could only move at the waist and knees, Jazz frantically did sit-ups to show the police that she was alive.

She barely recognized Tony's ragged voice as he yelled, "She's here!" Jazz went limp with relief. He'd come for her!

"Hands up, God damn it! None of you move!"

She heard deafening gunfire, and more shouts from her captors. "Run!" Cantini commanded. "Get to the boat."

Heavy footsteps hurtled past her and then she heard more explosive gunfire, followed by screams from both sides of her. Her heart jumped between her molars. Had Tony been hit? Killed? Oh, God, she couldn't bear the thought!

"I got one!" shouted a voice she didn't know.

"Bloody good shot, old chap," said her father's voice. "Hip, hip, hooray!"

What is Myles doing here?

She heard a groan next.

"Sinclair?" asked Myles. "Have you taken a bullet?"

No! Please, no!

"Just a flesh wound," Tony grunted. "Nothing bad."

The panic she'd been battling finally won out; she could no longer be brave with Tony shot on her account. Jazz screamed through her gag.

"They're getting away," the unknown voice shouted, accompanied by a sputtering boat motor.

"I don't care—I've got to make sure she's okay," Tony snapped. She heard his footsteps, running to her. A jingle indicated he was digging in his pocket for something. She prayed it was a knife.

Next she felt him untying the cloth over her eyes, and then he removed the gag.

"Tony!"

He scooped her up, covering her face with kisses. Tony smelled like desperate worry and musky man. His eyes burned into hers for a moment, and then he held her so tightly against him that she thought her ribs would crack. "Oh, baby. Oh, Jazz. It's okay. It's all over. Oh, Jazz, I love you. I love you so much. Marry me, Jazz."

Marry him?

All she could do was tremble and cry, and honk and gulp, and emit many other attractive, feminine noises. She was disgusted with herself, but couldn't stop. She pulled out of Tony's arms, but he began to stroke her hair, which turned the tears into a torrent.

So this was what being in love with a man did

to you—it reduced you to a sniveling puddle, rendered you entirely useless, and worse, exposed your emotional weakness in public. It made Jazz sob all the harder.

Marry Tony Sinclair? It was a nice fantasy, but it would never work.

He pulled her into his arms again, but she pushed against his chest. She had to scrape herself together, not indulge her pathetic dependent tendencies.

"I'm okay," she told her cop, wiping her eyes. "Go do your job, and be a hero."

Chapter 25

A SAVANNAH OFFICER WAS GRAPPLING AND rolling on the ground with Pug. Just as Tony ran to help, Bagel sat on the unfortunate crook and the two officers got his hands behind his back to cuff him.

Cantini's boat was getting away fast, churning up waves in its wake. Tony took aim at the thin man, who was farthest astern, and blew a hole in the sleeve of his expensive shirt. A faint howl of outrage could be heard from the retreating boat. He set his jaw and fired again, holding his arm rock steady and squinting in concentration.

Sinclair's next shot neatly removed the toupee from the crown of the guy's head, and sent it spinning into the waves. The man grabbed wildly for it, lost his balance, and joined it with a splash. The other occupants of the boat disregarded him and plowed on.

"Let's go, Sneller!"

Bagel was already struggling out of his shoes and shirt.

Tony blinked once at the sheer expanse of doughy white belly his partner revealed, and then followed him, running with a smooth dive into the water. "Call the Coast Guard, Myles!" he yelled over his shoulder. "Let's round them up." He launched into a fast crawl and easily reached the sputtering, coughing thin man first.

Bagel bobbed and dog-paddled behind him, but caught up with surprising speed.

They each grasped their captive by the collar and dragged him back to shore spewing an uncomplimentary stream of Italian. Tony couldn't understand a word of it, but caught the general drift.

Bagel began to read the prisoner his rights, while the man stared in horrified fascination at Sneller's looming, fish white expanse of belly. It gleamed in the sunlight like a Jell-O mold of the Himalayas.

Tony turned to Myles, who stood, unconcerned, on his remaining Gucci loafer and picked sand particles off the silk sock on his other foot. "Did you contact the Coast Guard?" he asked.

Myles shook his head.

"Why the hell not?" Tony grabbed for his cell phone.

"I'll call 'em," said one of the Savannah officers.

"Let them go," Myles suggested, his tone airy.

All of his companions swung around in shock.

"Myles," his daughter told him, "you're crazy! You could still go to jail for their crime. You have no alibi, and a past record."

Jazz's father ignored her. "Let them go," he repeated. He turned to the thin man. "Emaciado, old chap, or whatever your name is. Does Cantini have my little black book?"

The thin man's eyes snapped, and he uttered another few pithy words in Italian. Tony noticed that he didn't look nearly so elegant bald.

Myles smiled pleasantly. "But I don't *want* to have relations with my mother, if it's all the same to you. Now, really. What can it matter if you tell me about the black book? He's already taken off with it, hasn't he?"

The thin man glared at him, and then finally nodded.

"Thank you," Myles nodded. He turned to Tony and the others. "You see? Just let him sail off into the sunset. Everything will work itself out."

Jazz exploded. "You *want* to let him escape?

You just want to donate the world's art treasures of the last century to *Cantini*? Let him sell them for private gain? They belong to the public, Myles! How can you be so jaded? You promised me you'd retire. You promised to write me an essay on morality and justice! I can't believe you—"

"I have written," Myles pronounced with dignity, "an *Ode* to Justice. I've simply been polishing it for presentation."

Tony and Bagel groaned in chorus. "Please, no!"

"I am surrounded by barbarians," Myles said sadly. "Vulgarians. Troglodytes."

"We know," agreed Tony. "We're not fit to wear ascots."

"I do not deserve such a brutish son-in-law!" Myles mourned.

"Brutish?"

"Son-in-law?" Jazz stamped her small foot. "I'm not going to marry him!"

"Yes, you are," said Tony, looking mulish.

She ignored that. "And while you two yammer, the paintings are vanishing. Would you *do* something, please?"

Tony dialed the Coast Guard's number on his cell phone. His brows snapped together in astonishment when Myles grabbed the instrument and punched the END button.

"Let them go." His voice resonated with quiet

authority, instead of its usual plummy tones. "I've taken care of things."

Everyone stared at him.

Jazz was the first to break the silence. "What do you mean?"

"I mean that all is going according to plan." Myles, evidently tired of standing on one foot like a stork, peeled off his silk sock, rolled up his right trouser leg, and wiggled his toes into the sand with satisfaction.

"Myles," his daughter began in dangerous tones, "I'm going to hit you! What are you talking about?"

Her father yawned in a refined fashion, one hand covering his mouth. "I am a man of foresight," he stated. "Foresight, vision, and justice." He aimed a meaningful glance at Jazz. "*Poetic* justice.

"Being a man of perspicacious nature, I realized that Cantini wanted my international contacts quite desperately. What good are priceless paintings if one has no buyers for them? One cannot simply declare by bullhorn in the village square that one is hawking a Renoir.

"But Cantini is not a man of elegance or tact. Reluctant to introduce such a crass individual to my old associates, I simply made new ones." Myles bestowed a brilliant smile upon them all.

Tony folded his arms across his chest. "Pardon our stupidity, but could you explain a bit more?"

"A very nice bunch of fellows at Interpol," said Myles. "I never realized we'd rub along so well. I simply substituted their names for those of my old friends, and *voilà!* An entire new little black book was born."

"Are you saying," Jazz asked dangerously, "that when those thugs broke into my studio and stole the book, they stole a fake that you'd deliberately planted?"

Her father nodded with pride, and beamed at her.

Tony leaped for his throat and lifted him off the ground by his ascot. "You stinking, no good bastard! You knew they would follow you to your daughter. You deliberately put her in danger!"

Myles's eyes bugged out as Tony shook him, and he clawed at the silk noose around his neck.

"How do you explain that?" Tony shouted at him. "You put your girlfriend on a plane but sent Cantini after your daughter? How *could* you?"

"Stop it! Let him go," pleaded Jazz.

Tony gritted his teeth. "I'll kill him."

"Let him go. Please." She tugged at his arm.

Tony released her father abruptly, and Myles fell to the sand, clutching his throat.

"I never thought she was in danger. I knew—"

he coughed, "—that she could take care of herself. My Jazz has never needed any help doing that."

Disgust rolled off Tony in waves, and he brushed his hands together as if he'd just touched something contaminated. "Well, from now on she's going to *have* help, whether she wants it or not." He was shaking with protective outrage. If only he could turn back time and give Jazz the father she deserved—one who would have treasured her, and kept her safe, warm, and loved. If only her dad had been some nice boring executive with normal family values.

He looked at Jazz, a tide of emotions washing over him. Yet if her past had been different, she wouldn't be the woman she was today—the strong, courageous, independent soul he loved.

She stood unmoving, looking at her father with those big brown eyes of hers. After several moments, she stretched a hand toward him, and helped him to his feet.

Tony felt his heart turn over as she said with a sad, wry smile, "You're a piece of work, Myles. But you did the right thing, after all these years. I'm proud of you."

Chapter 26

"WHY WON'T YOU MARRY ME?" TONY ASKED Jazz.

He loomed in her studio doorway the next day, looking disturbingly handsome, all-American, and . . . devastated. Aw, Jeez. He wasn't going to make this easy on her, was he? Those blue eyes were hurt, and they were trying to x-ray her, and she didn't like it one bit.

"Tony," she sighed. "I can barely even say the word 'wife.' It gives me hives. It makes me break out in a cold sweat. It conjures nightmares of being smothered in a giant apron, or being boiled to death in a copper kettle, or being forced to whistle the theme from *Leave It to Beaver* while I dig my own grave."

"Jazz, that's ridiculous."

"It's not ridiculous! It's how I feel. That 'w' word involves Chantilly lace curtains, and rump roasts, and vacuuming!"

Tony stared at her, hands on his hips.

"Rubber gloves," Jazz ranted. "And coupon-clipping, and hospital corners!"

He blinked.

"Woven place mats, and daisies, and"—she felt her face blanch in horror—"*garden gnomes.* The very idea makes my skin crawl."

Tony shook his head and opened his mouth to speak, but she overrode him.

"I can't cook, Sinclair! I don't dust, and I've been known to stock up on new underwear just because all my other pairs are dirty."

"Jazz, I don't care if you can't cook. I can. We can both do the laundry and cleaning. And we don't even have to have a garden, much less gnomes."

"What happened to Tony Sinclair, Regular Guy? What happened to that nice Southern girl you wanted to meet?"

He shot her a crooked grin. "I guess my crystal ball malfunctioned."

"What about the houseful of kids?"

"Oh, I haven't given up on that, by any means."

"I can't be a *mom*," Jazz said. "I wouldn't have the foggiest idea what to do!" She had a brief flash of dozens of adorable little micro-Tonys rampaging through her studio. It was actually a very appealing image. Would they have his dimples? His blue eyes? His stubborn jaw? No, no, no. She couldn't go there.

They'd drool on her latex body parts. Chew on her spare noses and ears. Use her makeup for war paint.

They'd fall down the stairs, or get their diapers caught in machinery, or tumble headfirst into a bucket of alginate. She shuddered.

"I think you'd be a great mother," said Tony, grinning. "Think of the Halloween costumes you could make."

"You need someone who makes cookies, not monsters."

"I have confidence that anyone who can mix plaster can also sift flour and sugar."

"It's not the same thing," Jazz wailed.

"No, thank God; I never have developed a taste for cement. What are you afraid of, Jazz?"

"I'm not afraid of anything."

"Yes, you are. I think you're afraid to lean on anyone. You've been supporting your father for so long that you don't know how to accept any support in return."

"That's not true!"

"Yes, it is. But you have a career, Jazz. You wouldn't be dependent on me."

"That's right, and my career's going to require me to move to LA. So I can't possibly marry someone who's based in Atlanta." Hah, she had him there.

"Has it occurred to you that I could move, too?"

The thought of him uprooting his life for her sent panic shooting through her veins. God, what if they got all the way to California and it didn't work between them? How could she take on the responsibility for another person's happiness?

Her throat was starting to clog, and her eyes were prickling. He was too big, and too handsome, and had somehow gotten a powerful hold on her feelings. And there he stood in her doorway, blocking her exit. She felt trapped, and weak, and shaky.

He'd reduced her to a wet, weeping female dishrag down in Savannah, and she despised it. "You bring out all the weakness in me!" she shouted. "I can't afford that. I can't live my life like that."

"Weakness?" Tony's voice was dumbfounded. "You don't have a weak bone in your body, Jazz. Are you associating intimacy with weakness? Are you saying that because I can make you laugh, or cry, or climax, that I have too much power over you?"

"Yes!"

"Jazz, I think you've isolated yourself from feeling anything for so long that it scares the hell out of you."

"Don't psychoanalyze me, Sinclair," she warned.

Tony loomed over her, and she could see his frustration, wrapped though it was in a wrenching tenderness. He put his hands on her shoulders, but she skittered away.

"I won't abandon you, Jazz. I won't leave you holding the bag. I love you, and I thought you loved me. Did I read you wrong?"

She didn't answer.

"Did I?"

"No," she muttered. "Yes. No. Yes! I feel . . . affection for you. I was grateful to you for coming to my rescue."

"Affection?" He looked as if she'd slapped him.

She closed her eyes for a moment to block out the image.

A long moment passed before he said quietly, "I think you're lying to yourself. Are you really willing to walk away from love?"

"Tony, please go away," she begged. "I don't know what to say to you."

"Say yes or no."

"Then no!" she shouted.

"So that's your final answer?" In spite of his cool tone, his mouth had tightened, and the creases around his eyes were more pronounced than she'd ever seen them. He was in emotional agony, and she had put him there. A vise tightened around her stomach, and blood rushed to her ears. She wished he would shout at her, instead of throwing up the shield of male pride. Scream bad words, toss insults.

What he hurled at her instead was the truth.

"You've been working with smoke and mirrors so long that you don't know how to experience real emotion. You're an expert at makeup, but you don't know how to go any deeper than that.

"Life is more than a series of film stills, Jazz. It's more than creative success. It's about failures, too—and I guess I've crashed and burned in trying to convince the woman I love to spend her life with me.

"But you know what, Jazz? At least I've tried. I put myself and my love and my ego on the line. I don't know what the future holds, either. But I'm ready to meet it face-to-face—not hiding behind a mask."

Tears streamed down her face, blinding her.

"Go away, Tony—I don't want you to see me like this." She dashed at the tears with her hand. "I don't cry," she sobbed. "I never cry. I *never* cry . . ."

Chapter 27

*E*LLEN HESITATED BEFORE KNOCKING ON Myles's apartment door. She smoothed her hair, which had slipped out of the scarf she'd knotted around it. She locked her bare knees together to keep them from trembling. Then she rapped on the smooth, blank expanse of wood.

A moment passed before Myles opened the door, wielding an artist's brush. His green eyes flashed joy for the briefest of seconds, before his expression cooled into a mask of wounded pride. "Ellen," he said formally. "What a surprise."

"May I come in?"

He moved aside, raising his chin, and she walked past him only to be confronted with a horrific canvas. It depicted a woman's tortured face in the style of de Kooning, all teeth and wild hair and demonic eyes. The colors were acidic—greens and oranges and reds, violently exploding over browns and black.

In the upper left corner was tacked a snapshot of her own face.

Ellen swallowed. "Art therapy, darling?"

"Precisely. I'm going through an abstract expressionist stage."

She wished that the picture was a trifle more abstract and a trifle less expressionist, and averted her eyes from the revolting thing. This was not a promising start.

Myles stood aloof, arms folded over his chest. He looked so handsome, in dark trousers and an open-necked white-linen shirt with billowing sleeves. Not a speck of paint dared to mar his splendor.

Her eyes focused on his silvering hair and deeply tanned skin. She longed to run a finger along his stern jawline and trail it upward to his sensual mouth. But his stiff demeanor forbade such a gesture of affection.

She took a deep breath. "Myles," she began, "I was hoping that we could talk."

"Whatever is there to talk about, my dear Ellen? Will you regale me with tales of the straight-and-narrow? Have you written a tell-all book about your adventures with the Old Master? Do you want my blessing on a date with a stuffy, pin-striped stockbroker?"

She raised her chin and refused to let him intimidate her. "Myles, please. I want to . . . clear the air between us."

"Clear the air? Why, yes—it did become a bit polluted with suspicion, mistrust, and insult. But why should you concern yourself with that?"

"I'm asking you to hear me out."

"Very well, then." He rang a little bell on a side table. "But we must have refreshment."

Immediately the door from the kitchen opened, and a manservant appeared, bowing slightly. "Tea for sir and madam?"

Myles inclined his head. "Please."

Ellen stared at the man. He looked familiar, but where . . . ?

As she wracked her brain, the manservant returned bearing a silver tea service, which he set on the table, along with some delicate pastries.

"Thank you, McGraw."

Ellen did a double take. *McGraw?* Myles's vile cellmate? But . . . but . . . he had manners, and hadn't looked once at her breasts. He was paunchless, and clean, and hadn't burped. *McGraw?*

"Anything else you need, Sir Myles?"

"No, thank you. That will be all. Are you enjoying the Judith Martin book?"

"Oh, very much, sir. Very much." McGraw retreated once again to the kitchen and left them alone together.

"Is he medicated?" asked Ellen. "Or was he lobotomized?"

"Mr. McGraw has responded very well to obedience training," said Myles. "I needed to devote myself to a true raison d'etre, after being betrayed and trampled by the woman whose happiness—" he wiped a tear from his eye "—was my only concern."

Ellen blinked rapidly. Myles certainly wasn't making this easy. "Those are strong words, don't you think? I didn't betray you. I reacted to feeling swindled, and cheated, and foolish beyond measure."

He sprang to his feet. "You cast me aside like rubbish! Left me in a cell to rot! Threw money at my agony!"

"You weren't honest with me! Allow a seedling of truth to sprout from that melodramatic manure, Myles, and you'll recall that I gave you a chance to explain.

"And put yourself in my shoes. You were gone from my bed when the crime occurred, a Degas was found in your apartment, and suddenly the newspapers revealed a long record as an art thief you'd neglected to tell me about. What was I to think?"

Myles turned his back and folded his arms. "Interpol had sworn me to secrecy."

"That was all very well for you and Interpol, but I was left quite in the dark!"

Myles gave a great, miffed sniff. "You might have trusted me."

"Why? You had already violated my trust in the worst way!"

He paced to the far end of the room.

Ellen pressed her hands together to stop them from shaking. "Look, I don't want to have a row. I came to say that I'm sorry."

He didn't reply.

"I came to say I was wrong."

He said nothing.

"I came because," Ellen took a deep breath, "however ridiculous and dramatic and secretive you are, I love you . . . but that apparently doesn't matter to you."

Myles turned to face her, those green eyes flashed again, and she allowed herself to hope. But still he made no move toward her.

She swallowed the acrid misery that had risen in her throat and blinked back pinpricks of tears.

"Fine, then. I see it's no use. Good-bye, Myles."

Forcing her legs to remain steady, she stood up and put one elegantly shod foot in front of another until she reached the door. Her hand wrapped around the cold brass knob, twisted it, and pulled. Atlanta's summer heat slapped her face.

An elegant masculine hand reached around her and closed the door.

"If I ask you to stay," inquired Myles, "will you make an honest man of me?"

She stopped in her tracks, and her mouth trembled. *Oh, God. Could it be?* She turned slowly to find him wearing the beginnings of a smile. "That sounds like a very daunting task."

"I realize that. I haven't had much practice, you see." He shrugged.

Joy and tenderness surged through her and dawned into gratitude and exultation. "We have the rest of our lives to transform you into a fine upstanding citizen." She hugged him as if she'd never let him go and finally looked up through a haze of tears.

He grinned ruefully. "Fine, my dear Ellen, is one thing. But upstanding?" He shuddered. "I fear I shall never qualify. Sounds a frightful bore, anyhow."

"Oh, Myles." She giggled like a girl. "I love you."

"I must admit, I love you, too. It's damned inconvenient, however—gets in the way of my shallowness and greed."

"How devastating for you. Marry me."

"Why, you shameless hussy—that's my line." He tilted her head back for a deep kiss. "You realize that you'll have to make it worth my while to become an honest man, don't you?"

"Are you going to be difficult?"

"No, darling. Just expensive."

"Not *you*." She grinned.

"I want Narciso Rodriguez tails. And a custom-tailored trousseau."

"Done," she said promptly.

"I want a fabulous bloody circus of a wedding, and only the Ritz-Carlton will do."

She didn't blink.

"I want a twenty-tiered chocolate wedding cake festooned with truffles and marzipan, and a running fountain of Piper-Heidsieck Reserve champagne."

"All right," said Ellen. And she gave him a million-dollar kiss.

Chapter 28

AS JAZZ STOOD UNDER THE STREAM OF HOT water in her shower, she wished she could wash the cop out of her hair. She wished that cream rinse could untangle her emotions as well as her curls.

She turned off the taps and watched as the last of the water eddied and swirled down the drain. Why did it seem to be washing away her happiness?

"Stupid men!" she announced to her reflection in the mirror. Her father had played roulette with her life, and she simply wasn't ready to let another man take a spin.

True, Tony was a very different man—he was good, and true, and ethical. He had come to her rescue. He'd told her he loved her. He'd asked her to marry him. But how could she sacrifice her independence? She hadn't relied on a man since she was ten, when Myles went to jail.

Jazz threw her towel across the bathroom and sat on the toilet seat, putting her head in her hands.

Sinclair probably hated her, now. He thought she was some kind of emotional coward. But that wasn't true . . . was it?

She got up, walked slowly to her closet, and fished out a T-shirt and a faded pair of overalls. She should get over to the studio—she had plenty of projects to complete; deadlines she couldn't afford to ignore. A couple of Hollywood producers had been hinting that they could give her more work if she relocated to Los Angeles, and Jazz thought about it again as she pulled on a pair of boys' white tube socks with a hole in the left heel. She didn't particularly want to go through the hassle of moving, but it was necessary for her career.

Myles was an expensive relative, but she hoped that Ellen would marry him, now that the whole museum mess was over. She pulled on and laced up her shabby work boots. Why wasn't she angrier at her father for the role he'd played in the whole mess?

She supposed it was because he had actually kept his word to retire. And she'd spent a lifetime of forgiving Myles for various and sundry offenses. Any illusions she'd had about him had long since faded; her expectations of him weren't high.

Tony seemed different, but in Jazz's experience, men weren't altruistic. They got what they could out of you. Tony had said he wanted to take care of her and help her. Ha—he just wanted to patronize her and get in her way.

A small voice inside her head told her that she was being defensive and difficult. The voice got louder and more insistent as she fired up Floozie's engine and drove to work.

She entered the old warehouse and made her way down the hallways to her studio, where she heaved open the metal door and flipped on the lights. Donovan-the-dragon and all her other funky creatures greeted her. The space aliens huddled together on the wall above her, looking curiously forlorn. It took her a moment to realize that three of their orange-bulb eyes had burned out.

The poor little guys. Jazz went to the utility shelves for replacement bulbs and a ladder, and had them fixed up and happier within minutes.

As she put the ladder away, she wished it were as easy to put the light back into Tony's eyes. She sighed, looking at Donovan's big green scaly head. He looked right back at her, his expression serious.

She walked over and stroked his nose. "What should I do, buddy?"

His head cocked to the side under the pressure of her hands, and he gazed at her quizzically.

"Okay, so maybe I'm in love with that blasted, interfering, too-good-looking cop. But what can I do about it? I'm still not good marriage material. And this whole 'mom' concept is scarier and more grisly than any monster I've ever created . . ."

Donovan had white fuzz in his eyelashes, and she plucked it out with care. Then she wiped at his purple nostrils with a clean rag, and adjusted his forelock.

"It's true that I could get used to waking up next to him. And probably under him. Not to mention on top of him."

Donovan's head nodded on its hidden springs, and she had a sense, however nutty, that he was listening to her. God, maybe she *had* been alone too long, if she was having conversations with giant puppets.

But she and Tony were simply too different. He wanted a woman who ran a washing machine, not a studio. He would never get used to her odd hours, on-the-fly jobs, and lack of femininity.

Tony Sinclair, no matter how he set her hormones raging, was not for her.

As she reached this gloomy conclusion, she heard her phone ring. She lunged at it and was disappointed to find her father's voice on the other end of the line.

"My dearest Jazz," he began.

She waited.

"How are you?"

Myles had never asked that question of her—not once in her life. What had gotten into him? "I'm fine," she said.

"Truly? You're not suffering any ill effects from those ruffians?"

"A mild concussion. That's it."

"So you saw a doctor, my dear?"

Jazz was growing suspicious. "Yep. Myles, what do you want?"

Another long pause ensued.

"It occurs to me that I haven't always been the most . . . ideal . . . of fathers."

Her brows rose. "It does?"

"Yes. And, well, the thing is, though I know it's rather late in our relationship for me to have these revelations, I see that we've lived in many ways a role reversal of parent and child. I'd like to make that up to you."

Jazz stared at the receiver blankly. She shook it to make sure the phone wasn't malfunctioning.

"Are you there?" Myles was saying, when she returned the device to her ear.

"Yes. Go on."

"I want to apologize for thoughtlessly putting you in danger. It wasn't well-done of me. Not sporting at all."

"Not *sporting*?" She began to giggle weakly.

"I care very much for you, Jazz. You're my little girl who was never a little girl—always wiser than I. Can you forgive me?"

She was silent for a moment.

"I grovel in your general direction, my love, truly."

She collapsed into helpless laughter. "No, no, Myles," she gasped. "Don't get humble on me after all these years. I much prefer your studied elegance and self-absorption. If you want to make it up to me—"

"Tell me how!"

"You can get yourself married to Ellen Whitaker Northrop Banks."

"Quite coincidentally, my dearest, she has just accepted my proposal."

"Congratulations!" Jazz resisted the urge to whoop and holler.

Her father continued in his plummy tones, "So

I'd be delighted for you to meet her, Jasmine. Why don't you come out to dinner with us?"

She hesitated. "I'd love to meet her. But if you want me to do that, you'll have to take me shopping for an item which has never entered my closet: a skirt."

"You don't possess a skirt?" His voice was aghast.

"Not a one," she said cheerfully.

"We will away to Phipps Plaza posthaste! A skirt, you must have. And a pair of terribly sexy high-heeled sandals. Whatever do you wear to parties?"

"Levi's." Jazz grinned at the shriek from the other end of the line. "And as a matter of fact, I might even let you choose a devastating top for me."

"I'll pick you up in the Jaguar. I refuse to be seen in that hideous jalopy of yours."

"Of course," Jazz said, with a roll of her eyes. "I'll see you in a few minutes, Dad."

She heard a sharp intake of breath on the line. "You just called me—"

"A temporary lapse. It won't happen again."

"That would be rather a pity." He sounded crestfallen.

Jazz grinned. "Just teasing. It'll take me a while to get used to it, though."

* * *

Tony sat at ease in the captain's office, one leg crossed over the other. He struggled to keep his face bland.

His boss had gone through a metamorphosis. His fierce, jowly face had lost the rounded, pugnacious quality of a bulldog's. It had lengthened and drooped into the expression of a basset hound. It was as if someone had removed the stuffing from his cheeks.

The captain made a big show of shuffling some papers on his desk. "Sinclair," he muttered. "How are you?"

"Just fine, thanks." Tony nodded politely and folded his hands in his lap. "What can I do for you?"

"It's been called to my attention that you and Sneller made a very courageous rescue the other day. And took down a couple of Sal Cantini's top henchmen, to boot. Well done."

"Thank you, sir."

"I have here a copy of a signed award from the mayor, commending your bravery and thanking you for your service to the city of Atlanta."

Tony squelched a surprised grin. *Like some salt and pepper on that crow, Captain?*

"He also suggests, in an accompanying letter,

that you and Sneller be promoted and given suitable pay raises." His boss squinted at him across the desk. "Of course," he continued, "I saw no reason to share with him the results of our last interview in this office."

"Oh, no reason at all, sir."

"In fact, you may consider yourself reinstated with full privileges and duties, Sinclair. The promotion and award will be announced next week at a press conference. You will work with the PR department on acceptable comments."

"I'll be happy to do so."

Next came a long pause which Tony wasn't sure how to interpret.

"I also asked you to come back in today because . . ." His boss swallowed.

Tony waited.

"Because . . ."

Tony raised his brows.

The chief exhaled like a spent muffler, and growled, "Aw, hell!"

"Mmmmmmh," said his visitor.

"I have an apology—a partial apology—to make. My daughter, my little Britney, came to me in tears. Seems she's been hanging out with her older cousin, who's in college." The chief reddened, then purpled.

"I think I understand," Tony said. He really

should let the poor guy off the hook and ignore the evil imp inside that enjoyed watching the man squirm.

"Her cousin is more experienced in the ways of the world . . . Taught her some interesting things to do with—" the captain wheezed violently.

Tony couldn't take any more. "Stop—it's okay. Put it out of your mind."

"I blamed you. Of course I blamed you for what happened. No father likes to think of his little girl—" Naked agony mooned Sinclair from the captain's face.

Tony winced. "Forget it," he said. "Just give me this opportunity to clear up something else."

The captain nodded, his head now in his hands.

"I have never done drugs. The woman I was kissing in the police van—" it was Tony's turn to redden, "—is going to become my wife." *If she ever says yes.*

"Okay," said the captain. "Congratulations on your engagement."

"And one more thing," added Tony. "Though I do desire to live up to my father's name in the police force, he had a few more years than me to become a legend. I'd appreciate it if you'd judge me on my own merits, and not on Sam's."

The captain ruminated. "I see what you're saying. I guess I've been hard on you because he asked me to look out for you. Show you the ropes, that sort of thing."

"I'm not as perfect as he was, sir, but I'll do my best."

His boss let out a startled bark of laughter. "Perfect? Your father wasn't always a Boy Scout, you know."

"How do you mean?"

The captain leaned back in his chair. "We were in the Academy together, and he was full of piss and vinegar. Boy, I can tell you some tales . . ."

"Ellen, my love, we have a problem." Myles massaged his elegant beak with two manicured fingers. His signet ring glinted in the evening candlelight.

They sat on the cavernous screen porch of her Buckhead home, listening to the wind sigh through the trees. A platter of caviar and other delicacies remained untouched, as they only had appetite for each other.

"What is it, darling?" She rose to put a concerned hand on his shoulder, and perched on the arm of his chair.

"My dearest daughter has developed a *tendre*

for your churlish nephew—the one with the strangulating tendencies."

"Tony is *not* churlish."

"Very well, my love, but he *did* try to strangle me."

"No doubt," Ellen said with a meaningful glint in her eye, "he had his reasons."

Myles raised his chin in mild affront, but decided not to engage. "At any rate, my poor Jasmine is miserable and distraught."

"So is poor Tony. He asked her to marry him, you know."

"I do know. The girl has some peculiar ideas about the wedded state. These are mixed-up modern times. I assured her that marriage is quite blissful, or I wouldn't consider repeating it."

"And?"

"And I think she's very confused. But I have a plan. After all, I *am* the Old Master!"

Ellen fiddled with the diamond stud in her left ear. "Myles, darling. Perhaps you should tell me about this plan. Get the female point of view."

Myles got up and poured them some sherry. Handing her a glass, he began, "My idea was born this afternoon, when I took her to purchase some evening clothes . . ."

* * *

Jazz was to meet them at a quiet Italian restaurant called Basil's. Myles had offered to pick her up, but she'd opted for her own transportation. She climbed into Floozie wearing a white-silk shantung camisole embroidered with pale yellow dahlias and dotted with tiny, clear bugle beads resembling dewdrops. The matching skirt was short, slit to mid-thigh, and made her feel self-conscious.

Floozie didn't seem to recognize her owner, choking and sputtering when Jazz turned the key in the ignition. Jazz got out, muttering, and fiddled with the fuel pump, blackening her fingers and the pale pink polish her father had chosen at the manicurist's. She wiped the worst of it off on a rag and climbed back into the driver's seat.

Myles had taught her how to mince delicately in the strappy three-inch sandals, to the great amusement of the Neiman Marcus shoe salon staff. However, he hadn't taught her how to drive a stick shift in the things. By the time she pulled into the restaurant parking lot, she was as rattled as Floozie's motor.

She climbed gingerly down from the old van, pulled her skirt as far down as possible, and took a deep breath. Armed with only a tiny evening bag and a modicum of her normal attitude, she teetered to the door. She really hoped Ellen was nice.

Once her eyes adjusted to the dim light, she scanned the nearly empty room for her father, but didn't see him anywhere. The only person in the restaurant she recognized was . . . Tony Sinclair. He was perusing a menu at a quiet corner table.

Jazz flushed as Tony raised his head and simply stared at her. The menu dropped from his hands, and his eyes darkened, moving over every inch of her body. Her knees began to shake.

"Jazz." Tony's voice was husky, and filled with admiration.

The maitre d' appeared and hovered, his face a question.

What was Sinclair doing here, damn it? And why was she both pleased and discomfited by his reaction to her tonight? She'd give anything for her baggy overalls and a nice, soft cotton men's undershirt.

"I, uh," she said gracelessly. "I was supposed to meet Myles and Ellen here."

"So was I." He stood a little awkwardly as the light dawned on both of them. "It occurs to me that we've been tricked."

Damn Myles! She was going to throttle him.

The maitre d' gestured to Tony's table. "Your party, *signorina*?"

"Yes," said Sinclair. His gaze pinned her, challenged her.

Though she wanted to flee, she wobbled forward and settled in the opposite chair. She wondered why she had dressed to the nines, and in clothing she could barely sit down in. This was so not her. She was unsentimental, and practical. She never dressed like a Southern belle. *Double damn Myles.*

"You look—spectacular," said Tony. "Beautiful."

She looked down at the tablecloth and fiddled with her silver.

"I've never seen you in a skirt."

"I haven't seen you in one, either," she returned with a grin, to break the ice.

He laughed. "You're not likely to."

She was unable to look away from the handsome grooves on either side of his determined mouth, the lines of humor radiating from his eyes.

This man who was not for her had the despicable charm to order a bottle of red wine. A pinot noir, her favorite. She told herself that it would help her relax; take the edge off the uncomfortable situation.

Jazz gave silent thanks that Tony, unlike Myles, did not make a production out of sniffing the wine, swirling it in the glass to determine its "legs," or questioning the bottle's label. He merely sipped it, nodded, and let the waiter pour for them both.

Once the man had retired from their table, Tony held his glass up in a toast.

"To the woman I'm going to marry."

Oh, no. Not this again. "Lucky her. Who is she?" Jazz kept her voice steady, though her heart insisted on flopping about like a landed fish.

He didn't miss a beat. "Well, for starters, she's adorable. Generous to a fault. Smart and brave."

Jazz focused on ignoring the pinpricks behind her eyelids. Fine—she'd drink to the woman he'd someday marry. She would make monsters until she was ninetysomething, alone in her studio; collect cats; and leave her money to a society for the study of space aliens.

Jazz let the delicious light wine slide down her throat to seduce the nerves in her stomach.

Tony watched her, wearing a speculative expression. "Let me tell you more about my fiancée."

She could have sworn that the loose knot of curls on top of her head was tightening, creating a prickling sensation all over her scalp. "That won't be necessary," she assured him, and picked up her menu. Bruschetta? Or insalata caprese?

"I disagree."

For some reason, the print blurred under the *Antipasti* heading, and she was forced to move on to the entrees. But there, too, the letters swam out of focus, and she found herself reading the same description of a penne pasta dish over and over.

"The woman I want to marry," he continued, "is creative by nature. She's a brilliant and successful businesswoman. She has a lot of pride."

Penne pasta, cooked al dente, topped with a light marinara sauce, mushrooms, minced onion, and capers . . . Jazz read.

"She pretends a calm, pragmatic disposition that hides her truly passionate nature. When she loves, she loves with a fierce loyalty that amazes me."

Penne pasta, cooked al dente . . .

"She has few flaws, and they stem from the very qualities I love about her. Her loyalty to those she loves causes her to support her deadbeat father, for example."

. . . Mushrooms, minced onion, and capers . . .

"It's fear and pride, however, that I'm having to battle at the moment—"

Jazz put the menu down and took a large swallow of wine.

"—mostly fear. This woman I've fallen for faces thieves and murderers with her chin up and her fists swinging, but tenderness sends her into a panic. Kisses and caresses disarm her, expose her raw nerves. My darling hasn't had a lot of kisses or caresses in her life, and we all fear the unknown."

Jazz attempted to tune him out, but couldn't.

She also couldn't seem to find her tongue to make him stop.

"You're still making your monsters to keep the bogeyman away, sweetheart: The bogeyman of trust, of intimacy, of love. But love doesn't have to be a monster, Jazz. Love can be warm and humorous and tender . . ."

"Tony, stop," she begged.

"No. You want me to stop because I'm getting under your skin and whispering down your veins, and pretty soon I'm going to get into your heart. And once I'm there, I'm never going to leave."

Tony reached out and took her hands across the table, warming them in his own, caressing her palms with his thumbs.

"You're unconventional. I fell in love with you even though you weren't what my mind's eye had always told me was the ideal woman. You crafted a *new* ideal for me, one that blows the doors off the old one. The things I can learn from you, the things we can accomplish together, are extraordinary. I see us moving to a different city, becoming partners in the fullest way, designing and building a new studio together."

Jazz went very still, her gaze riveted to Tony's face.

"I can't put aside who I am or what I stand for," he said softly. "I'm a regular guy. But I *can* put aside my pride one more time, and ask the woman I love to look beyond her own.

"Don't mistake this for humility, sweetheart. "Don't mistake it for weakness. This is courage, me asking again. It's strength—strength that I want to share with you."

My God, he was right. He humbled her.

"Love isn't tangible, Jazz. It's built on faith. It's built on trust. I can't offer guarantees, sweetheart; nobody can. But I want to marry you more than anything in the world. I want to spend my life with you."

Jazz stared wordlessly at this man who was not for her. At least, he hadn't been for her a moment ago. Now she was no longer sure. Blast him, why did he have to be so perceptive? Her fear and pride *did* go hand in hand. She'd always been, well, *proud* of her pride. It had gotten her through life. She'd looked upon it as a virtue, not a flaw or a stumbling block.

Jazz pulled her hands from his and frowned at him.

He waited.

She frowned some more, and excused herself to go to the ladies' room. Once inside, she made her way to the small window and raised it, taking deep gulps of night air. Could she do this? Could she marry Tony Sinclair?

Chapter 29

"A PENNE FOR YOUR THOUGHTS," TONY SAID, when she returned.

Jazz groaned. "You're not allowed to disarm me with humor after broadsiding me emotionally. You're playing dirty."

His smile was both tender and wicked. "I know. But you kinda like it dirty, don't you, sweetheart?"

To her annoyance, her lips twitched.

The waiter chose that moment to approach and ask them if they'd made their selections. Jazz pointed to the penne; Tony never took his eyes off her.

"Surprise me," he told the waiter. "Now please go away."

The poor guy vamoosed.

Jazz pursed her lips and looked down at the wavering flame of the candle between them. "So you've got me all figured out," she said, folding her arms. "I've just got a bad case of fear and pride—kind of like gas."

His eyes twinkled.

"The problem is, I don't know what to do about it. Naming it doesn't make it go away, Sinclair."

A long pause ensued, and she rubbed at her left arch with the mama toe of her right foot. She hoped the inventor of the high heel was roasting on a spit in hell, with an apple in his mouth.

Then, gathering up her courage, Jazz looked across the table at this man who was not for her, and decided that even with a bad case of fear and pride, she'd have him anyway.

Sinclair was ... true blue. He was honorable. He was, for some unknown reason, obsessed with her.

She'd unwillingly fallen in love with his protectiveness, his humor, and his damned stubborn streak. And he was one of that rare species of men who could be humble on occasion.

She loved those cop blue eyes of his, and the way his skin glowed bronze in the candlelight. Besides, wearing this short skirt was making her horny.

She wondered how Tony's broad chest would

look decorated with marinara sauce. Yes—she repressed a smile—tonight was an excellent night for *mani*cotti . . .

"What are you smirking about, you provoking woman?" Tony asked.

"Well," she said demurely, "I was just wondering if you could help me recover from this bad case of fear and pride."

He narrowed his eyes at her.

She put a pink-tipped nail to her lips. All innocence, she inquired, "Do you suppose they can be massaged out, like a muscle cramp?"

Tony went very still.

"Or," she ran her tongue around her lips, "do you think they can be *sucked* out, like snake poison?"

His eyes dilated, and he took a deep breath. "You're not a nice woman," he said in strangled tones. "We're in a public restaurant."

"The other alternative," she continued, trying not to laugh, "is to *pump* them out, with a big, rigid tool."

"That's it," Tony growled. "We're leaving." He erupted from his seat, grabbed her by the hand, and dragged her past the maitre d'. "Here"—he said, flipping a plastic card out of his wallet at the man—"is my Visa. Charge the meal on it, and I'll be back to pick it up tomorrow."

Once outside the doors, he pulled her to him. "I'm going to *love* the fear and pride out of you," he rumbled into her ear. "Then I'm going to do everything else you suggested until you beg for mercy." His mouth descended upon hers, and he kissed her breathless. His lips were demanding; his tongue tumultuous, his arms masterful.

It's all so politically incorrect, she thought wildly, *and I love it.* She loved *him.*

The cotton of his dark slacks rubbed against her bare calf; her nipples tightened against his chest; and she wanted to climb him like a tree.

"Easy, there, Jazz." He pulled back and grinned at her. "I see Floozie over there, but I'd rather not make it in a van. That means we've got a long drive to your place or mine, though."

"The studio," she said. "It's the closest."

He picked her up and walked with her to his car. "Now, let's clarify something," he murmured, with another kiss. "Are you just using me, or are you going to quit being stubborn and marry me?"

Though she was sure he could read the answer in her eyes, she pretended indecision. "Hmmmm . . . I don't know."

He grunted and tossed her into the passenger side of the MR2. While he drove, she unfastened the straps of her sandals and removed the instruments of torture. She put her bare feet up on the dashboard and wiggled her toes in the wind.

When they reached the old warehouse, Tony squealed into the parking lot and had her out of the car before she could blink.

"Keys," he demanded.

Since she was hanging upside down over his shoulder, it was a little difficult to maneuver, but she located them in her beaded handbag. In no time at all, the door was open, the hallway had passed in a blue streak, and she was lying, bemused, on a pile of costumes under the belly of Donovan the dragon.

Tony stripped off his shirt and advanced on her, undoing his pants. "Now, where were we? I believe I had asked you to marry me, and you gave me some weak put-off."

"I—"

He kissed her. In the meantime, his hands were busily at work unzipping the back of her camisole. "Oh, yes. First, I'm going to massage away the pride." He eased her over onto her stomach and began to stroke her neck, dropping light kisses on it as he moved down to her shoulders.

He seduced her the old-fashioned way, rubbing all the way down her spine with his thumbs, and loving every inch of her back with his big, warm hands. He created a symphony of sensation all over her skin.

He slipped his fingers under the waistband of her short skirt, and she ached for them to move lower.

As her breath began to come in pants, he started at her feet and ankles, tantalizing her, working his way up her calves and thighs. Those lean, strong fingers came creeping under the fabric again, shimmying up to cup her bottom, and slipping under the flimsy barrier of her panties.

Jazz became almost incoherent when he found the secret folds between her thighs, then gasped in disappointment when he took away his hand. "Please," she whispered.

In answer, he slipped the panties down her legs and turned her again to face him, then took her breasts, one at a time, into his hot mouth.

She writhed and moaned, moving frantically under him. She was going to go mad if he didn't come inside her.

"I know you're restless, darlin'," he murmured, "but I'm working on the fear, now. And it can be a little stubborn." He continued to suckle and lick, squeezing her breasts together.

His eyes were hot and blue and knowing—so sexy as he devoured her flesh. "You afraid of me, now, Jazz? Hmmmm? Do you want to run away when I do this?" He slipped two fingers inside her and caressed the essence of her femininity with his thumb.

She arched against him, climbing the slope of climax already.

He spread her thighs and kissed her intimately. "How about when I do that?"

Deliciously impossible to answer. Rough stubble, hot seeking tongue, flashes of pulsing need: all at the very core of her, rhythmically swirling into one thought. *I love this man, I love this man, I love this man.*

A zipper finally rasped, she felt his bare flesh against hers, and then at last, he entered her.

"Let me in, Jazz. Let me deep inside you, so deep. Let me come all the way in. I don't ever want to leave, baby." He stroked forward and then back, and forward again.

She began to tremble and shudder around him.

"Now, sweetheart," he whispered, with a tremor of laughter in his voice, "will you marry me?"

"Yes, yes, *yes!*" Jazz shouted, collapsing into shattering sensations. "Oh, yes . . ."

"Good," said Tony. "I'm glad that's settled."

Chapter 30

JAZZ WAS SPLATTERED FROM HEAD TO TOE with plaster and green paint when she opened the studio door for Tony.

"Hi," she said, greeting him with a lingering kiss.

"You've created a monster," he told her. "I can't get enough of you." He began to unbutton her overall straps.

She sidestepped him, laughing. "Actually, today I *have* created a model for a new dragon. Female—with hot lips. Danzer Studios wants a girlfriend for Donovan! Isn't that great? They've got a script for a sequel."

"Wonderful. But where are you going to put her?"

"That does pose a problem," admitted Jazz. "We'll have to build that new studio in LA soon—but the wedding will be expensive."

"We could elope to Vegas and do that drive-through wedding chapel," Tony teased.

"Can you imagine Myles's reaction?" Jazz shuddered.

While she went to scrub her hands, Tony perched on a wooden stool and watched the evening news on the studio's small television. He shook his head as the announcer detailed a number of traffic accidents, a hit-and-run, a drug bust, and a kidnapping with an unexpectedly happy ending. His gaze sharpened at the next item.

"Known mobster Salvatore Cantini was indicted today on charges of grand theft, international smuggling of stolen goods, and racketeering. Two Atlanta police officers and one civilian resident of the city were responsible for apprehending a co-conspirator of Cantini's in the burglary of the High Museum of Art. If you will recall, the theft occurred a month ago during the exhibition *Collecting Impressionism*. Over twenty high-profile and extremely valuable paintings were stolen. Cantini was apprehended in a sting operation when he tried to sell these works of art overseas. The prosecution is confident that its case against the mobster is strong."

"They got Cantini!" Tony called to Jazz.

She emerged from the bathroom, wiping her hands on a towel. "I hope they can keep him behind bars. He's not someone I'd relish meeting again."

The news anchor continued with the story. "All twenty-three paintings have been recovered and restored to their rightful owners, most of which are museums around the world."

"I think they'll win their case," Tony assured her.

They were both riveted to the television at the announcer's next sentence. "The High Museum has retained the expert services of former cat burglar and art thief Myles Taylor, who has graciously agreed to consult on security issues in the building."

"What?" gasped Jazz.

"Taylor, known in the seventies as the Old Master, is engaged to marry High Museum trustee Ellen Whitaker Northrop Banks, and has shown a sincere desire to atone for his past actions. We go live now to Buckhead and MariBeth Downey, standing with Myles Taylor. MariBeth?"

"Hello, Steve, and good evening to all. Myles Taylor, how do you see your new role with the museum? Do you find it ironic that the art establishment has hired you, considering your background?"

Tony and Jazz watched Myles smile in a self-deprecating fashion and adjust his ascot. "I'm simply happy, after all these years, to use my . . . unusual knowledge for the greater good of the city of Atlanta."

"I'm going to be sick," muttered Tony.

"As for the question of irony, isn't all of life ironic? I have written an ode upon the subject, which I'd like to share with our viewers tonight." He produced a piece of fine parchment and flourished it for the camera. "Irony is as irony does," he began.

"Oops, time for a commercial break, folks." MariBeth Downey flashed a professional smile. "Join us next for coverage of the new Flea Market on I-20 . . ."

"I'm glad Myles and Ellen are reunited. I like her a lot," Jazz told Tony that evening, as they ate dinner by candlelight. "She's very elegant. Reminds me a little of Wallis Simpson."

"Don't tell Myles that, or he'll start having delusions of martyred royalty."

"Too late—he's been doing genealogical research to try and prove that he's a direct descendent of the house of Windsor."

"No!"

Jazz nodded, biting her lip.

"Sweetheart, if you don't mind my asking, how did you turn out so normal?"

"One of us had to be grounded, and it sure wasn't him. But Tony, a lot of people don't consider what I do normal. Making monsters is not on everyone's daily "to do" list."

"My little Frankenstein," he murmured. He reached out and took her hand. "Speaking of making monsters, how many little ones should we have?"

"Two or three, I think. But let me get more used to the idea, first." Jazz smiled, took a sip of wine, and then handed her future husband a small, flat box. "I remembered you'd had a hard time finding this stuff. My neighbor's a pharmacist, and he gave me some for you."

Tony stared down at the box of Nicorettes with a wry smile. "Thanks, sweetheart, but I think I've managed to quit. It's been forty-nine days, four hours, and"—he glanced at his watch—"thirty-two minutes since I've had a cigarette."

He produced a box of his own, pushing it across the table at her. "I've been waiting for the right time to give you this," he said.

"Oh, Tony!"

"It's not what you probably think it is," he told her quickly. "I had it custom-made."

She kissed him, then slowly lifted the hinged lid to see what was inside.

"We'll go pick out an engagement ring together, but I wanted you to have this immediately."

Jazz stared down, her eyes awash with tears and laughter as she lifted out a gold pendant on a serpentine chain. It was a delicately molded Cupid—and instead of a bow and arrow, he held a nail gun.